SK
OVER
THIN
ICE

JEAN MILLS

Red Deer Press

Published in Canada by Red Deer Press
195 Allstate Parkway, Markham, ON L3R 4T8

Published in the United States by Red Deer Press
311 Washington Street, Brighton, MA 02135

2 4 6 8 10 9 7 5 3 1

Library and Archives Canada Cataloguing in Publication
Mills, Jean, 1955-, author
Skating over thin ice / Jean Mills.
ISBN 978-0-88995-561-5 (softcover)
I. Title.
PS8576.I5654S53 2018 jC813'.54 C2018-900411-8

Publisher Cataloging-in-Publication Data (U.S.)
Names: Mills, Jean, author.
Title: Skating Over Thin Ice / Jean Mills.
Description: Markham, Ontario : Red Deer Press, 2018. |
Summary: "Music, performing arts, sports and hockey collide in this young adult novel about family, commitment, and friendship set against coming-of-age social issues of two exceptionally gifted young adults who are both facing uncommon pressures to succeed." – Provided by publisher.
Identifiers: ISBN 978-0-88995-561-5 (paperback)
Subjects: LCSH: Gifted teenagers – Juvenile fiction. | Belonging (Social psychology) – Juvenile fiction. | Bildungsromans. | BISAC: YOUNG ADULT FICTION / Coming of Age.
Classification: LCC PZ7.M555Sk |DDC [F] – dc23

Design by Tanya Montini
Edited for the press by Peter Carver
Printed in Canada by Copywell

Red Deer Press acknowledges with thanks the Canada Council for the Arts and the Ontario Arts Council for their support of our publishing program. We acknowledge the financial support of the Government of Canada through the Canada Book Fund (CBF) for our publishing activities.

www.reddeerpress.com

For my parents, missed always.
They gave me a happy childhood that included
Hockey Night in Canada and, one special Christmas,
at last, a piano.

CHAPTER 1

THE END

I never know how to describe it, but maybe like this: It moves the air.

It's impossible to explain with words. We've talked about it a lot over the years, Père and Papa and I. They both nod when I describe it like that, because they know. It's the same for them, when we're performing and the sound—the *music*—is rising up from our fingers and billowing out over the audience like a wispy net that hangs in the air over their heads and then drifts down to capture them all.

That's when it's good.

But that August night in Scotland ... that night when something happened and the net got caught in Père's fingers and snagged, just for an instant. Okay, maybe two instants. That note. My eyes were closed and then they were open, looking over at Père, who caught my eyes and nodded, and then the net was whole again and drifted slowly down to cover us all again.

But I was listening now, too. And looking over at Père, whose eyes were closed. Maybe he was looking for that wrong note inside himself.

I think that was the beginning of everything. The beginning of the changes. Of the end.

CHAPTER 2

LITTLE IMOGEN, THE WEIRD GIRL, IS LEFT BEHIND

I'm on the stairs, shivering in my pajamas, sitting with my left side pressed against the wall, my left leg too, and my feet all twisted around each other. Père and Papa are talking quietly in the kitchen and they think I'm upstairs in my bed, sound asleep.

Who can sleep when our house is being ripped apart? No, not literally ripped apart. But even little Imogen can tell when the air is vibrating with storms. People storms. The parent storms. Again.

"How can I do this?" my father is asking my grandfather. There's music in his voice and my seven-year-old self tries to identify it. Something tragic. Rachmaninoff. The c-minor piano concerto. Fierce and angry and tormented.

"You will go forward because you have to do this." My grandfather is the placid bass line of a Bach chorale. "For Imogen."

A pause. Two silent men. Father and son. But their silence is so loud, it's deafening to my sensitive ears, and I put my hands over them, but very carefully so they don't hear me.

I've sat like this before, listening to my mother and father hissing at each other in the kitchen, all fierce and spitting with anger, circling each other, trying to strike and injure.

Really, do they think I can't hear them? Me?

My mother walked me to school this morning and hugged me goodbye, and then went home, packed a couple of suitcases, took her car, and drove away. She left a note. Père found it when he brought me home from school that afternoon, but he left it, unopened on the kitchen table for Papa to read when he got home from the university later.

She might be dead. I'm not sure, because at bedtime, my father just says she has gone away. Sounds very much like other words for "dead" to me.

"When Geneviève died ..." Père is talking about my grandmother now, his wife. She died. I lean in harder to hear them, thinking I know where this is going.

"When Geneviève died," he repeats, "I mourned. I still mourn. You will mourn. And then, like I did, you'll stand up and walk again. Because you must. For Imogen."

What is that odd sound? I think my father might be crying. I'm about to rise from my perch on the shadowy staircase and run to him, but then I hear him say:

"I can imagine a woman leaving her husband. I can. But her child? What could make a woman leave her child behind?"

My breath won't come for a moment and I see sparkles, even though my eyes are closed. What is he saying? She left us? She's not dead? She left us—me—behind?

I know why, too.

She left me because I'm weird. It's that simple.

I'm weird and everyone knows it. Even Père, even Papa. The nervous kids at school who don't want me in their social studies group, my kind teachers who try to see that I'm included, even when Eve Gagnon rolls her eyes and sighs, and pokes me under the desk so that I can't sit still. It might be the music that makes me weird, I'm not sure, but I am weird. And everyone knows it.

Since that first day of school, in kindergarten, when everyone sat in a circle singing, and all those voices clanged together like a glockenspiel on crack, and I put my hands over my ears and loudly sang a B-flat to bring them all into alignment.

Except that to everyone else, it probably looked as if I were screaming some weird sound. Everyone fell into shocked silence and my B-flat raced around the room—like a conductor waving his baton in front of the orchestra—and brought all the sounds into order again. I stopped singing and took my hands away from my ears. Opened my eyes. Saw them all staring at me with speech bubbles over their heads filled with the words: *Wow. Who is this weird kid?*

Back to the shadowy staircase and my seven-year-old self, listening to Père and Papa.

"What could make a woman leave her child behind?" my father has asked.

I freeze and listen, afraid of what I will hear next. I picture Père placing his hand on my father's shoulder. Father to son.

"A woman who is at the end of her rope," says my grandfather.

Her rope ran out, I tell myself with relief.

It wasn't me after all.

CHAPTER 3

A NEW BOY ARRIVES

When Nathan McCormick walks into the room—Grade 12 English, homeroom with Mr. Norton at Hillside Academy—the air changes. I hear it.

I hear it before I see him, actually.

I'm doodling. I do that when I need to retreat from the buzz in the air around me. Or when I'm rehearsing in my head. It works like this: instead of having the notes in front of me, I'm staring at a page and the music takes form in shapes flowing from the end of my fountain pen. Perfect black lines all weaving together, just like my piano and Papa's cello and Père's violin. Today it's the Korngold D Major. Just those few bars near the end of the Finale. Difficult, but sweet. Sweet. Doodle, doodle.

The air today is full of voices. Conversations range from this weekend's proposed trip to some concert in Ottawa, to the scores from the baseball game last night, to the deliciously horrible end somebody succumbed to at the hands of a criminal horde on that deliciously horrible criminal horde TV series.

"Good morning," says Fredrik, dropping his pack on the desk beside mine, and I smile at him. A moment later, he's off to the front to talk to Mr. Norton.

I sit in my spot in the back corner by the window and watch the show. Listen to the vibrations created by a group of teenagers living away from home at boarding school at 8:30 in the morning on a school day.

Mr. Norton is at the front and he's talking, too. Talking with Fredrik.

Fredrik Floren, the Swedish ambassador's gay son. Probably my best friend. Fredrik is awesome. Also much admired for his tech savvy. Need a hack? Ask Fredrik. Need help with your failed disk drive? Want to download stuff without paying for it? Anything at all. Fredrik is your man. Security tricks, how to hide stuff, find cool tech equipment? Oh, yes, that would be Fredrik. He has his own show on YouTube with thousands of followers.

He is also a beautiful boy, with that tall, golden-haired Viking vibe. Girls fall all over him, which is very entertaining because they don't always realize at first that falling all over Fredrik is a sad waste of their time and efforts. I love Fredrik—no, not like that. I just love him because having someone like

Fredrik nearby makes everything interesting. And I feel safe with him. And he gets me, I think.

I can't say that about someone like, say, Victoria Hanson-Massey, the daughter of the Prime Minister's advisor on something-or-other. She is beautiful in a classic clear-skinned, long-hair-long-legs-long-arms-long-neck kind of way. But I can tell she's unhappy here. She dabbles at schoolwork, just enough to survive. And she thrives on everything not to do with school. I predict a highly successful career in marketing. Something that involves looking beautiful (no denying she has that covered) and talking to people (also covered). She talks to me because she's not an unkind or excluding kind of person. Not at all. I don't dislike her. But she's no Fredrik.

We're an odd assortment of high-school students here at Hillside. Children of parents who are in busy jobs requiring international travel or brutal hours, many from Parliament Hill. Some students are from other countries and are used to being sent to schools here and there around the world. They must wonder what planet they have landed on when they arrive at Hillside Academy in little Brick Hill: population 2,000—about 200 right here at the school. Children of diplomats. Children of business scions and television personalities. We're all here because Hillside is a little hiding place for us, away from the glare and public lives of our parents. Or ourselves. Protected.

So Fredrik is talking to Mr. Norton at the front of the room, and my doodles start to include not only Korngold, but also Fredrik's questions about the upcoming group project that will form forty per cent of our final grade in this year's English/Media major assignment. I'm mildly interested in this because I hate group work.

Doodling. I hear Fredrik say "video," and then Mr. Norton says something and the air changes.

I look up from my doodles and see this boy standing just inside the door, a paper in his hand, a backpack in the other. He's tall, big, dark. Quiet. Not happy, I think. He's looking at Mr. Norton, not at us. But pretty well everyone is looking at him.

And the voices are talking rapidly, urgently. The air is so loud with excitement I can hardly stand it.

I haven't got a clue what's going on. It's like that time we arrived in Elora to play the Schubert 99 and found out from the program that they were expecting the 100. Oops. Moment of panic colored by comedy. Père and I giggled helplessly while Papa asked for a practice room, and we all dug in to pull it out of our memory banks. Someone ran to the Festival office and found the score, and I had to keep the music in front of me, which was distracting at first, but after a few pages I didn't need it anymore. The whole concert went by in a blur, but the audience enjoyed it, and we laughed about it afterward on the way home to Montreal.

Back to the boy in the classroom, and the voices, and the air.

"Oh, please come in, Mr. McCormick," says Mr. Norton,

always formal with newcomers. He shakes Mr. McCormick's hand and takes the paper from him, doesn't glance at it, turns to us, watching.

"Please welcome Nathan McCormick to the class," he says, and a few people say, "Hello," wave, smile, make other socially acceptable welcome motions.

Nathan McCormick looks at us all, nods. Doesn't wave. Doesn't smile, which is perhaps not quite socially acceptable. I look around and no one seems to mind. Everyone is looking at him with such energy and interest, I realize that something is going on here that I don't understand.

Mr. Norton directs Nathan to an empty spot in a group consisting of mostly the rugby boys. Big athletic boys with manly voices and muscles all over. Nice boys, all of them, who always ask me to play their fight songs on the piano during pre-game pep rallies. But sometimes fierce and unapproachable. This seems like an odd choice to me, but I notice they are making room. They're happy the new boy is sitting with them.

And then Mr. Norton calls the class to order. The air settles a bit, and soon I discover who Nathan McCormick is and why he is here.

CHAPTER 4

MORE ABOUT THE NEW BOY

He is a famous hockey player, apparently.

I've never heard of him but that's not surprising, although I do know a little about hockey because Père and Papa are dedicated followers of the Habs—the Montreal Canadiens.

My mother, however, was not a fan. Of the Habs or hockey in general.

She came from England and preferred football, which was her name for soccer. She also liked tennis and once tried to coax little Imogen onto the courts at our local Montreal West Tennis Club. A fail of epic proportions. I don't like showing my bare legs. I don't like running. I don't like hitting things. My tennis career ended quickly.

She would banish Père and Papa to the TV room in the basement on hockey night. I'd hear them cheering and complaining and discussing in loud voices the exploits of their heroes on the ice while, upstairs, my mother turned up the recordings of Elgar,

Finzi, and Vaughan Williams that were her drug of choice. I would try to settle in the kitchen with my homework or my drawing spread out on the table. The air was saturated with competing choruses—"Pass the puck, you moron!" versus the delicately ascending lark. Eventually I would retreat to my room and put on the bulky headphones that Père had given me. Silence.

Although Père and Papa loved hockey and watched it regularly, they didn't include me in their devotions. And when I was old enough to be left alone, they made the pilgrimage into the big arena to watch it live. I turned on Hockey Night in Canada to watch a little and see if I could spot them in the crowd, or hear Père shouting to the morons to pass the puck, but I never did (that is, see or hear them). I would watch, mesmerized, without knowing a thing about what was actually happening in the game, because I found the patterns made by the players on the dazzling white ice thrilling.

So I knew about the Habs. The men in *bleu, blanc, et rouge.* Père's and Papa's hockey heroes.

But the larger hockey world, the place that inspires animated discussions in the media (professional and social) about winners and losers, and what this or that coach or player said or did that caused a storm of reaction from the French and English newspapers throughout the city? Or what actually happens in the games and on the ice? No. I don't know much about that. Only that it was important to people.

So. The hockey boy.

At lunch, I hear Victoria Hanson-Massey talking *sotto voce* to Melanie Arsenault and Polly de Cormier. They're standing at the salad bar in the dining hall, dithering over croutons. I'm in the line behind them with a head full of Korngold, but Victoria's whispering has an element of excitement that intrudes on the phantom score I'm rehearsing.

"He literally beat the crap out of that guy."

Well.

Korngold fades into the background in light of this comment. Who did this literal beating of that guy? And who is "he"?

"I don't care," says Melanie Arsenault (daughter of bank president-financial guru). "He's gorgeous."

Who? Who is gorgeous? The beater?

"Agree," says Polly (daughter of head honcho at major media outlet in Ottawa).

Long, silky hair swishes around three long necks, diamond earrings flashing quickly on three sets of perfect ears, as the girls glance behind me to the tables in the corner where some of the boys are sitting.

Where Nathan McCormick is sitting.

Ah. I have my answer. The who of the beating is the new boy.

The girls have turned back to the croutons. I am glad I'm not starving or in a hurry, because apparently this is going to take some time.

"There's a video on YouTube," Polly is saying. "Tons of hits."

The girls giggle at this.

"He beat the crap out of that guy from Sweden," says Victoria. "That's why he was kicked out."

Sweden? Kicked out of what?

"Right off the team, out of the national program. Gone," Victoria says.

"You're very well informed," Polly says.

"Hard to avoid." Victoria rolls her eyes. "It was in every paper. All over the news."

"All over YouTube," Polly reminds them.

They have assembled their salads and selected their croutons and, still talking, drift over to a table not far from the boys. Not far from this boy Nathan who beat someone, got kicked out, and is all over YouTube.

With my salad and soup (tons of croutons in both), I move away, looking toward my regular table by the window where I often sit alone.

I don't mind. Sometimes Fredrik joins me. Sometimes others. On occasion, Victoria has even sat down with me—when her entourage is busy on the field hockey pitch, or wherever, and she needs company. Victoria does not do alone very well.

I look over at the boys, lounging in their chairs or stuffing their faces. They're talking and trying to bring Nathan into the conversation, but the new boy is eating (with impressively good table manners for someone who beat the crap out of somebody) and nodding a bit, but not talking much.

The room is buzzing. Not the buzzing of what voices are saying. The buzzing of what people aren't saying.

In fact, there's so much buzzing, I have to know what, why. It's like listening to the second movement of the Fifth and desperately hanging on for the *andante con moto* to end and the *allegro* to begin.

Berit Sodersen (Norwegian ambassador's daughter) and her boyfriend William Cowling (everyone says his mother works for M—is that a thing, or only in spy movies?) are sitting together nearby, so I join them and they smile in greeting.

"Hi, Genny," says Berit with that mellow accent that reminds me of water lapping on rock. Maybe that's a Norwegian thing.

William nods hello. He's tall and thin and always seems to be eating. His mouth is full and he's very polite, so not speaking while he chews.

"I was wondering," I say. "About the new boy."

The two of them glance over and then back at me, nodding.

"What are you wondering?" asks Berit.

"I heard the girls talking about him, about how he beat the crap out of someone," I say, expecting—I don't know—some reaction from them. Surprise?

Instead they both nod and get that look that people get when they want to tell a good story.

CHAPTER 5

WHAT HAPPENED IN PERTH LAST SUMMER

The Scottish tour took up most of August. It rained. A lot. But we didn't care, we three ...

The people are nice, with their indecipherable accents. The halls are spectacular. Stepping off Buchanan Street, with its looming brick facades, into the space of the Glasgow Royal Concert Hall, all pale wood and acoustics so sweet that you never want to stop playing. That place in Edinburgh swimming in red—Usher Hall. And churches, too—cathedrals, really. All over Scotland. Stony, cool, whispering churches with people sitting bravely on bum-crushing pews to listen to us.

"Shall we stay here forever? Become Scots?" Père asks me one afternoon, an off day before our final concert, as we wade into tea and scones at a corner table in the dining room of our hotel in Perth. "You're having fun, I think."

My mouth is full of biscuit and cream and jam, or whatever

they call it here. I know he's teasing me but I look around, as if considering. The comfortable low chairs with their muted upholstery—flowers, swirls, birds—and the tables covered in white linen. China pots, hand-painted teacups, and delicate saucers. Silver spoons and little knives with some clan- or hotel-inspired insignia, laid out in perfect, precise tempo.

Order.

I shake my head.

"Too tidy," I whisper, leaning toward him so that I don't disturb the room's unruffled air. So that no one around us might hear and be offended.

So what does he do? He laughs out loud and people look at us anyway. The air is now ruffled. So much for being inconspicuous.

Two ladies of an age—older than Papa, younger than Père—are watching us from a table by the window. I can see past them to the drizzle outside. The glass is fogging.

"Too rainy," Père is saying. "Too much dodging of raindrops." Agree. We nod at each other.

The tea is strong and has more flavors than my regular, familiar, bagged Red Rose at home. Five weeks into our tour and I don't think I have tasted the same tea twice. Another reason to go home and leave Scotland behind.

The ladies at the window draw my attention again. They are clearly plotting. I can tell by their whispers and glances that they know who we are. Who Père is, anyway. Sure enough, a moment later, they lean toward each other and exchange a call to arms, rise ceremoniously, and cross the room toward us.

"Excuse me," says one, all silver-haired and blue-eyed, wool suit and pearls.

And we're off!

Père is gallant and courteous, as always. He rises and speaks, makes them laugh, asks questions, and does the accepted conversation dance that is required in these situations. He introduces me and I rise, brush away the crumbs, shake hands. Try not to think of my rapidly cooling tea.

"You're such a wonder," says Lady Number 1. I think that's what she says. It might be "Your suits are under," which, of course, is gibberish. I nod and smile.

After a few minutes, the conversation winds down and they make moving-away noises. Père and I shake their hands and wish them well. They tell us they are coming to our concert tomorrow. Smiles and thanks all round and they are gone, back to their window table.

I take a sip of tea and put my cup down with a sigh. I know Père is watching me but, for some reason, I do not want to look up. It's part of our job, I know, to be nice to the people who buy tickets and recordings. Papa and Père and Alain, our publicist, have been reminding me of this since I made my first public professional performance at the National Arts Centre (I was six. I played Clara Schumann). I am not great at it.

He knows me very well.

"Shall we request more hot water?" he asks.

I look up at him, my darling grandfather. He winks.

The concert is a well-received, standing-ovation success that will have Alain rubbing his hands in glee back in Montreal. The BBC Scottish Symphony Orchestra plays Brahms. We play Korngold and are brought back for two encores by a thundering, cheering audience. The reception afterward is glittering, noisy, exhausting, and I know I'm going to crash soon, as I always do. I'm swaying on my feet.

In the cab on the way back to the hotel, snug between them, I lean my head back against the seat and let my eyes fall shut.

And then Papa asks Père what happened.

A long pause, and Père says: "One moment it was all there under my fingers, and the next it was gone."

I feel him shrug.

Gone. What does that mean?

"But it came back," I remind him. "We were fine."

Père says nothing. Then, "Yes."

"This time," says Papa.

"Yes, this time," agrees Père. He pats my knee and I realize I am shivering.

CHAPTER 6
PHOTO SHOOT

On the morning of the photo shoot, I lie in bed for a long time.

Soon I'll have to ease out from under the warm duvet, cocoon myself in my old red plaid flannel robe, and join the parade to and from the washroom down the hall, where various beautification rituals are underway.

My rituals are simple, since all I really care about is being clean. Although Victoria once told me she could do a "makeover" any time I wanted. I'm not sure why she would think I want that.

My room is dim, shadowy. It's early, not even seven o'clock yet. The blinds are shut and the window closed, so only a little birdsong sneaks in from outside. I can tell from the way the light spills in around the edges of the window that it's going to be another brilliant October day.

Perfect for the photo shoot. Alain will be happy.

I pull the duvet up to my chin and stare at the shadows on the ceiling. Thank goodness, I don't have to talk to anyone yet.

I'm one of the few Hillside students with a single room. This is partly because I'm in my last year of high school, and we can ask for our own rooms if we want. Most of the girls in my grade have always been in large rooms of two or three, a setting that fills me with dread. Perhaps Papa knew that when he registered me at Hillside for Grade 9.

"Imogen is sensitive to sound," he says to Mr. Colville, the headmaster, as we sit in the office during my entrance interview, discussing whether I should leave my public day school in Montreal and try this out-of-the-way, safe haven here in Brick Hill, Ontario.

Papa doesn't mention the shaking or the headaches or the mornings I need Père to come with me on the Métro and walk with me along the busy, slippery, noisy sidewalks, my guardian through the too-busy, too-overwhelming city galaxy. Right to the door of the school, where I have permission to enter early and go to the gym. There's a piano there, on the stage at one end of the echoing, hardwood-floored cavern. Père kisses my cheek, pats my shoulder, and sends me inside to settle myself with Mr. Chopin and Mr. Brahms. He's there at the end of the day, too. If he weren't, I might end up sleeping on the gym floor.

"She needs a space of her own," Papa says to Mr. Colville, who nods at me.

"Imogen will have her own room," he assures us. "And of course she can use the piano in the chapel at any time—except during services," he adds. Then he smiles at me. "Unless, of course, you'd like to play for us on occasion, Mademoiselle St. Pierre?"

This is a deal-maker for Papa. A piano for practice. Opportunities for performance. Away from the city and the growing interest in the girl who plays the piano, the people asking for interviews, asking for photos.

But also away from Papa. Away from Père.

In my shadowy little room at Hillside, I pull the duvet up over my face and settle myself in silence to hear what might float through my head this morning. Ah. A few measures of "Jupiter, The Bringer of Jollity." I need to go have a shower and get ready, but not yet. Not yet. Soon.

Of course, soon comes soon enough. It always does.

Like that moment before we walk on stage, when the three of us stand, close but separate, in the wings or, in some cases, in a narrow auditorium hallway, or the Rector's office, or whatever space happens to be available. Each in our own space before the music starts. When my head is full of absolutely nothing but a musical blankness waiting to be filled, and always those tiny flitting thoughts just beyond words that *soon my fingers will be on the keys,* and *soon we are going to fill this space with music,* and *soon we will play the last notes and it will be done.* Père will sometimes whisper in my ear, "See you on the other side," as he leads me out, always behind him and in front of Papa. Our parade formation.

So, soon enough, I pull the mental plug on Holst. I crawl out of bed and make myself presentable. The camera crew will arrive at nine o'clock, Papa's email says, and I'm to meet him and Père and Alain at Mr. Colville's office for the formalities.

It's not our idea, this shoot. It's Alain's, our agent and publicist and trio-plus-one. Alain is all about the publicity and the social media and the advertising. He and Papa work together on our tour dates and venues, and on the interviews with media, like the classical music magazines. Alain manages our Facebook page and Twitter feed. Alain is the marketing guy.

Père goes along with it because he knows it's "part of the game," as he describes it to me. But he's like me. He just wants to play his violin and let the music speak for us.

"Not the way it works anymore, I'm afraid," Alain explains, hands turned up in a charade of helplessness. Alain is about the most un-helpless person I've ever met. He needs to meet Victoria. They are from the same planet. The planet of Beautiful People and Now, Now, Now!

Soon has become now. I'm walking across the quadrangle toward the main building and the school's administrative offices, pulling the cold, moist, October morning air deep into my lungs and squinting against the effect of the autumn transformation of birches and maples against blinding blue sky. Autumn in Ontario. Soon, snow.

"Good luck, Genny!" Fredrik dashes by, late for class, taking the shortcut across the quadrangle from the residence exit toward the classrooms. He knows how I feel about this photo shoot idea.

"Hey, it's part of the game," he tells me at breakfast earlier, echoing Père.

"You know how much I love games," I say.

"You must be used to it, though. All the concerts and media and stuff."

I shrug. Yes, I'm used to it.

Alain, dressed in black with a gray scarf and leather jacket, is in the hallway on his cellphone and waves a greeting as I arrive. Alain is very stylish, with his gray hair carefully tousled and his expensive sunglasses. (I'm being hard on Alain. He is nice. But he pushes us hard. Sometimes Père steps in and pulls him back, as if Alain is a poodle straining the leash and wanting to get to the dog park, *now*.)

"Bonjour, Genny," he mouths and points at the phone, rolling his eyes. With a tilt of his head, he indicates that I should go into Mr. Colville's office.

Père is sitting in one of the comfortable chairs, but Papa is at the window with the headmaster. They are talking weather, and the fall trees, and how spectacular the school grounds look this morning.

"Just perfect for the shoot," he says and Mr. Colville jokes about doing his best to arrange the weather for us.

I glance at Père, who winks and rises to brush both my cheeks with his.

"Ah, Imogen, my love," says Papa, stepping around the desk to kiss my cheeks, then standing back to see what I'm wearing. "Good girl. Just as Alain told us, hmm? All in black."

All three of us are in black, Papa and Père in their perfectly fitted shirts and sweaters, me in my black jeans and a long turtleneck that feels like a hug. Apparently we will look fabulous against the backdrop of autumn in Brick Hill. So says Alain.

It's not so bad, once we get underway. The photographs are for a story that will be published in *Classical Music Magazine*, but Alain also has something cooked up with *Maclean's*, so we need lots of variety, he says.

Variety means posing along the fence out by the woods, Père standing, Papa leaning, and me in the middle, sitting (precariously) on the top rail. And strolling along some of the trails by the river. And standing on the grassy lawn leading down to the pond. Père keeps up a running commentary that makes me giggle and the photographer—a gaunt man who makes me think of Ebenezer Scrooge, with a silent boy, his assistant, holding up the reflective white boards and extra lights—loves it.

And soon it's over.

Actually, no. It's not.

Papa and Père have disappeared down the tree-lined drive, Papa driving. Back to Montreal for Père's master class at the university and Papa's rehearsal with that visiting chamber orchestra from Toronto. ("A musician must wear many hats," he always says.)

Alain and I are standing in the little parking lot just outside the main administration building, and I expect he will say goodbye and take himself and the photographers back to Montreal to work their magic on the fruits of our photo shoot—but no.

Instead, he says this:

"So, Genny, I asked your headmaster if we could take some inside shots for a story *Maclean's* is doing."

The air around me does that thing where it seems to get thicker, close in, grow, thrum.

Papa's car has disappeared down the road now. I try to remember what the *Maclean's* story is all about.

Oh, yes. It's about ten young over-achievers, including me. Girl pianist. Girl performer. Learning from those who came before. Or something. In other words, that weird girl.

"Oh," I say to Alain. "Do I have to? Don't you have enough?"

"No, we need something a bit different. Kind of sassy," he says, then notices the look of horror on my face. I don't do sassy. "Oh, now, come along, Genny." He's using his hearty marketing guy voice. "Mr. Colville says your English class is in session now. That will be perfect!"

He has taken my arm—gently, because he knows I hate that—and is steering me across the yard toward the block of classrooms. Mr. Colville and Ebenezer trail behind us with the silent assistant.

First instinct? Pull away and run.

But I don't, of course, because as Papa says, it's part of the game. I'm getting better at it, this game of our musical life. But the air around me is so thick, and the noise of the trees in the wind, and our footsteps on the flagstones of the quadrangle, and Alain, chattering along about this beautiful building, and and and ...

I'm proud of myself. I keep walking. I don't think about soon. I think about Papa and Père driving away and leaving me here with Alain.

Did they know?

We arrive at the classroom, our little procession, and Mr. Colville opens the door and enters, stepping aside as we come in. First Alain, smiling around at my English class with that speech bubble over his head that says, "Hello Everyone! I'm Here! This Is Fabulous!" He shouts, even when he's not speaking. Then me, making my feet go, looking at an uninhabited spot in the air somewhere between me and the window.

I am about to walk on stage, I tell myself. It's the same.

But of course it's not.

Mr. Colville has been speaking to Mr. Norton and Alain about the photo permission forms that have to be sent out before photos of Hillside students can be used anywhere. But he's done, and now he nods at everyone, smiles at me, and leaves.

"How can we help?" Mr. Norton asks, and Alain and Ebenezer are all over it, suggesting moving the desks and where people can sit. Setting the scene.

"By the window, I think," says Alain, so Ebenezer and Silent carry equipment to that side of the room, herding students out of the way.

"This is fun," says Polly. "A photo shoot. You're so lucky, Genny!"

I don't look at her or anyone. I'm trying hard to keep the air from closing in on me or, worse, breaking apart and leaving me with nothing to breathe.

Mr. Norton is called on by Alain to direct everyone to move the desks into a semicircle. Hideous scraping and scuffing noises ensue. Laughter.

I hazard a glance at my classmates. Maybe Fredrik will throw me a lifeline, a look, anyway.

But he's busy, too, rocking his desk into position, swearing a bit in Swedish as he avoids getting his fingers pinched by Victoria's lack of awareness that she is pushing her desk dangerously close to his. Polly has maneuvered herself beside Victoria, to the front. They are hoping for lens time, obviously.

Mr. Norton is pointing, directing, as if it's the school play. Playtime. Alain is right in there, joking and making suggestions. Ebenezer is taking light readings.

Soon turns into now and Alain says: "Okay, Genny."

Everyone looks at me.

It's like walking onto the stage at the NAC, that time when I was twelve, and I'd been sick for a week with an awful sore throat, a coughing, achy, hurting illness, and hadn't been able to practice properly. I knew every note of the Chopin. Knew it as well as I knew my name. But still, that moment when you think: there is a barrier between me and perfection.

"You do not have to be perfect," Père whispered to me then, his hand warm around mine as we stood in the wings. "You only have to be present."

I am present, I tell myself, standing in that classroom, waiting for Ebenezer and Alain to tell me where to stand and where to look and what they want from me. It will not be perfection. They can ask Victoria Hanson-Massey to pose for them if they want perfection. She'd love it.

"Here, Genny," Alain is saying, and off we go.

First a few shots of me alone, standing by the window, sitting on a desk. Then Ebenezer calls in the chorus. My classmates sit. Stand. Cross arms. Look the other way. Hold books up to their faces so that only their eyes show. They laugh. Alain is like a crazy pre-school teacher and they adore him, as I stand with my back to them all and look directly at the camera.

Thank God, Ebenezer doesn't ask me to smile. Just my usual face. My usual eyes and mouth. Looking into the camera and being blinded by the lights. Trying to ignore the shufflings and movements and laughing behind me. A break from studying *Hamlet*. Obviously this is way better.

And then Alain says, "Okay, one more."

A fun one, he says. The story for *Maclean's* is called "On the Shoulders of Giants." How about some of the students holding Genny like a sports hero, on their shoulders. You know, like the guy who scores the winning touchdown.

The rugby boys are all over this. Alain and Mr. Norton are directing again, moving desks, picking out who will provide the shoulders.

The air starts to vibrate.

"I don't want to," I whisper to the space in the air between me and Alain, but I'm not sure he hears.

I look over at him and he's coming forward with that marketing guy "Let's do it" smile on his face. *C'mon Genny, my love, just this one more and we're done.*

No. I tell him without speaking.

Alain hears me, but he gives me the typical adult "I am disappointed in you" look. Head slightly tilted to one side.

Mr. Norton is hesitating. "Genny, I'm sure you'll be safe," he says. He thinks I'm afraid of falling.

No. Not falling. At least, not falling to the floor.

I just don't want to do this. It's very simple, Mr. Norton. I do not want to leave the ground and have these boys' hands on me.

"It'll be fun!" Alain says. He has me by the arm now, leading me to the group of boys standing together, goofing around, flexing muscles.

"We'll be your giants, Genny, don't worry," says Braedon Korduk, one of the rugby boys. They are so ready for this.

"No. Really." I am pulling back now, and Alain lets go of my arm.

"Now, Genny," he says, and I can hear the frustration in his voice. He really, really wants this shot. Wants to show the world that tidy little Imogen St. Pierre has a sassy side.

Ebenezer is getting impatient. He opens his mouth to say something.

"Well, if Genny really doesn't want to ..." Mr. Norton begins. I look toward him, hopeful.

But someone else has stepped forward, inserted himself between Alain and me.

"She doesn't want to do it," says Nathan McCormick. "She shouldn't have to do it if she doesn't want to."

Silence in the room as we all stare at him.

He's looking from Mr. Norton to Alain, who blinks up at him, mouth open. I cannot imagine what's going through his marketing-guy head.

The air is vibrating and cocooning me as I step away, away from Nathan McCormick and Alain and Mr. Norton and the rugby boys and my classmates, who are enjoying this. The crazy hockey boy who beat the crap out of that guy is going to beat the crap out of this marketing guy. Maybe.

"I agree, actually," says Mr. Norton. "I feel we shouldn't expect Imogen to do anything she's uncomfortable with." He says it to Alain, but he also gives me a confirming nod, and a nod to Nathan, who hasn't moved. Who is watching Alain as if he expects him to pull a knife or something.

And then it's over. Alain shrugs, gives in, laughs it off, tells everyone, oh well, they have to get back to work now, gives me a little smile and his helpless (not helpless) shrug, and then it's madness as everyone starts to move the desks back into normal formation, talking, chattering like birds. Nathan doesn't chatter, but he turns away and picks up a desk, moves with the crowd. Ebenezer and Silent are packing up equipment; Alain is turning toward me to speak but I turn away from him and go.

Out of the classroom, down the hall to the first exit door, across the quadrangle, and over the parking lot to the chapel. Walking quickly. Don't run, I tell myself. Just walk and breathe. Go to the piano.

It's all about Bach preludes until the lunch bell, and even then I can't shake the feeling that the ground isn't solid under my feet.

CHAPTER 7
YOUTUBE

He beat the crap out of that guy.

That's what the girls said. They also said it was all over YouTube.

I'm in my room much, much later. Curled up with my duvet, with my computer on my lap.

"Now, Imogen, my love, I had no idea that's what Alain had planned," Papa is saying on Skype. His face is enormous and distorted, his eyes hooded and strange in the pixels on my screen. He's at the dining room table at our house and, every now and then, Père walks by in the background, wearing his striped dressing gown, carrying a mug, leaning in to blow me a kiss. A typical evening when there is no rehearsal or performance.

"I'm sorry." Papa is trying very hard. He knows the photo shoot was bad for me. I should be more generous and tell him it's okay, I'm okay, it's all okay now.

But it isn't.

"But you know Alain," I say. It sounds like whining, even to me. "He has crazy ideas."

"Crazy!" Père agrees, from somewhere off-screen.

"It was only supposed to be a simple little photo shoot." Papa sounds both sorry and impatient.

I'm being needy. High-maintenance. Silly.

"I know. It was. It was just his idea for this group shot, with the class, and ..." I trail off, embarrassed to admit not wanting the boys to lift me in the air, like a star athlete with the winning goal. Basket. Home run. Whatever.

Papa has already talked to Mr. Colville, who had the story from Mr. Norton. Yes, all the grown-ups are talking about me.

"But in the end, you didn't have to do it," Papa soothes. "So it's all done, all over, right?"

He's right. It's over.

I sigh. Père's face suddenly appears on the screen as he squeezes Papa off to the side.

"Brave girl," he says. "Standing up for yourself. I salute you." He raises his mug and nods his affirmation.

How can I not smile at that?

Later, after we've said goodbye and disconnected, I stay propped up in my bed, staring at the screen.

I wasn't so brave, Père. It wasn't really me.

And then I remember: YouTube.

Within seconds, the site has loaded and I'm trying to decide what to type into the search box.

Nathan McCormick hockey fight

Instantly, a list of video titles appears. Almost all have the same screen image: two hockey players surrounded by other players and stripe-shirted officials, one player in red and white, helmet off, fist drawn back; one player in yellow and blue, on the ice, helpless. Frozen like that.

And words in the titles. *Best hockey fight ever. World Juniors McCormick and Andersson. Crazy hockey fight. Violence in junior hockey. Canadian hockey player goes berserk. Nathan McCormick gets thrown out of World Junior final.*

Do I really want to see this? Well, yes, actually, I do.

I look for the one with the most views and click on the link.

It's footage from a television broadcast. Fast action and fast commentary describing the play. A player in red and white chases a puck toward the boards, behind the net. A player in yellow and blue follows him in and hits him hard. So hard the boards shake and I can see the fans beyond the glass draw back in surprise.

"A hard hit by Andersson on Charette and Charette is down," says the announcer.

Charette is down, all right. Face down on the ice and not moving.

The player in yellow, Andersson, just bounces off and skates right into ...

McCormick. His name is on the back of his jersey and he's already dropping his stick and tossing his gloves and launching himself at Andersson, who goes down before he has a chance to do the same.

Nathan rips his own helmet off, as if he can't breathe inside the cage, and now Andersson's helmet has come off and the hitting starts.

Nathan is pounding him. Pounding Andersson in the head. Andersson is trying to get his arms up but Nathan has him pinned, overwhelmed. He's pounding, pounding.

Players from both teams are trying to get at them. The officials move in and try to haul everyone out of the way, trying to get to Nathan, but he seems unaware of everything going on around him. He's still pounding and Andersson is just reacting, trying to get an arm up to protect himself, trying to move his head away from the furious pounding of Nathan's fist.

There's blood everywhere.

The officials get through the crowd and pull Nathan off, but he's acting crazy, wrenching himself out of their grasp, trying to get back at Andersson, who's staggering to his knees, bleeding, holding his nose, and swaying a little. Players are grabbing each other, wrestling.

There aren't enough officials to keep them from pairing off. The officials have their hands full trying to hold Nathan.

A doctor or trainer slides into the scene, holding onto the

arm of a Canadian player, and kneels beside the unmoving body of Charette.

The camera zooms in on Nathan, being pulled away from the scene, being yelled at by the referee, by the other players. Everyone is looking at Charette, or bloody Andersson, being helped to his skates by two teammates.

The officials pull Nathan away. He's shouting at someone.

"McCormick is incensed," says the announcer. "The officials need to get him off the ice."

Before he kills someone. That's what the announcer is not saying, but I hear it as clear as anything.

And then it shifts to a different camera angle, and the camera catches him full on, shouting at Andersson, screaming at him.

But the officials have him now. It's almost over. I can see the other players relaxing their grips and cautiously stepping away. One of the Canadian players skates over to Nathan and the officials and says something to him, puts his hand on Nathan's back and skates alongside him, talking, talking him down as he is shepherded across the ice to a gate leading under the stands. To the dressing room, I suppose.

And Nathan—it's as if the air goes out of him. He gives up, gives in. Clomps off down the walkway and out of sight. It's over. We don't find out what happens to Charette who, at last view, was still lying unmoving on the ice. We don't find out what happens to Andersson, whose blood is everywhere.

The announcers are discussing the cause of the fight. The hit on Charette from behind, aimed at his head. How it's not the first time Andersson has targeted Charette, the Canadian captain. How McCormick and Andersson have a history. How McCormick and Charette are teammates back in Ottawa, longtime friends. How McCormick is the biggest and probably most skilled player on the ice.

End of video.

I lie curled up under the duvet for a long time, staring at nothing, waiting for the scene of violence to dissolve and the thud, thud, thud of Nathan McCormick's fist on Andersson's face to fade ...

The sounds do go away, after a bit.

But Nathan's face doesn't go away. Nathan McCormick beat the crap out of that guy, yes he did.

And even when I close my eyes, his face is still there.

CHAPTER 8

FRIDAY DEPARTURE

On Friday afternoon, I'm packed and standing under the portico of the old house that is now the main building of Hillside, waiting for Papa to pick me up for our weekend of rehearsals.

The Christmas tour in the UK starts in just over two months, and we still have a lot of work to do on the Messiaen before the first concert in London in mid-December. Anthony Clapperton has come from Cambridge to perform a few Canadian concerts but mostly to practice with us. Clapperton, the next big thing in woodwinds, say all the classical magazines and media, introduced to us by one of Père's old friends from McGill. He's the clarinetist who will make our trio a quartet for this one piece.

Quartet for the End of Time. What can I say? I love it. Love the piano score because it's so dark and dense and solid. I could just crawl into the music and live there for a while, underground.

In fact, I've noticed, whenever I'm practicing, it's hard to climb out again afterward.

Père says that is exactly what Messiaen intended and exactly what he was living when he wrote it in a prisoner-of-war camp.

Shivery stuff.

Also shivery is the wind today, as I stand waiting for Papa. Most students stay on campus for the weekend, so the front door and parking lot are quiet, but I can see some of the girls jogging purposefully toward one of the playing fields where a group of boys is already tossing a Frisbee. Right. There's an Ultimate Frisbee challenge this weekend. Everyone, even the not-so-sporty people, has spent the week signing up on teams and picking names and colors. The school has organized the distribution of shirts and printing of logos.

"Can't you stay, Genny? Just this once?" Berit asks on Tuesday, the day after the photo shoot. "It'll be fun."

"Great exercise," adds Fredrik, not previously known to be sporty. "You don't get nearly enough exercise. All those hours in the chapel with the piano. You need fresh air."

I love Fredrik. He sounds like someone's mother, a bit.

"Don't nag, Freddie," says Berit. "But he's right, Genny. You need to get away from homework and that piano, girl."

"You could be on our team," William offers, which is very generous, because they all know I'm about the last person to make any kind of contribution to a team.

Basically, I'm terrible at sports. I know it. They know it.

So it's really kind of them to ask, but it's still Messiaen who wins.

"*Désolé*. I'm rehearsing all weekend," I say.

I can see them now. They've recruited one of the Grade 11 girls to make up their team, and they're trotting across the field in big green T-shirts over school hoodies. Big Green Machine, they call themselves. This morning before assembly, all the teams showed off their shirts, a sort of informal pep rally. It was raucous. I'm not sorry to be escaping.

Now I look the other way, out past the school gates, and my eyes follow the road that runs up the hill through town. A flash of sunlight on a black car. Papa? Yes.

We haven't talked since our Skype conversation on Monday night. I wonder if we should or shouldn't. My eyes stray to the field where the Frisbee players are assembling. Maybe I should have said yes to Berit and Fredrik and William after all.

"Not sticking around for the weekend?"

I turn—Nathan McCormick has come out of the door behind me. He's wearing a blue long-sleeved T-shirt with "Blue Lightning" written on the front, with a lightning bolt shooting through the words.

He is very big, very tall. I don't look at his face.

"No, I have to go home," I say, looking over at the fields, thinking how those words make me sound as if I'm in kindergarten. I take a quick glance at him.

The last time I saw Nathan's face close up, it was on YouTube. How does this boy compare with that one?

This Nathan, the tall boy who sits several rows over in my English class, not the one who beat the crap out of that guy, has an Ottawa Senators ball cap pulled down low over his thick brown hair, and he's squinting down the driveway into the sun, where Papa's car is visible now, just turning off the road and starting up the drive.

He nods.

"You're a musician, right? Do you have rehearsal or something?"

My turn to nod. Watching the car.

"Well, make it a good one."

He's moving away as he says it, breaks into a relaxed, athletic lope, and heads across the yard toward the path that leads to the playing fields. Victoria and Polly, also in Blue Lightning shirts and wearing very tight black leggings, appear from the door at the end of the classroom wing and catch sight of him. (No, Nathan McCormick is not wearing tight black leggings. He's wearing something that looks like black pajama pants, loose-fitting and athletic.) They wave, laugh, toss their abundant and unnaturally shiny hair, join him in a jog toward the fields, the other teams, the competition.

I gather up my weekend bag and backpack and, as the car pulls up, I see that Père has come along for the ride, which means

(I hope) that we will stop at the *patisserie* in town for croissants and a big cup of tea (for me) and coffee (for Papa) and café au lait (for Père) for the drive home. We'll listen to rehearsal recordings Papa has put together and discuss notes for each piece, each movement, each bar, sometimes even each note.

No conversation about the photo shoot. I'm just fine with that.

Instead, I will escape into Papa's playlist and, maybe, think about Ultimate Frisbee, and what it might take to develop an easy athletic lope and wear tight black leggings with confidence.

Fredrik might be right. I need some exercise.

CHAPTER 9

MEDIA ASSIGNMENT

The air in the Monday-morning classroom is humming.

Wait, that might be me humming. The *Quartet* has buried me so deeply inside my own inner concert hall that I've been having trouble finding the exit.

I'm not complaining, though. I love this part of the process, especially with a piece like the *Quartet*. It's still just a dark space with dark, magical music seeping so much pain. Pain and longing. My fingers twitch a little, searching for the keyboard that is nowhere near, so I clutch my black pen and doodle, doodle, doodle. Stare at the page and hear Clapperton's clarinet—like a voice, pleading and crying. Exquisite pain.

Papa and Père are not sure about Clapperton. Clapperton is not backward about coming forward, says Papa, who manages not to show his frustration at the frequent stops to discuss points of interpretation during the two long days of rehearsal.

Père, patient and calm, keeps us moving along, paddle in the water, steering us past the worst of the rocky sections, the unexpected dangers.

We are nearly there and I love this part of the journey. But my problem is that I can't get out of the boat, even when the music stops. It just keeps flowing, pulling me along.

"Imogen, my love," says Père on Sunday afternoon. I'm standing in the kitchen during a tea break, looking out at the leaves falling in our backyard, unaware that the kettle is burbling so hard it might erupt. He stands in front of me and drops his hands gently on my shoulders, leans forward a little to look into my eyes. "Come back."

Blink. I'm in the kitchen. The kettle is boiling. We smile at each other.

"It is very powerful music," he says. "But we mustn't allow ourselves to drown in it."

I blink again, in the classroom on Monday morning, and tune in to the humming around me.

Lots of excitement, mostly to do with the Ultimate Frisbee competition, won by Yellow Fever, a team made up of two rugby boys and two extremely tall girls from the basketball team. They defeated Purple Rain, a team of Grade 11 upstarts, apparently, and it was a near thing.

"If I hadn't lost my contact lens," Victoria says, in a voice that declares she was somehow unfairly treated by the Frisbee gods, "we would have won that semifinal."

Braedon, who was on the winning team, gives her a look that says what everyone is thinking: *Um, nope*. Followed by: *You're so full of yourself, Victoria.*

Clapperton is very full of himself. That was clear to me the moment he arrived at our front door. It's his scarf that gives him away. A red scarf flecked with bits of black and white, the long ends trailing from a loop at his neck. It's supposed to look artful and blasé, but he's trying too hard. I imagine him standing in front of a mirror, arranging it around his neck to achieve the GQ effect. Fail.

He stands just inside our front door, tall and languid, with longish dark hair, as he slips his sunglasses off. The clarinet case and briefcase together in one hand, standard musician accessories. But the scarf ruins it.

Père sees it, too, but he is as gracious and polite as always. If it weren't for all the interruptions and his need to discuss everything, Clapperton might be just another in a long line of Trio St. Pierre musical collaborators—but he is so needy. So *talk talk talk*.

He can play that clarinet, though.

Victoria, however, despite her contact lens complaints, isn't much of an athlete, so her success in the Ultimate Frisbee contest is doomed from the start. I wonder if Nathan McCormick knows this when he signs on to play with the Blue Lightning, or if he is just one more in a long line of Hillside boys drawn to the glittering jewel that is Victoria Hanson-Massey, only to discover there's not much there. Except for glitter.

I'm being mean to Victoria in my head, which is all the more unfair of me, because not only is she basically a nice person, but also the reality is that I couldn't throw or catch a Frisbee if my life depended on it.

"Good morning. Let's get started, shall we?" says Mr. Norton from the front of the room. I had forgotten for a moment that I'm in a classroom.

General rustlings and settling of bodies and books as we turn our attention to the screen at the front of the room where Mr. Norton is starting a slideshow of something.

An assignment.

Media Assignment, says the first screen. Victoria raises her hand.

"Mr. Norton, I was wondering," she begins.

But Mr. Norton has been here before.

"Victoria, please hold questions until I ask for them."

"But, sir, I was just wondering if we could work in groups ..."

Slide number two clicks onto the screen.

Group Assignment, worth 40% of final grade.

"Mr. Norton!" She's relentless. Her hand is in the air. Mr. Norton is ignoring her. The entertainment value of having

Victoria in the class is impossible to measure. "Do we get to pick our own groups?"

She's already exchanging looks with Polly. Flicking her eyes over to where Nathan McCormick sits on the far side of the room.

Slide three: *Groups will be assigned at random. Time will be given in class to work on this assignment.*

Victoria slumps in her seat. If she had a speech bubble over her head, it would say: "Please, God, don't let me be in the same group as Imogen St. Pierre."

We did a group presentation together once last year, in Geography. I hate classroom presentations. Strange, since I can play the piano in front of hundreds of people in an audience and not even notice them.

A classroom is very different. Our presentation didn't go well. She stepped in and took over, which earned us a low mark for group work, which then resulted in appeals of "Not fair! Genny just doesn't do anything!" Which is so not true.

It was ugly.

Slide four: *Create a short (5-10 minute) film, podcast, or audio performance (music or spoken word) on a subject of your choosing. All members of the group must contribute creatively and/or technically. Technical instruction and possible topics will be discussed with the teacher.*

Silence in the class now. But also a current of excitement. The humming is getting a bit louder.

Slide five: *Your finished product will be presented to the class for peer assessment, as well as assessment by the teacher, using the distributed rubric.*

We haven't even finished reading this yet and Mr. Norton is already passing out the handout with the rubric and, on the second page, the list of groups.

Frantic reading as everyone searches for his or her name.

I wait a moment, savoring this last bubble of freedom and peace before being thrust into the maelstrom.

Group work is my life, as long as the other members of my group are Père and Papa. Maybe a Clapperton or someone like him. Otherwise ...

Deep breath, open eyes, scan the page.

Imogen St. Pierre. Fredrik Floren. I stop there and let it sink in.

Saved!

Imogen St. Pierre. Fredrik Floren. I read it twice and look up to see Fredrik grinning at me, thumb up.

But the other names. I didn't read the other names.

Just one other name. Nathan McCormick.

We are a trio: Fredrik the techno wiz. Imogen the weird girl. And Nathan who beat the crap out of that guy.

I exhale. Maybe I will survive this assignment.

"What a waste," I hear Victoria mutter as she pouts in my direction.

CHAPTER 10

FLASHBACK: SUNDAY DINNER WITH PAPA AND PÈRE

After Clapperton leaves on Sunday afternoon, Papa says: "I am not cooking tonight. Get your coats, everyone."

We walk through the dusky chill to our favorite diner, Chez Viau.

We're known here. We're barely through the door and there is Monsieur Viau himself, waving us to our table in the back corner by the long side window overlooking the side street and the park. Wine glasses are filled while the men exchange news—a new grandchild in the Viau household, our upcoming Christmas concerts in London. Meals ordered—pasta, soup, bread, salad that we share—Monsieur Viau moves away and we are alone.

Père sips his wine, relaxed. Papa sips, too, leans back and lets his shoulders drop a little, as if he's been held up on a coat hanger and now he's free to sag.

I glance at him. His face is sagging a little, too. The past two days of rehearsal have been difficult.

First Clapperton, with his need to analyze and question every bow stroke and every breath.

And then Père.

We all see and hear it. Père has to reach further to grasp notes that have always simply fallen into place under his fingers. His fingers, a little creaky, he says. A little bent. A little stiff sometimes.

Papa is worried but Père simply shrugs.

"I am old, Maxim." He smiles. "And these fingers are tired."

When he says this the first time, on Saturday night after Clapperton has left in a taxi for his hotel, I am so frozen with dread that I have to retreat to my room, distract myself by visualizing my way through the second movement of Brahms No. 2, playing phantom notes with my hands on my thighs.

There is a knock on the door before I reach the shift to major mode and the third theme. My silent music crashes to a halt.

"Imogen, my love," says Père. "Come and have a cup of tea with me."

I sit and watch while he assembles everything on the table, boils the kettle, spoons Buckingham Palace Garden Party into the little tea egg he uses when Red Rose tea bags just won't cut it. He moves slowly, gracefully, purposefully around our little kitchen. Smiling a little, humming under his breath. As if making tea is the most enjoyable thing he's done all day. As if he has nothing on his mind but making tea for me.

"All is well," he says, pouring from the china teapot left behind by my English mother. "You must not worry about me."

We sip. Père doesn't mind silence and neither do I.

Also, he is a mind reader. I glance at him and he is smiling at me. These are the words he isn't saying: *I know you are worried about me and our music. About your music. But I am not worried. And neither should you be.*

"Just drink your tea," he says.

Now, sitting in the restaurant, he smiles at me again, sipping his wine. And then he asks:

"Have you thought about next year?"

This question has been lurking, hiding, for a long time. I want to keep it hidden in its little dark corner a while longer, mostly because I don't have an answer. I don't even want to look for an answer, just as I don't want to hear Père's fingers falter on the violin strings or see Papa's face sag with fatigue.

I look out the window.

"University applications have to go in soon," says Papa. He's been talking to Mr. Colville.

A trio of squirrels is dashing through the leaves under the maples in the park across the road. Playing a game? Or terrified and trying to escape from some menace? A woman pushes a stroller down the sidewalk toward the houses further down. She's in a hurry, deep in thought. Maybe she doesn't know what she will make for supper. Maybe she has money troubles. My imagination doesn't reach any further than that.

"The UBC program is excellent," Papa says.

The streetlights are on now and they throw light into the moist air, making cones of faint fogginess at intervals up and down the street.

"Or you could stay home with us," Papa continues. "Go to McGill and be stuck with me or Père as your teacher, for History of Western Music, that is."

"Though perhaps not the best plan," adds Père.

They wait. I look out the window and see, not trees, squirrels, sidewalk, streetlights, but the chapel at Hillside two weeks ago.

Mrs. Silverstone from the guidance office is standing at the front of the chapel, where the entire Grade 12 class is assembled for a session on the university application process. I am at the back, with a good view.

Victoria, Polly, and Melanie are rapt. Clearly, getting to university and leaping into a whole new social soup presents thrilling possibilities. Most students are busy scribbling notes and, for the most part, paying attention. Fredrik has his head tilted to the side, as if weighing everything Mrs. Silverstone says against his own knowledge of the subject, and, knowing Fredrik, he has it all figured out already. The rugby boys are listening but appear bored. Nathan McCormick is looking down, maybe sleeping.

I half-listen to Mrs. Silverstone's advice and instructions. The truth is, I don't have a clue what I want to do next year when I leave Hillside.

No, not strictly true.

I know what I want to do. I want to play piano with Papa and Père from morning until night, and go to sleep with music in my head. Then wake up and do it all over again the next day. And the next. It's simple.

But now, sitting in Chez Viau, it doesn't seem so simple.

"Imogen, my love," says Père, gently. His hand closes over mine so that we are both holding my tea cup. "Look at me."

I do. His sweet smile.

"We will figure it out together," he says. "Yes?"

I glance at Papa, and he's watching me and nodding.

"Do you want me to go away?" I take my hands off my teacup, slip them out from under Père's, and clasp them in my lap. "Do you think I should go away?"

To UBC, or Western, or maybe Wilfrid Laurier, the three music faculties that Mrs. Silverstone mentions to me in our one, brief, guidance session. Universities with good music programs, where Papa and Père have friends and colleagues. Or maybe the programs even further afield. Julliard. The Curtis Institute. The Peabody.

"I think you should go where you're going to experience something new, not just the same old dreary rehearsals with your grumpy father and dotty grandfather," says Père. He winks at me.

"Grumpy. Who's grumpy?" asks Papa.

"I'll think about it," I say after a moment.

"You could apply to those three, maybe, and see whether you're accepted," says Papa. "Then make up your mind."

"Keeping your options open," Père adds.

"Or I could just stay home. Go to McGill. Or not," I say. "That's an option too, isn't it?"

Père smiles, nods, finishes his wine, and holds out his glass for Papa to refill.

"Now we're looking at all the options," he says. "That's all we ask."

No one mentions Alain and his plans and schemes.

Options. I can live with that. When Mrs. Silverstone takes us to the computer lab to walk us through the online applications process, I will apply to those three programs. And McGill. That will make Papa and Père happy, and then, if those schools accept me, I can go. Or stay. No need to decide right now. I have options.

Later, walking home along the dark sidewalks, I match steps with Père, our arms linked. Tomorrow morning, early, Papa will drive me back to Hillside, in time for my first class (English with Mr. Norton). I wonder how the Frisbee tournament went. I wonder if the Blue Lightning won.

CHAPTER 11

AN INVITATION

An email arrives from my mother:

Dear Imogen,

I see that you will be in England over the Christmas season. Although I doubt I'll be able to make it to any of your concerts, I do hope we can meet for tea on one of your free days. I don't expect you to make the trip to Oxford. I will take the train to London. If this sounds like something you would like to do, let me know the day and time you're available and I'll make the arrangements.

I hope your school year is going well and that plans for next year and university are in progress. Your musical career is certainly blossoming. The reviews from the Scottish tour were outstanding.

Gavin and Annabel are growing so fast (now aged seven and four) and both show talent for the piano, although, of course, they do not have a gift like yours.

I do think of you often and hope you are well and happy over there in Canada.

See you soon,

Mother

Yes, my mother's emails are very formal.

The best part of this message is the news about my half-brother and half-sister, Gavin and Annabel. I've never met them, so they're like some fairy tale creatures to me.

The worst part is the invitation to have tea with her.

"You don't have to go," Papa says when I tell him about the email invitation. "But, of course, it would be nice for your mother to see what a beautiful and accomplished daughter she has."

I don't want to look at him because I know what I will see there.

"And it would be nice for you to see your mother," he says.

But I don't want to see her, this woman who left us. Who sends me a birthday card every year with her formal good wishes. Who made my father cry.

I have seen her, of course, a number of times over the years. Usually with Papa there to protect me. A meal in a busy restaurant in Montreal or in London. Awkward conversation as my mother, always formal and radiating disapproval and disappointment, makes small talk with Papa and asks me a few general questions about school and my piano studies. Photos of her new children, her new house, her new life. It always takes me hours to breathe normally again afterward.

"You must do what feels right, Imogen," says Papa. He squeezes my shoulders and leaves me sitting at my laptop at the kitchen table. He knows how I will respond.

Dear Mother,

Thank you for your invitation to tea in London. I would be happy to meet you on one of our free days: December 18, 20, or 27. We are staying at The Landmark and will be there from December 12 through 30, when we fly home.

I'm happy to hear that Gavin and Annabel are learning to play piano.

Let me know what arrangements you make for our visit.

See you soon,

Imogen

There. I can be formal, too.

CHAPTER 12

IN THE CHAPEL

On Tuesday, in gym class, I faint.

One minute, I'm doing very slow, unathletic laps of the field-hockey pitch with the other girls, and the next, there are sparkles around everything and the loud sound of nothingness in my ears, and then ...

"Genny? Genny?" Miss Bucher, the gym teacher, is kneeling beside me on the damp grass and the faces of the other girls are coming into focus, her chorus, standing behind her against a backdrop of low October clouds, heavy with rain.

She looks worried but the others just look interested. Something exciting to break up the tedium of another gym class.

I could just lie here forever on the cool grass. I could just close my eyes and sleep for a while.

But of course Miss Bucher is all business, has me sitting up, and is looking at my eyes, asking me questions about breakfast and what time of the month it is. She is thinking fuel, body chemistry, health, fitness (and how lacking I am).

I am thinking how much I hate gym class and especially how much I hate running laps. Running is the worst exercise ever—so jarring with its thud, thud, thud as each foot makes an impact against the ground. I've tried thinking of rhythm, of tempo, but no—running just feels so awkward and plodding.

Eventually, Miss Bucher decides I'm not about to expire on the field.

"What do you feel like doing, Genny?" she asks, after sending the other girls off to finish their laps. "Do you want to sit on the bench? Or you can go to the dining hall and get a drink of juice. Just check in at the office, please, and tell them I sent you."

She sends Berit with me. We tell Mrs. Folkard in the office that I've been excused from gym and why, and receive the official instructions about sitting in the office so that they can make sure I'm not about to fade away again.

Berit gets me a bottle of juice from the cafeteria and returns to the joys of gym class, leaving me perched on the uncomfortable pew inside the office.

Mrs. Folkard is eyeing me over the screen of her computer.

"The chapel is empty this morning, Genny," she says after a moment. "If you'd rather recover there."

I'm already standing, smiling my thanks, when she adds:

"Just be careful, dear. I'm not sure if you were in there

this morning, but it will be dark. The admissions office did a presentation last night and the curtains are all pulled shut."

"Thank you," I say, both for the warning—I didn't get up with enough time to fit in an early-morning practice today—and for the sudden spurt of joy I feel when picturing myself playing music in a dark room.

A few minutes later, the heavy chapel door clangs shut behind me, and my juice and I navigate the aisle to the piano, just off to the left in the sanctuary.

Sanctuary. Yes, it is that.

I click the light on the music stand and a little cave in the darkness opens up, with just room enough for me and the keyboard.

I start with a few stretches while listening to the silence in the chapel and decide to start with fainting music—scales going down. Then arpeggios falling from treble to bass. I wonder what I looked like, collapsing to the grass. I wonder if anyone who saw me wondered if I was dying.

Dying music. Minor key, slow chords rising—then falling again, down, down on the keyboard.

I take my hands off the keys. Sip my juice. Close my eyes. Put my fingers back on the keys and wait for it to start.

It's what I do when I know no one is listening. When Papa and Père are teaching or rehearsing somewhere else and I have the house to myself. I just let my fingers go into their own place on the keyboard, anywhere they want to go. My eyes are closed, my ears are closed, too, because the music isn't coming from outside. It's coming from somewhere inside—I don't even know where.

But I do know. It comes (today) from fainting. And from the email from my mother. And from Père's missing notes and tired fingers. And from that YouTube video of blood and violence. And from the university applications that we're doing in class this afternoon. It all rises up and spreads itself out on the piano keys.

I keep playing, even when I feel a sudden change in the air. There's a sound at the back of the chapel, the door opening. Still playing, I glance over my shoulder and see that someone is going out, someone is momentarily framed in the doorway.

But I just keep playing. Nathan McCormick carefully holds the door handle to close it gently behind him and leave me in the dark chapel alone.

CHAPTER 13

OVERHEARD IN THE LIBRARY

"So what about the draft?"

A sound, maybe a grunt.

"You going?"

Pause. "Maybe. Have to see what my agent says."

"Sucks, eh? Especially in your draft year." It's Braedon.

A third voice: "You can't play, right?"

Another pause.

"I can work out. I can still skate," says Nathan.

I should be reading *Hamlet*, but that angry Danish boy and his dysfunctional family are not nearly as intriguing as this conversation.

Since watching the YouTube video, I've done some research—easy research, since the story pops up on all the online news outlets.

McCormick suspended for a year after vicious attack on Swedish player

Swedish Hockey Federation asks for lifetime ban for McCormick

Charette to miss rest of season with concussion

McCormick will miss entire season, says Hockey Canada

"Unacceptable," says IIHF president

Hearing for McCormick scheduled for November 28

November is a few weeks away. What hearing?

CHAPTER 14

INTERRUPTIONS

"So? What do you guys want to do?" asks Fredrik.

We are having a group meeting in Thursday's class. Mr. Norton has given us time to plan our media projects. It's a welcome break from *Hamlet*, a sad, scary play that I am cautiously beginning to find interesting.

Fredrik is just being polite for the sake of Nathan. Fredrik knows exactly what we're going to do and he will shortly tell us.

He looks at me, face neutral. Looks at Nathan who is slumped back in his chair, arms crossed.

"Genny? Any ideas?"

Fredrik, the video blogger, is all about film.

"Maybe a film?"

He nods. Pauses. Turns to Nathan. "What do you think?"

Nathan sits up a bit, shrugs. "I'm not much into media stuff, so yeah, a film sounds okay."

"Right. We'll do a film."

We were always going to do a film, are you kidding? YouTube video sensation Fredrik Floren?

And now YouTube video sensation Nathan McCormick.

The air is disturbed by a sound as Mrs. Folkard puts her head around the classroom door and catches Mr. Norton's eye.

"Sorry to interrupt, but Imogen," she says, catching my eye, "could you come to the office, please?"

Everyone looks at me. A trip to the office is usually something to do with bad news, or bad behavior, or bad consequences. The air around me positively throbs with expectation—my classmates', not mine.

I am packing up my computer, moving as slowly as possible to keep the air unruffled. It's not working.

"But, Mr. Norton, we're just getting started," Fredrik protests.

Mr. Norton, of course, ignores him and nods at me in that wordless language that teachers use to give instructions.

Papa and Père are standing in the waiting area just inside the office door, and I quickly look around to see if Alain is somewhere nearby. No. Just we three.

"Get your overnight things, my love," says Papa. I see the car keys dangling from his hand. "We are going to the doctor."

The doctor?

In our post-fainting conversation on Tuesday night, Papa mentions going to the doctor, a check-up, or a follow-up, or something. I had no idea he would actually go ahead with it and I am suddenly filled with horror.

"No, Papa. I don't need a doctor." I am prepared to run back to class if necessary. Naturally, Père reads my mind and is smiling at me, shaking his head slightly in what could be admiration at my effort to put up a fight, however meager.

Papa glances around at Mrs. Folkard and Mrs. Gerrard, at Mr. Colville's office door, where the principal can be seen on a phone call.

"Come, we'll talk out here," says Papa, and I allow myself to be led outside to the parking lot. We stand by his car with a stiff October breeze tossing the falling leaves in all directions.

"I don't need a doctor," I say, as forcefully as I am able. Which, to tell the truth, is not very forcefully.

"But fainting, Imogen. In class."

"We were running. I hate running."

"All the more reason not to faint," says Papa. "Good healthy exercise and there you are, dropping to the ground like a sack of potatoes."

I know Papa is trying to persuade me without showing how worried he is.

But he's worried. I can see that very clearly, and suddenly the wind is biting cold and the falling leaves are swirling around like fingers pointing at me in blame.

"A visit to Dr. Bertrand," says Papa. "Just to check that you aren't coming down with something ..."

"Something like being a teenager who doesn't eat or exercise enough," mutters Père, and when we both look at him, he raises his hands in the air as if to say, *Did I say that out loud?*

They've driven all the way from Montreal to pick me up. Papa must be very worried. Maybe I should be worried, too. I glance at Père and he is watching me.

So I go back to my room to pack a weekend bag and my schoolwork, while Papa looks after signing me out until Monday.

As we pass the edge of town and speed up toward the highway, I text Fredrik (who is the only person, outside of my father, grandfather, and Alain, who has my cell number):

Going home for weekend. Sorry. Film project?

Fredrik will check his phone when he gets out of class and let me know what he and Nathan have worked up for our media project.

No. He'll let me know what he has worked up for our project. I have a feeling Nathan McCormick is not going to be making much of a contribution.

But it's only a few minutes later that I receive his reply:

still undecided. need your input. on hold until monday.

Then a moment later:

think about it ur the soundtrack.

I text back:

It? What is It?

He replies:

not sure yet but prob includes hockey.

Hockey. Nathan McCormick must have had some input after all. That's something to think about all the way home.

CHAPTER 15

SATURDAY REHEARSAL

Clapperton is flying through Montreal on his way back to England from New York, so he arrives at our house for a rehearsal on Saturday afternoon, scarf and attitude in place.

"It's coming," says Papa, after two hours of hard work.

While the three of them discuss a section close to the end that Clapperton is unhappy with, I close my eyes and roll my shoulders and wrists, bend my head, and try to ease some of the tension out of the back of my neck.

The truth is, I've hardly been aware of my muscles and joints or anything other than my fingers on the keys for the past two hours. After Messiaen and the *Quartet*, it's not easy to wake up in the world and feel real again.

"I think if we spend a few more hours on it once you get to London, we should be ready," says Clapperton. He's standing and whisking his hands around, as if flicking away beads of water.

We will play the *Quartet* on December 17. It's not jolly Christmas music, of course. We're playing it at a concert to commemorate veterans, or wars, maybe. Something historical and meaningful. Apparently we'll be meeting members of the Royal Family during our time in London, too, so Père has told me I should practice my curtsy, just in case.

"You've been to London before?"

It takes me a moment to realize that Clapperton is speaking to me. Papa and Père are in the kitchen now, putting the kettle on, pulling out wine glasses to offer our guest a restoring sip of something before the taxi comes to take him to Mirabel.

I nod, still rotating my neck, trying to ease the tension.

"Did you like it?"

I nod again. I wish he'd stop talking to me.

Awkward pause. He's looking at me.

"Have you always only played with those two?" he asks suddenly, in a different voice—a stifled, secret-telling voice.

It's such an odd change, I actually turn to look at him. He's asking something different from what his words are asking, although I'm not sure what, and it's making the air vibrate a little.

I nod. A third time.

And then he shakes his head and, very quietly, so that I can hardly hear him, says: "You could do *so* much better."

"A glass of wine before your car comes, Anthony?" calls Papa from the kitchen.

"Thank you, Maxim, yes," says Clapperton in his normal voice, but he turns back to me briefly.

And, to my horror, winks.

CHAPTER 16

HOCKEY NIGHT IN CANADA

Papa and Père are watching the hockey game and I join them, tucking myself into a corner of the couch and covering myself with the brown-and-beige zigzag afghan, knitted by my grandmother long before I was born. My hands are wrapped around a mug of hot tea.

The sounds from the TV fill the room, making music with the rise and fall of the announcer's voice and the thrumming bass of the crowd.

"Suddenly a hockey fan?" asks Père. He raises his eyebrows. "What took you?"

The Habs are playing Boston. The *bleu, blanc, et rouge* against what looks to me like a swarm of bees—noisy, violent yellow-black bees. Papa is berating the referee for missing penalties. He and Père analyze the action, sip their wine, cheer, and groan. They love this.

I love watching them. Like two excited little boys instead of two famous musicians. (Says Alain in all our promotional material. He's not exaggerating. They *are* famous, and accomplished, and important. Take *that*, Clapperton.)

The Habs score and I nearly spill my tea at the explosion of their cheering.

I'm tired tonight. We all are, I think. The Clappertons of the world do that to you.

I settle back into the cushions again and watch the moving shapes and colors on the TV. Random, undisciplined forms reel and sweep and bounce together, change direction, stop abruptly.

"Four on four," says Papa.

Penalties have been called. Players from each team go to the penalty box and glare at each other, spit, wipe their faces with towels, look both manly and boyish at the same time. (Those helmets ...!)

And now the movement on the ice is completely different. Long ribbons of colors as players swoop against the dazzling white, one end to the other, passing, swirling. There's so much more room now. Space to move. Room to skate without thumping into each other. Flow. Like wind or water.

And just like that, I have a vision of myself flowing like that—swooping across the white ice (no stick, no crazy padding, and, please, no helmet), wind in my hair and eyes and ears. Motion and speed. Freedom.

Dr. Bernard, in our brief and unproductive consultation on Friday, didn't find any signs of illness. I'm perfectly well.

"You could probably eat a bit better," she says. "And you need to play more, Imogen," she adds. "And by that, I don't mean piano."

She threatens me with supplements and blood tests until I agree: I will eat more, and I will find something to do for exercise.

"Try yoga," she suggests. "Lovely apparel."

Tight pants and T-shirts. Bare feet. Maybe not.

Now, safely tucked up on the couch with tea and Grandmère Geneviève's afghan, I imagine something that I could do. Something with movement and motion. There is a problem, however.

Dr. Bernard might approve but Papa will not.

Still ... when I get back to school ...

I could maybe learn to skate.

CHAPTER 17

AFTERNOON OF A SLEEPING GRANDFATHER

I'm standing at our front window, watching the leaves drift down and waiting for Papa to get off the phone with Alain. I can hear long pauses in the conversation, then Papa making sounds of agreement. They are reviewing the itinerary for the English tour. Business.

Outside our window, the scene has turned from bright autumn midday to fading afternoon. The color is draining from the streets, the brick façades of our neighbors' houses, the grass. Only the trees still cling to a few blots of red and yellow.

Autumn isn't my favorite season. Other people think the chill in the air and the transformation of the leaves are the highlights of the year. No, no, no. It's as if the trees know the extreme self-indulgence that was summer is nearly over, so they throw one last party to ward off the long, cold, inevitable winter. Of course it never works.

Soon Papa will drive me back to school. He and I enjoy this Sunday night routine. We'll stop for supper at the diner perched on the side of the 417 at the Brick Hill exit. It's hardly Chez Viau, but it is a favorite of ours, and a ritual transition from our life together at home to my exile at school.

I would like to play the piano while I wait but, behind me, Père is sleeping in his chair. One moment we were talking about the tour, and the next, the rhythmic sigh of his sleeping breath. A repeated measure, in and out, up and down. "Les Barricades Mystérieuses" starts looping in my head.

I turn away from the window and watch him, my grandfather, with his thick silver hair brushed back from his high forehead. Bony brow and nose, the cheekbones jutting out over slightly sleep-sunken cheeks. He sleeps neatly, with his mouth closed. Smiling a little. Dreaming maybe.

As I watch, there's a pause—a moment when no air is going in or out. He's suspended in sleep.

"Breathe," I whisper, and wait. What if he doesn't?

Is his chest rising? No.

"Breathe, Père," I whisper again.

I will ask him to come with us on the trip back to school, to join us for supper at the diner. To talk about the English tour, and the *Quartet*, and Alain's plans for us. And other things, too, like Papa's invitation to fill in for the cellist with a string quartet in Ottawa who is going on maternity leave. And my university applications. So much to talk about. He should be there.

He makes a snuffling sound, twitches a little but doesn't wake.

His hands are folded on his stomach, long fingers laced together. The fingers that are losing the notes, he says. His tired fingers.

I hate Sundays.

CHAPTER 18

SKATING LESSONS

I've only been in the arena once. Okay, maybe twice. It was during the fiddle and step-dance competition, Labor Day Weekend, during my first year at Hillside. Instead of ice, the surface of the rink was checkered with tables, and people drinking beer supplied by the local micro-brewery, and people dancing. Dancing loudly to superbly rhythmic violins. Fiddles.

A long time ago, when my mother was still with us, we had a neighbor with a fiddle. M. Duval. He's from the Gaspésie, and his playing is nothing like Père's playing, but I love it, so compelling and urgent. So percussive, with his feet clicking and stuttering in a rhythm as precise as a team of ticking clocks.

Père likes it, too, and he visits M. Duval, sometimes bringing me along. They get out their violins and M. Duval, with his missing teeth and a cigarette burning to ash in a random china saucer he uses as his ashtray, pounds out tunes on his beat-up fiddle, tunes that Père (to my astonishment) can play by ear.

"What's the difference between your violin and M. Duval's fiddle?" I ask him one evening, on our way home from one of these visits.

"M. Duval plays 'Pays de Haut' the way I play my Brahms concerto." Père says. "That's what you should do, too. Whether it's in a concert hall or on the back step of a little house in Montreal, it doesn't matter. Just play your music, little Imogen. And be happy doing it."

There's ice in the Brick Hill Memorial Arena now—I can smell it as I cross the cement floor to the one wide window that overlooks the ice surface. If I push on one of the pairs of heavy doors on either side of the window, I'll be shivering in the walkway around the boards. So I stay where I am.

But on one of the doors, I see what I'm looking for: a noisy poster that announces: *CanSkate begins October 22! Register now!*

CanSkate.

"Can I help you?" A man's voice, and I turn around quickly.

Faced with a real person, and with the actual prospect of having to explain myself, my thoughts collide and splinter. So I point at the poster.

"I was wondering ..."

"Oh, the skating lessons? CanSkate?" The man, in his fleece jacket and work boots and Ottawa Senators baseball cap, smiles, nods. "For you?" I nod. "Well, there's an adult class on Saturday morning, early."

He waits, expecting me to respond. I'm thinking that Saturday is not good, since I'm often at home, rehearsing.

"Or the kids' classes are on Tuesday and Thursday afternoon." He pauses. "You're from the school, aren't you?"

I nod. Clever man.

"Thought so. I know most of the kids who grew up around here," he says. He's very chatty and friendly, and I start to relax a little. Still, I wish I'd brought Fredrik with me.

"I want to learn to skate," I say, and hope I don't sound on the outside like the infant I sound like to myself on the inside.

"Oh, okay, so you're looking for the adult class, then," he says and nods.

"Actually, I think I'd rather be in a kids' class." And as soon as I say it, I realize how true that is.

The man is surprised, but he waves me toward the office.

"Well, let me get you signed up, then. You're an absolute beginner, are you?"

My mother didn't mind the tennis experiment, but skating is beyond her tolerance.

"Learning to skate is a rite of passage for children in Québec." Papa tries to convince her. "The little rink in the park down the road ..."

"And who will be the one who has to stand there in the cold, watching?" my mother says.

"Well, I will, of course," says Papa.

"And if she falls? And breaks a finger? Or a wrist?" My mother's voice is turning on its edge, getting thin and sharp, starting to bite a little.

"She will hurt for a while and then she will heal," says Papa.

My mother sniffs, turns away, walks from the room, leaving something vibrating in the air. The skating question is all about the music. The piano. My little fingers on the keyboard. I know what it is.

Already my mother can hear that there's something in my fingers that she doesn't have and will never have. Trio St. Pierre is already changing and I'm barely five years old.

If you want Imogen's fingers instead of mine, then you had better look after them (she says without speaking; I have excellent hearing).

So, no skating for little Imogen.

Until now.

The man gives me a registration form and a pen, and I sit in his little office and fill in the spaces with the information. Name, age, address. There's a permission section, which stumps me for a moment, but then I realize I'm old enough to give myself permission. I don't need Papa to sign the form. The freedom I feel is almost overwhelming, and I lift the pen off the paper and look around the office for a moment.

"Okay?" asks the man, looking up from his computer. He's waiting for me to finish.

"Yes, fine." I look down at the form and finish filling it out. Hand it to him. Wait for instructions.

"Okay, you've signed up for beginner skating, so that's CanSkate Level One. That's Tuesday afternoons." He pauses, looking at my form, thinking. "Actually, I think Polly—you know Polly, probably? Polly de Cormier? She's the instructor."

No.

But it's too late.

"Oh," I say.

"And you probably know Nathan, too," the man is saying, nodding at me, smiling. "Nathan McCormick? You know, the hockey player? He's teaching the pre-level at the same time."

Nathan. Polly. And me.

"He has to do it for his community service or something," the man is saying. "You know, because of the thing that happened at the World Juniors last year."

I just smile slightly, look at my form, look at him, look down. Oh, yes, I know all about the thing that happened at the World Juniors. *Blood on the ice. The sound of a fist connecting with that other player's head.*

"Yes."

"Well, Polly's good with the kids and, since you know her, you'll have some fun out there." He's saying this in a hearty, friendly, encouraging way, and I don't know how to tell him that learning to skate from Instructor Polly probably wouldn't be my first choice.

But never mind. I'm going to learn to skate. Yes, I am. I pull out my debit card and we seal the deal, and, before I know it, I'm crossing the Brick Hill Memorial Arena parking lot toward Main Street and the twenty-minute walk back to Hillside Academy.

Am I thinking about fun, fun, fun with Polly de Cormier? Or stepping out (and probably falling) on the same ice as Nathan McCormick?

No. I'm thinking: I'm going to need some skates.

Oh, yes—and something to protect my hands.

CHAPTER 19

HOCKEY EQUIPMENT

I find Nathan McCormick in the library on Wednesday afternoon during a spare. He's bent over his history textbook, reading and making notes.

When I pull out the chair beside him, he looks up, and I can see he's still inside History somewhere, doesn't register that I'm there. Then the History fog clears and he sees me.

A beat.

"I wonder if you can help me," I say in my library voice.

I've rehearsed this speech the way I would rehearse anything. In pieces, slowly, then putting it all together so it flows together smoothly. But of course it comes out in a rush.

"Sure." He looks around to see if anyone else is listening to us.

Not sure about listening, but there are many sets of eyes rotating like lighthouse lanterns all over the library. I ignore. This is something I'm good at. Focus on Nathan McCormick and try not to see that face from YouTube.

(Which is easy, actually, because this face is pale with a little dark stubble along the jaw line, and dry, not red and sweaty and gargoyled in fight mode.)

He's waiting. So I ask about hockey gloves, and fingers, and falling on the ice.

He squints a little as he processes my question.

"Well, I guess hockey gloves could probably protect you from breaking a finger if you fall," he says, quietly, also in library voice, and also as if he doesn't want anyone else to hear. He's frowning a little and looking off into space at some imaginary glove-encased finger. Clearly he's never thought about this before. "Nothing will protect you if you go down hard, or suddenly, the wrong way. Or get hit with a puck. Or a stick. But, yeah, I think hockey gloves protect the fingers, generally."

I nod. That's exactly what I wanted to hear. I start to rise.

"Why?" And now he's looking at me, perplexed. Trying to figure it out.

"I'm taking skating lessons at the arena," I say and wait. He's still looking at me. He's waiting for an explanation, and I'm waiting for him to laugh. He doesn't.

"I can't hurt my hands, so I thought maybe hockey gloves." I shrug.

Lightbulb moment. *You're a musician, right?* He nods.

"Yes, then. Gloves might be a good idea."

"Thank you." I rise and go, and I know he's probably looking at me walking away and thinking: *Well. That was weird.*

CHAPTER 20

SHOPPING TRIP

Once a month on Wednesday afternoon, there's early dismissal and the Hillside Academy bus is organized to go to one of the Ottawa malls—Orleans, Rideau, St. Laurent. Today the bus is heading to St. Laurent and I'm on it.

Victoria, Polly, and Melanie are sitting near the back with Braedon and the rugby boys. Nathan is back there, too, but when I glance quickly, I see that he's staring out the window with his ear buds in.

I'm near the front. Berit and William are across the aisle, one row up from me, talking quietly to each other. Berit smiles over at me. I know I'm welcome to join them, but I just smile in reply, turn my eyes to the window, plug in my earbuds, and stay where I am.

Lots to think about. Conversation with others not required.

First, the *Quartet* has taken over most of the space in my audible brain, thanks to hours of intense rehearsal with Papa and Père over Thanksgiving weekend. Even without Clapperton's clarinet, we are waking some dark, dormant thing inside the pit of Messiaen's score, but it's so hard to climb back out. Here it is Wednesday and I'm still haunted, still hearing it.

We've left Brick Hill behind, and the bush that lines the side of the 417 flashes by. Green and the colors of autumn emphasized on this bright October day. Soon it will be all white, gray, messy with snow and ice.

I watch the farms and trees and fields speed by and think about skates and hockey gloves. When we get to the mall, I will go to the sports store and buy them. Just like that.

Papa and Père are speechless when I tell them over Sunday's turkey dinner that I have signed up to take skating lessons.

Papa actually puts down his knife and fork, leans back, furrows in his forehead.

"But, Imogen, is that a good choice?" he asks.

Père reaches for his wine glass, takes a sip, watches me with that unreadable smile of his.

"Yes," I say. "It looks like fun." (A kindergarten reply if I ever heard one.)

"But ..." Papa pauses. I wonder if he is remembering that conversation with my mother all those years ago. "If you fall. Accidents can happen on ice. And we have the concert tour."

"It's okay, Papa. Just a beginner class," I say. "I just want to try."

I don't tell him it was watching his Habs floating and flying across the white ice that propelled me toward this idea of skating.

"And I will wear gloves," I add.

"Gloves?" Papa is confounded. "You think *gloves* are going to help?"

"Hockey gloves," I say and decide to lay it out. "I asked one of the boys at school, a hockey player, and he says gloves are good protection."

Papa and Père. Speechless. Either because of the idea of hockey gloves protecting my hands, or the idea that Imogen spoke to a boy. A *hockey-playing* boy.

"But what does this hockey player know about protecting a musician's hands?" Papa asks, finally.

"He knows I'm a pianist," I say. *The dark chapel, the momentary silhouette. Was he there the whole time I was playing?* "So he gave me this advice. Hockey gloves."

"Imogen, my love," Père says, takes a sip, smiles broadly. "How lovely. Skating."

After that, they start discussing skates. Hockey skates or figure skates? Two pairs of warm socks or one? A helmet? Yes, of course a helmet. I draw the line at a mouth guard.

"No one will be using a hockey stick," I tell them. "It will just be me and a bunch of little kids in a beginner class. And the teacher is a girl from my class."

I add that last part because it will make them think I will have a friend there, looking after me. They don't know Polly de

Cormier, and it's so far from the truth I can't even explain, but I say it all the same and they both nod in approval.

"Dr. Bernard said I should get more exercise," I say. That's the kicker, the *coup de grâce*, the big final crash on the bass notes.

There's nothing Papa can say to that except to pat my hand and tell me to be careful. To have fun.

I'm twitching now. The idea of walking through the mall to the sports store and finding someone to help me buy skates and gloves and, I suppose, a helmet is suddenly as daunting as stepping out onto the National Arts Centre stage by myself, without Papa and Père.

And we're there. The bus lets us out at one of the entrances, and I hang back a little so Berit and William will go ahead without me. Victoria and her posse emerge from the back of the bus and, momentarily, I'm in their midst, although they don't know it, swimming around and past me as if I'm the toad on the lily pad and they're the sleek trout. Silver, beautiful trout, of course. I stay with them until we're through the doors and into the mall and then I dart out, off current, an escapee, free to swim away. To find some skates.

I've been in this store before, once or twice in late summer, getting ready for school and needing running shoes for gym class, and shorts (from the boys' department, long, loose basketball shorts that need safety pins in the waistband to stay up around my skinny middle). I find the hockey department and stand in front of the skates that sit on the display shelves in orderly fashion.

Orderly is not exactly what I'm feeling right now. Where to start? I think about the skates, my skates, me skating, and picture the white ice, and the long lines of color and motion during that Habs-versus-Bruins four-on-four. All drawn together near the boards, then bursting apart and flowing in the other direction. That will be me, flowing.

Well, maybe not. But I want to feel it. And maybe I will, after ten or more years of CanSkate Level One.

"Are you okay?" A boy's voice.

I open my eyes and there's a salesperson—a boy not much older than me, probably—standing beside me (with a speech bubble over his head that says: *Weird.*) He wears a nametag that says his name is James.

"Skates," I say. "I'm taking skating lessons."

James nods, back in his comfort zone now that we're speaking his language and his commission is assured.

And we're off. Hockey skates or figure skates? What size am I? Have I ever had skates before?

"Hockey skates," says a voice behind me.

James looks past me, blinks. I see on his face the exact moment when he recognizes Nathan McCormick.

"Oh, okay then." James is fumbling a little now as he reaches for one of the skates, lifts it off the shelf.

Bauer Supreme, it says on the side. It looks like something a knight would wear, like a weapon. I might be having second thoughts.

"What size are you?" James asks, so I tell him my shoe size.

Nathan has stepped forward now and he's pointing at another skate, another shelf.

"Try this in 5½," he says. "Maybe bring a 6, too."

"Sure, okay. Right," James nods as if he's had some input into the decision and marches off to the back room.

I look up at Nathan. He's wearing his Senators ball cap over his thick brown hair, a gray hoodie (hands stuffed in pockets), and jeans. He looks like every other boy wandering around St. Laurent.

"Hope you don't mind." He shrugs and I shake my head and look away, then back at him. "I thought maybe you could use the help."

He smiles. I smile. This means he has followed me here. Separated himself from the beautiful trout and swum here instead of flowing off to Starbucks or wherever.

I look away. It's hard not to see the face from YouTube when I look at him.

"Are you shopping for anything?" I ask him. Stupid question.

"No, not really. Just came along for the ride, I guess. Get out of the school."

James is coming back with big boxes and heads toward a bench, sets them down and opens one.

"Here," says Nathan. He takes the other, lifts the lid and picks up a skate, sits on the bench and nods me over. He's undoing the knotted laces and is starting to fit them through the holes. "Take your shoes off and try these."

James is trying to be helpful, too. He's working the laces of the other pair and glancing at Nathan. Clearly he's dying to start a conversation.

Which is perfect, because it means neither boy is watching me slip off my leather boots and sit, sock feet exposed, quivering a little.

Nathan is done first, which, I suppose, isn't surprising. He's probably dealt with the laces on many, many skates. He hands me one skate with a "Try it on" nod.

It's unfamiliar and awkward. I get my foot into it and reach for the laces but James is there.

"Here, let me help."

So I sit and watch as he draws the laces together, tightening expertly as he goes. Nathan hands us the other skate and starts working on the other pair, but I see James glance over at him. Any minute, there will be a break in the long series of full-measure rests.

"How does that feel?" James asks after both skates are laced up.

I don't know how it feels. Yes, I do. It feels comfortable. And weird.

"Here." Nathan puts down the skate he's working on, stands up, and reaches out to take my arm. Pauses with his hand out toward me. "You'll be able to feel the fit better if you stand up."

"Okay." I push myself off the bench and feel his hand under my elbow to steady me.

I'm taller now. My feet and ankles wobble just a little. Good thing Nathan is here or I'd be over like a downed tree.

Moment of terrible awareness: how am I ever going to stand alone in these skates on ice?

CHAPTER 21

FOOD COURT

The box with the skates has its own little handle, so it's easy to carry. I also have a bag for the helmet and gloves. As I put my debit card away, and before I can reach for them, Nathan lifts both box and bag off the counter and turns toward the exit. My helper.

The helmet and gloves weren't as easy as the skates.

"Looks like you need a kid's size," James says.

I put it on and picture myself in the penalty box.

"Can I just ...?" Nathan asks me and I nod. He puts his hand on the top of my head—well, technically, my helmet—and pushes down, moves it around. My neck is immediately compressed and I shrink, but the helmet slips a bit. "Probably need a smaller size."

I try on three before he's satisfied the padding will hold the molded plastic armor in place around my fragile skull. Then we move on to the gloves.

James isn't sure about the gloves, though, and I can tell

Nathan isn't either. They actually have a conversation at this point. James is in heaven. He's going to get off work later and tell all his friends he was discussing the safety implications of hockey gloves with Nathan McCormick.

"I need the gloves or my father won't let me skate," I say finally, which draws twin expressions of doubt. I shrug.

"She's a musician," Nathan says to James, who nods as if he understands how being a musician and wearing hockey gloves in a CanSkate Level One class are related. So he's willing to buy in. If Nathan McCormick says it, it must be true.

Later, at the food court, I join Berit and William, who can't hide their astonishment when I appear with my Bauer Supreme box and big shopping bag. And, very briefly and in the distance, Nathan.

"Wow," says Berit after I drop my stuff on the floor under the table. "You and Nathan McCormick. Shopping together."

"For sports equipment," says William.

"I'm going to learn to skate," I explain, turning away to find a cup of tea. Desperately needed tea.

It was a bit of a walk from the sports store to the food court. Nathan carries my Bauer Supreme box and awkward big bag (awkward for me, nothing for him. I expect he's used to carrying one of those big hockey bags.) We don't talk much. He says I'm ready for my skating lessons now. I say yes, and thanks for his help.

Three boys are walking toward us. Slouching. Sauntering. Ball caps and baggy jeans and oversized hoodies. They see us. I think for a moment they're going to stop and talk to us, but I feel the tempo change and Nathan keeps walking, so they pass by. And as they pass, they nod at Nathan and one boy says something in French—not the French that we speak at home. The French of the street, the coarse language of boys—and Nathan replies. We keep walking.

I'm still inside this conversation as I stand in line at Tim's, waiting to order my tea.

Into private school girls now, eh Nate? Moving up in the world. Guess it pays to beat the shit out of Swedish goons.

Fuck off.

And just as we get to the food court, he hands me the box and bag and turns away.

"Sorry about that," he says, and is gone.

CHAPTER 22

GUY WITH A CAMERA

We're standing with Mrs. Callandar, in little groups and pairings, waiting for the Hillside bus to arrive.

It's dark now and I'm tired. The excitement of my skate-buying adventure has worn off and all I want to do is retreat to a single seat on the bus, plug in my ear buds, listen to Angela Hewitt playing Bach, and stare out the window for the fifty-minute drive back to school.

I keep seeing those rough boys in my mind. Hearing their rude words. Nathan's reply.

He's by himself, leaning on the wall behind us all, apart from us all. Listening to music with his head tipped down so that the brim of his ball cap hides his face. Everything about him shouts, "Go away."

Go away.

When I was nine, we performed in Toronto at Roy Thomson

Hall. It was my first Toronto concert, and the newspapers and media were churning in anticipation. I don't know this, but Papa and Père do. They're worried for me, that I'll find the attention overwhelming, that it will affect my playing, scare me, tire me out, suck the air out of the room, and leave me suffocating.

Alain has arranged a media event and it's the most frightening thing I've ever done. The lights flashing and people like robots—half-human, half-camera—standing a few feet away and aiming at me. Shooting. That's the word and it's the right one. Shooting me.

"Imogen! Miss St. Pierre! Genny, can you look this way for moment, please?"

Who are these people? Papa is on one side with his arm around my shoulders. Père holds my hand.

Go away, I'm saying in my head. Not shouting. More like a whimper.

"What's it like being a professional musician at such a young age?" someone asks me.

Père squeezes my hand and leans down to whisper.

"Would you like us to answer the questions?"

Yes, I nod. Looking down. The media people keep asking, but Papa and Père—and Alain, too—do all the talking. As long as I am looking down, I'm invisible and unavailable.

That's Nathan McCormick right now.

Victoria, Polly, and Melanie are getting impatient and ask about the bus, but Ms. Callandar just shrugs and checks her phone again. Delayed, on its way, whatever. We wait.

"Did you buy skates, Genny?" Victoria asks, nodding at my purchases. I sense a stir behind me.

"I'm taking skating lessons."

"Oh! At the arena?" asks Polly, all interested and fairly loud. That draws some attention. I glance back at Nathan and he looks up briefly.

And at that moment, a father and son walk by, into our group, right by Nathan, on the way to the parking lot. The father sees him, recognizes him—I know the signs: the pause, followed by a straightening to attention as the realization sinks in. *Hey! I know you!*

Nathan quickly ducks his head but it's too late.

"Hey, excuse me." The man stops, still holding his son's hand. "You're Nathan McCormick, aren't you? Ottawa 67s?"

I'm holding my breath. Why?

Everyone has stopped talking and watches as Nathan stands up from his slouch, looks at the man, nods, takes the ear buds out.

Waits.

"My son is a huge fan of yours," says the man, reaching into his jacket pocket for his phone. "Could I take your picture with Marcus here?"

The little boy trembles with excitement, standing on one foot then the other, looking up at Nathan and his dad. He's wearing a Sens ball cap.

"Sure," says Nathan.

He looks down at the boy, puts out his arm, and motions him to come stand in close next to him. Two hockey boys, a big one and a small one. Both in their Senators gear.

"That is so adorable," Victoria whispers to Polly, next to me.

"Adorable," Polly breathes.

Nathan tips his cap back a bit so his face shows more. We're all watching as if it's a public performance. Nathan doesn't seem to notice. He's done this before, I can tell.

"Okay, Marcus, ready?" says the dad to the boy, who looks at the phone camera and smiles hugely.

Nathan smiles, too, his arm around the boy's shoulder, leaning in a little bit, and for a moment the two hockey boys are frozen there. A flash, another, and the scene unfreezes. Nathan stands up to his full height again, adjusts his cap, looks down at the boy.

"What team do you play for, Marcus?" he asks.

"Gloucester Rangers," says Marcus. "Novice."

"You a forward?"

"Defense." The boy looks as if he's going to faint.

"Me, too," says Nathan, smiles again.

"We're fans," says the dad and reaches out to shake Nathan's hand. "We wish you the best, son," he says.

"Thanks very much." But he says it so quietly that I have to read his lips to be sure. The dad and Marcus are moving on.

Nathan slouches back against the wall, Sens cap pulled down, ear buds in. *Go away*.

The bus comes shortly after.

CHAPTER 23

MEDIA PROJECT

"So I'm thinking we'll film Nathan skating with a soundtrack of you playing something freewheeling and action-packed on the piano," says Fredrik.

We're in English class on Friday afternoon, and Mr. Norton has given us a free period to plan our media project. We're in the back corner near the window and, while I listen to Fredrik elaborate on his vision for our movie, I'm watching leaves drift down to join the brown and yellow carpet spreading across the expanse of grass that leads down to the pond. The October sky is fiercely blue, but the air is moving, just the tiniest shifting of currents. Every now and then a diamond leaps off the pond and immediately disappears.

"No hockey gear. Nothing that says hockey," Fredrik continues. "Just skating. Maybe all in black. Or whatever Nathan wants, doesn't matter."

I look away from the window and consider Fredrik for a moment. His Viking blonde hair is spiky and tousled, as always. His beard never seems to grow or change. I've known him for four years now—he was one of the first people I met at Hillside when I arrived in Grade 9.

("Hey, pleased to meet you. Love your playing. Here, I'll introduce you around." Like a guardian. I wondered if maybe it was arranged between Papa and Mr. Colville, but when I asked Fredrik, he scoffed. "Never. I heard you were coming and wanted to be the first to greet you." Fredrik. My hero. My friend.)

Now his eyes are closed and he's using his hands, as if to frame the images he sees taking shape on Planet Fredrik: the skating boy, all in black.

"Have you asked Nathan about this?" I say, and he opens his eyes and looks at me. Comes back to Earth.

"Yes, briefly," he says. "Briefly on that first day, when you had to leave. I said we needed to make a film about something we knew about, and he said, all I know is hockey."

"But you don't want to do hockey?"

"No," says Fredrik. "Nathan and hockey. Everybody knows about that, don't they? We want to tell a new story."

How I love Fredrik. He and I speak the same language, and what I hear him saying is: *Everyone knows Nathan McCormick is an amazing hockey player who beat the crap out of that guy. But we know Nathan McCormick is a lot more than just that.*

I nod.

"This is going to be a film that starts with movement and music," says Fredrik. "And how beautiful that can be. Nathan skates. You play the piano. I create the film." He grins at me then. "And it's going to be something special. Top marks. We'll nail it."

We are able to have this conversation—talking about Nathan as if he's not here—because, in fact, he's not here.

"That big SUV in the parking lot this morning? Guy from Hockey Canada," Victoria tells everyone at lunch. Actually, she's just talking to her posse and some of the rugby boys, but she only has one volume (*mezzo-forte*) so we all hear. Which is her intention, of course.

"He had his stuff with him," she continues. "Obviously gone for the weekend."

"How do you know the guy was from Hockey Canada?" Braedon asks.

"Crest on his jacket. He was talking to Mr. Colville just inside the office and I had to see Mrs. Folkard about something," says Victoria.

Something imaginary, of course. She was on a mission. Spying.

"So what's up? Something about the hearing?" asks one of the boys.

The hearing. In November.

"Don't know. The guy just said he needed him for the weekend. He gave a letter or something to Mr. Colville." Victoria is running out of information to feed us. There's much nodding.

"Probably meeting a lawyer," says Jeff.

"Or his agent."

"Maybe it's about the draft. He told me they were working out the details on that," says Braedon, and the boys nod as if Nathan has told them everything happening in his hockey life.

I'm alone at my table by the window, sipping soup and listening to the discussion, but my eyes are on my computer. My email, to be exact.

Hi Genny,

Quite a familiar opening for someone I've met only twice.

Further to our little discussion at the last rehearsal ...

That was no discussion. It was something, but it wasn't a discussion.

Just wondering if you've given any thought to what you're doing next year. I know this is your last year of high school.

The reason I ask is that I'm in the early stages of creating a new ensemble of exciting young musicians, some from the Ottawa–Montreal area, next year and I think you'd be a perfect fit. It would give you some new musical opportunities, too, which is always a good thing.

Looking forward to chatting about it when you get to London in December.

Cheers,

Tony

Clapperton. I wonder how he got my email. Alain, probably.

Another three leaves drift through the air and Fredrik is now writing notes in a red Moleskine hardcover journal. Other groups are planning and laughing. Or maybe just talking and laughing, it's hard to say. Mr. Norton circulates and, when he comes close, everyone sits up a bit and looks focused and industrious. So far he hasn't checked in with us but then he knows, as everyone knows, that Fredrik lives for this stuff, and that I will just do whatever I'm asked to do as long as it involves my piano.

"Nathan has to agree, though." I turn to Fredrik and he stops writing. Looks at me with his kind and clever eyes.

"Of course," he says. "And I think he will. We'll make sure he enjoys it, too. We all will." Nods at me in affirmation. Smiles, then turns back to his writing. "And your job, Happy Music Girl, is to start thinking about the soundtrack. The perfect soundtrack to accompany Happy Skating Boy."

I turn back to the falling leaves and push Clapperton out of my head, thinking: *Couperin? Bach? Ravel? Shostakovich?*

What will make me happy?

CHAPTER 24

CONCERT

We have a performance on Saturday night and it happens again.

We're in Redpath Hall at McGill, on stage with the huge organ looming over us. Of course, I don't see the organ, or anything other than Papa and Père and Ravel's notes forming and filling the air.

But a sliver of something slices through, opens a wound in the smooth surface of our playing.

Père stops and rests his instrument on his knee as if he's waiting for his entry, smiles calmly and nods at Papa, who keeps going, who nods at me, and I keep playing, too.

And then Père raises his violin and joins us. The wound closes and we are whole again.

At the reception afterward, Père sips wine and waves off questions.

"A momentary lapse," he says and shrugs. He looks unconcerned, chatting with students and other members of the small audience, who have come to hear us as part of a concert series organized by the university.

I stand with Papa, a glass of red wine in my hand, although I've yet to take a sip. Music students come up to chat and I listen and watch them, imagining myself in their place. It could happen next year if I stay at home and go to McGill. Many of them are my age, accomplished and well-trained, looking forward to a career in performance—or teaching, or composing, or writing film scores.

They eye me, the daughter. The pianist. The prodigy. The weird girl.

Papa tries to include me in the conversation but I have nothing to say, and besides, they are all about sucking up to Dr. St. Pierre, their professor and mentor, the man with the connections. The man who evaluates and assigns grades and can produce a free ticket to an orchestra audition or career opportunity or agent.

Enough. I feel my post-concert crash approaching so I excuse myself, wander away, and pretend to examine the food spread out on one of the tables, while trying not to think about Père. Impossible, of course.

"Imogen, isn't it?"

A youngish man has joined me, looking at me with that slightly leaning posture that says: "You don't know me but, too bad, I'm going to talk to you anyway."

Père's and Alain's training kicks in.

"Imogen St. Pierre," and I put out my hand for the inevitable wet-fish musician handshake. (Has to be a musician. Upper year student, most likely.) I'm not disappointed.

"Hi, I'm Richard Bezic, a friend of Tony Clapperton's," he says. "I'm in fourth year here. Oboe."

Bells ring. Richard could be Clapperton's blond twin. Same height, hair, and forced air of confidence, as if he thinks he's a GQ cover model. (I'm being mean to Monsieur Bezic. He's a nice-looking guy, if a bit thin and colorless.)

I'm not sure how I'm supposed to respond. If Richard Bezic is expecting enthusiastic acknowledgement of my bond with Anthony Clapperton, he doesn't let his disappointment show.

"Yeah, so Tony said he spoke to you about L'Avenir," he says, waits for my reaction. Gets nothing. Plods on. "The ensemble he and I are putting together? Mostly McGill grads but some big names on the emerging classical music scene, too." (He sounds just like Alain for a moment.)

He names two or three musicians. Yes, I've heard of them, so I nod.

"He thought you might be interested." Give Richard Bezic some credit here. I'm not giving him much to go on. In fact, I'm giving him nothing, because my thoughts are swirling around the image of Père sitting there on stage with his violin silent on his knee. "So, I just thought I'd connect. What do you think?"

What I think, M. Bezic, is that my grandfather is losing something, and if he loses that something, then I will lose something, too. And down we go.

And then what?

Richard Bezic is waiting. I imagine a speech bubble over his head that says: *What the hell were you thinking, Clapperton?*

"Well, I'm not sure what my plans are for next year," I hear myself saying. It sounds halfway intelligent and actually relevant, too. "I may be at UBC."

Richard Bezic jumps in right away.

"No reason why you can't be studying at the same time," he says, nodding enthusiastically, now that I've actually given him something to work with. "We'd have a very small concert schedule to start with, so most of us would be doing other gigs or studying as well."

I don't say anything because it sounds like an impossible arrangement to me. Me, out there in Vancouver, the other musicians in Montreal. I mean, really. How is that going to work?

Richard Bezic appears to be able to read speech bubbles, too, because he's all over it.

"You would have the score and some of the rehearsal recordings, too," he says. "We have the technology, right? You can prepare, using the recordings, and then when you come in for performances, we'll have a chance to fine-tune in rehearsal."

I'm looking at him, thinking: *Really? You really think that's how an ensemble works? It's just about playing the right notes at the right time?*

Because it's not. An ensemble is a creature, a living thing, with each part dependent on the others—skin, sinew, breath, blood. All bound together to create the body, the music.

Like Papa and Père and me.

I look away and try to take a sip, but my hand trembles and the wine spills a bit. Fortunately, drops of red wine don't really show on a black dress.

Richard Bezic doesn't notice, or pretends not to, gives me a card with his email and phone number, and tells me to please think about it because L'Avenir would love to have me at the piano. Then he excuses himself.

Deep breath, Imogen.

I turn and face the room again. Père is watching me, smiling a little, and beckons me over with a wink.

"A new boyfriend?" he murmurs when I reach his side.

"No, not a chance."

"Excellent oboist, Monsieur Bezic." He takes a sip of his wine. "A friend of Tony Clapperton's, I believe."

I turn to look at him, my grandfather, with his innocent smile.

"Yes, apparently."

"Ah, yes. Well. Always good to keep up connections," he says, giving me a quick, gentle hug. "You never know."

"Oh, Mon Dieu," he whispers then, out of the side of his

mouth. “Imogen, my love, please stay close by. Here comes one of the university’s patronesses and I simply can’t face her alone. I suspect she has marriage on her mind.” Then more loudly: “Bonjour, Madame Boucher, how lovely that you could make it out to our concert. Have you met my granddaughter, Imogen?”

“Félix!” gushes Madame Boucher, diamonds glittering on outstretched hands, silk scarves trailing like streamers.

And we’re off.

Later, alone in my room, I find Richard Bezic’s card and drop it in the garbage. After a minute I retrieve it and put it in my desk drawer. I’m not sure why.

CHAPTER 25

SKATING LESSON

"So, everyone stand in place and just squiggle your blades side to side on the ice, like a windshield wiper on a car," Polly says in her chirpy kindergarten-teacher voice, watching as eight small children and I attempt to stay upright while following her example.

I'm astonished that I'm still standing. Fifteen minutes into the class and I haven't fallen yet, although there have been a few close calls, including my first step onto the ice after our warm-up and safety talk. I pause in the entrance with both hockey-gloved hands on the boards and have to take a few deep breaths. Off balance, leaning forward a bit, I push off gently and glide.

My ankles stay firm. (Thank you to a nice mom who helps me lace up my skates: "Here, let me help," she says after watching me try it twice on my own. "These need to be tight or your ankles will cave. There. How does that feel?")

"Good!" squeals Polly, giving us the thumbs-up. Nobody has

fallen during the exercise, which is a victory. "Can you do it with both skates, Abigail?"

Abigail, an anxious child who walks across the ice with her arms extended wide, seems to think she's going down any minute and wants to be sure her hands will take the brunt of it, not her freckled pale face behind the full cage of her helmet. She's fallen several times and I have a feeling the next tumble will bring the tears. Even now I see her lips trembling, eyes fixed on the toes of her new white skates. Her mother is sitting in the seats where the heater is, with a couple of other moms, all wrapped in down jackets, all clutching their large coffees from the café on Main Street.

No one is here to watch me, thank goodness.

"Are you a hockey player?" Abigail asks as we clomp into formation along the boards before stepping onto the ice. The kids are eyeing my Bauer Supremes and hockey gloves. Most of them have white figure skates with toe picks.

"Oh, you guys!" laughs Polly. "Genny's learning to skate just like you!"

Polly uses a cloying primary-school voice that would irritate me if I weren't so focused on staying upright and keeping my weight evenly distributed and my knees soft. At the first step from terra firma onto the ice, I feel the change—right up through my feet and legs and spine.

Ice. It sounds different. It has a smell. It feels *hard.* Using my safely gloved hands, I push myself away from the boards and glide briefly, just enough to hear the slight rumble under my skate blades. My momentum fades out and I come to a stop. Push off with one blade, teeter a little, and then glide again.

Awesome.

Polly makes it look easy, of course, in her tight black leggings and fitted teal jacket, with her long dark hair tied back in a ponytail. She darts in and out of our group, showing us what to do, picking up the fallen, modeling the actions she wants us to copy.

Once she skates all the way to the other end of the rink to ask Nathan something. The kids and I stand still and watch as she flies across the ice, circles, weaves, stops in a shower of snow, then starts a short conversation. Nathan appears to say one word: “No.” He shakes his head, hardly looks at her. He’s busy with a group of very young beginners in snowsuits, who spend most of the class lying on the ice or being lifted back onto their skate blades, and then tipping over again a few minutes later. So she swoops back, as if she’s competing in the Olympics and is about to throw herself into the air, turn multiple times, land, and strike a pose. I think she may be expecting applause, too.

Thirty minutes into our fifty-minute class, my legs start to wobble. *(You see, Papa? Excellent exercise! I’m tired already!)*

I start pushing and gliding my way toward the boards, where I plan to prop myself up for a few minutes.

“Genny, what are you doing?” Polly calls. “We’re not done yet. Twenty minutes to go!”

I turn awkwardly and see the kids all lined up like soldiers, watching me. Polly, their commander, wears an expression both matronly and disapproving. Obedient Imogen. I push and glide back to the troop.

Two more activities and I feel the backs of my knees starting to shake with fatigue.

"Now, everyone follow me," Polly says after forty minutes, and we fall into a snaky line and follow her around the pylons. I'm at the end. Kids are dropping to the ice and tripping over each other, then awkwardly clambering to their skates and laughing. Polly skates backwards and beams at us. "You guys rock!" she calls.

And then I'm on my back, looking up at the giant fluorescent lights of the arena.

"Hey, Genny!" Polly calls over from several pylons away. "You okay?"

I raise a hand and wave. Lie on the ice for a moment longer. I'm not hurt but there's no doubt the ice is hard, and it came up to meet my back fast. I think my feet must have gone out from under me, sending me backward, but as I review the sensations of the past few seconds, I realize that everything happened in slow motion, and my rear end and hands—my hockey-glove-protected hands—took the force of it. And not much force at that.

Now I'm just tired. Lying down feels good.

I hear blades approaching, cutting through the ice, slowing down near me.

"You okay?" Nathan is standing over me, bending down. "Did you hit your head?"

"No, I'm fine." I sit up quickly, embarrassed.

"Ditch the gloves," he says and, when I do, he reaches down, takes both my hands and pulls me back up on my skates in one swift movement. Bends down to retrieve my gloves and gives them to me. "You should take a break if you need it."

"Maybe I'll just go sit on the bench for a minute," I say and push-glide away from him. I notice that his lesson is over, his little snowsuit army no longer on the ice.

Polly has joined him and she thinks I can't hear her, but I can.

"God, she's useless." She snorts it a little. Like she's saying it out of the side her mouth, a joke they share.

Another girl might turn around and glare at her, or protest, or defend herself.

Not this girl. No, this girl pushes and glides jerkily toward the safety of that opening in the boards where the players bench is. I sit and try to settle the air around me so that I can breathe again. Everything is buzzing but not from the fall.

"Hey," says Nathan to Polly before he skates away. "Be nice."

He's a beautiful skater. Polly, the kids, and I watch him power all the way to the other end of the ice where he begins to glide backwards, picking up and stacking the orange pylons in a fluid, graceful rhythm.

"Wow," says little Abigail. "Can I switch to that guy's class?"

CHAPTER 26

HALLOWE'EN

"I'm sorry, my love, but this meeting came up very suddenly and I'm afraid I must go to Ottawa," says Papa. "I could perhaps stop in on Sunday on my way home and take you out for supper—how would that be?"

Père has a cold, apparently, and is content to stay at home alone with his tissue box, tea, and Radio-Canada. He has instructed Papa to tell me the germs are monstrous and angry and I wouldn't like them.

No, maybe not. Still, I'd rather be anywhere but here at school this weekend.

It's Hallowe'en at Hillside. I don't do Hallowe'en.

Little Imogen, six years old. My mother dresses me as some small spotted animal (a Dalmatian? A rabbit? A cat? A cow?), a costume she sewed herself, and I feel ridiculous.

"Don't you look cute!" she cajoles me. I'm lying on the kitchen floor in protest. Papa and Père are there, too, offering support, although I'm not sure for whom.

It's bad enough that I have to survive a day at school zippered into this ridiculous, hot flannel outfit, complete with hood (ears!) and a tail. But the chaos created by my costumed classmates is exhausting. I've had my supper and now I want my room. I want *pianissimo*. I want my headphones. But my mother insists I head out with her into a dark, cold October evening and walk the streets of the neighborhood in this unspecified-animal get-up and chant at strangers for candy.

Père kneels on the floor and whispers in my ear—my human ear, that is—"Go out into the jungle and bring me home some candy. And then I'll sing you to sleep."

The best treat. I go and it's hellish, although my mother seems to be enjoying herself, talking with other parents huddled together on the sidewalk, as over-excited children race door-to-door, clutching pillowcases growing heavier and heavier with teeth-rotting treats.

"Imogen is so well-behaved," I hear Mme Foster say to my mother, who snorts a laugh.

"Yes ... well ..." she says. That's all. I walk beside her, hold her hand, dutifully approach the front doors of our neighbors' houses, and hold out my bag. Do it over and over, thinking: *Soon I can go home and Père will sing to me.*

One year later, my mother is gone and I'm free from the hideous ritual. No, not my favorite day.

And the Hallowe'en buzz at Hillside is deafening. I've been able to avoid it mostly, retreating behind my headphones when the conversations about the dance start. I'm going home, after all. Another weekend at home, rehearsing for a November concert in Ottawa. Korngold again, so not a lot of work needed, but still. I expected to be home rehearsing and, instead, I'm shipwrecked. At Hallowe'en.

"How is Père?" I ask, changing the subject so that I don't let Papa hear how disappointed I am. "It's a bad cold?"

"Yes, bad enough, but he's in good spirits and just needs to rest," Papa says. He doesn't sound worried, and I know he's trying to tell me not to worry either. But of course I will. "So what will you be up to this weekend, then?"

"It's Hallowe'en," I remind him.

"Ah," says Papa. We understand each other. "I'm sorry, Imogen. Will you be able to hide away somewhere until the madness is over?"

That is my plan exactly.

In the lunchroom on Thursday, the conversation is all about the Saturday night dance. No one is going home. Why would they? A boy in Grade 11 has taken over the DJ gig and is soliciting suggestions. His name is Anson and he stands up on a chair to get everyone's attention. Braedon and the rugby boys throw grapes at him but Mr. Norton walks over, crosses his arms beside Anson's chair, and stands like a knight protector until the announcement is over. No one dares throw a grape at Mr. Norton.

Hallowe'en madness is everywhere. Victoria, Polly, and Melanie have decided on their costumes (the Sirens from *Ulysses*) in keeping with the theme of the evening ("Myths and Monsters").

"My mother knows this lady who sews custom-made costumes," Victoria told the room during English class a few weeks ago. "We'll be in this mermaid-y kind of green shiny fabric. With shells. And seaweed. It's going to be fabulous."

It will be fabulous. They're perfect for the role.

Berit and William are coming as King George (Berit) and the dragon (William) and have been giggling over their "cross-dressing": William, as a Brit, should be the king, of course. And Berit, from mythological and folklore-packed Scandinavia, should be the monster. Nevertheless.

"Not so odd," says Fredrik. "I'm going to be King Arthur." Instead of Odin. Or Thor. Or Eric the Red.

"Too bad you're going to miss it, Genny," says Berit. "It really is a lot of fun. And it's our last year, too."

"Hallowe'en isn't really my favorite day," I say.

"Yes, we figured that out," laughs Berit. She is kind, though. "Oh, well. We'll get Fredrik to text you photos."

I have a niggling feeling that I should be honest with them, even though I know it might lead me into trouble. But they are good to me, these three. They are probably the closest friends I have ever had in my life (which, I realize, sounds terribly pathetic).

"I'm actually going to be here this weekend," I tell them, scrolling through a playlist on my phone so I don't have to look at them. "Our rehearsal was canceled."

"Perfect!" exclaims Fredrik. "You can be Guinevere."

And that is what you get for being honest, Imogen.

Fredrik picks up his phone, taps in a number, and starts talking in rapid Swedish.

In English class we discuss *Hamlet*—"Does anyone else think this guy is a bit of a wimp?" asks Victoria, and for once I think I might agree with her—then Mr. Norton turns us loose for the final fifteen minutes to get into our groups for more media project planning. We are the first stop on his round-the-classroom tour.

"So, Mr. Floren, Mr. McCormick, and Miss St. Pierre. Where are we?" he asks, pulling up a chair.

Fredrik takes over, of course, and outlines our loose plan—skating and an accompanying musical soundtrack—with the precise and perfectly chosen words that teachers love.

Themes, symbolism, expression, personal journeys, creativity ...

Fredrik knows how to work the system.

Our ultimate goal. Using the strengths of each group member. Working together ...

Nathan and I just listen. I'm in awe. Mr. Norton is not awed, but he watches Fredrik as he speaks and nods occasionally.

"All good, Fredrik, but of course your other group members are going to have some input into this project?" He looks at Nathan and me and we both nod our assurance, although I'm sure neither of us knows what our input is or how it could possibly top anything Fredrik will come up with. I hope I'm not asked to express my musical vision because I haven't really discovered it yet.

"Fine. I have high hopes for this group," he says, lowering his voice a little, leaning in. "You're the one group I put together on purpose," he adds. "No need to repeat that. Carry on." And he's off to the next group.

"How very godlike of him," says Fredrik after a moment.

And then he turns to me.

"And since we're doing the mythical thing, I just want to confirm that you're coming to the dance as Guinevere and there will be no dodging it this year," he says. "I've already got my father's executive assistant hunting for a costume. It should be here tomorrow night. Or maybe by Saturday morning."

"Fredrik, no." I try to sound assertive but I'm not succeeding. Fredrik is employing full Viking force today. "I hate Hallowe'en. And you don't know what size I am."

"Easy. Tall and thin, right? You can wear anything. And you'll be with me and Berit and William," he says, and turns to Nathan who has been following this exchange with a grin on his face. "Are you coming? Do you want to join us?"

"Ha. No. Thanks, though." Nathan looks at me. "Guinevere, eh?"

Arthur's romantic, adulteress wife. That's me all over. I'm sure what Nathan actually sees is Imogen in her helmet and hockey gloves, lying on the ice. *Pavane pour une infante défunte.*

"You should come, too," Fredrik says to Nathan. "You can be Bors or Gawain or one of the tough guys."

Nathan actually laughs at that. "You think I'm a tough guy?"

Best hockey fight ever. World Juniors McCormick and Andersson. Crazy hockey fight. Violence in junior hockey. Canadian hockey player goes berserk. Nathan McCormick gets thrown out of World Junior final.

Fredrik doesn't believe in awkward pauses, because if he did, this would certainly be one.

"Not at all," he says to Nathan. And then he says something in Swedish. Something that includes the word "Andersson."

Nathan's face changes. He's been grinning at us, but now it's as if a door closes. Firmly. I'm sure I can hear it swinging shut, and I think maybe Fredrik hears it, too.

"Relax," says Fredrik. "I said, 'Every hockey fan in Sweden knows Lars Andersson is a complete asshole.' I was cheering for you."

Fredrik. A hockey fan. Who knew?

"Not my finest moment," says Nathan and he shrugs.

"Not his, either," says Fredrik. Then, after a little pause: "When can we get out on the ice and do some filming?"

CHAPTER 27

PRACTICE, ANYWAY

The piano in the chapel is mine every morning before assembly. Except for rare occasions—when Alain has organized a photo shoot, for example—I'm in the chapel before breakfast, practicing. Playing. Dreaming. Thinking.

I'm running scales today because I don't have to think much about them.

Although ...

My first teacher, my mother, would disagree. Every movement of every finger requires attention, she believes. Every pressure on the keys. Every change of position of my wrists and forearms. My back. My neck. She is fierce, adjusting my height on the bench, holding a ruler under my wrists until I feel as if I'm tied up tight, like one of those Christmas trees before the man snips away the trussing and lets the branches flop and expand and make a tree, not a pencil.

When she goes away—to make supper, to answer the phone—I am able to relax and play again. She's always angry with me.

That's what I'm doing this morning, Friday. I'm playing. Running scales, just letting my fingers and hands move where they need to go to maintain the tempo and the even dynamics. Even-tempered. That's me. Eyes closed. Major, with flats, with sharps. Minor scales. Never-ending. Trance-inducing.

I need this today, the trance. Too much is happening around me and I need this place—the chapel with the curtains open and the late October early morning dimness dampening down the shadows. I don't even turn on the piano light. Don't need it. My eyes are closed most of the time, anyway. My fingers know where to find the keys. They don't move around, those constant keys.

Constant. So much is changing. (Up, up, up. Down, down, down.)

This ridiculous Hallowe'en dance. No, not ridiculous, but looming. Fredrik will look after me, though, I know. And Berit and William. Up, up. Down, down. Switch to A-flat. University. Maybe moving away, traveling home for concerts, meeting up with Papa and Père for rehearsals, for performances. And Clapperton and his little friend, Bezic. And tea with my mother during the Christmas tour. And skating, where Polly thinks I am useless and no doubt I am. (What was I thinking?) Switch to D-flat. Up, up, up. Down, down, down.

I lift my hands off the keyboard, shake them. Rest them on my thighs. Stretch my neck. Breathe.

Messiaen or Korngold? Or that Mozetich we'll be playing in London on the Christmas tour. I need to pick one of them before Mr. Jamieson, the custodian, opens the side door to give me my five-minute warning. Soon it will be time for breakfast, then assembly, then Friday classes. We have a concert next weekend in Ottawa. Korngold. There: decision made. I run through the Korngold and hear Papa's cello and Père's violin, no missing notes. Perfection.

CHAPTER 28

HALLOWE'EN COSTUMES

The three of them are staring at me.

Correction. Two of them—Berit and William—are staring at me. Fredrik is simply looking me up and down and nodding.

"Told you," he says.

My Guinevere dress is delivered on Saturday morning by courier, and Fredrik texts me to meet him in the Lounge for pick-up.

I try it on in my room and send him a selfie for quality control purposes.

"Approved," he texts back. "Lounge, ready to go, at six."

By six-thirty I'm fading, but King Arthur has me by the arm and won't let his queen escape back to her room.

"Great costume, Genny!" says Victoria, Queen of the Sirens, pausing to admire the deep blue floor-length dress that Fredrik's father's executive assistant has dug up from some Ottawa theater company's costume department. Complete with gold-braided headpiece. (Arguments over whether hair should be up or down. Down. Not tied back with a band, or pulled into a long braid, as usual. Just falling down my back, over my shoulders, in natural curls. It feels like bedtime. It feels unnatural. Fredrik, my king, insists. Berit and William agree. I go along with them, but I'm self-conscious and trying hard to fight the urge to push stray strands out of my eyes every few minutes.)

When I arrive at the Seniors Lounge, Berit (the big red cross on her tunic looks like a target) and William (dragon tail over his arm like a bride's train) stand open-mouthed, but Fredrik just nods approvingly.

"Told you," he says to the others. "Perfect." He offers me his arm, always the gentleman. In formation, we progress royally to the dining hall where the action is just getting underway. People are looking at me, but Fredrik just holds my arm and chatters into my ear.

But by nine o'clock, *fading* is no longer the right word. More like spinning. Hurtling. Shattering. The cracks are beginning to show. The music is loud, the lights prickling, the voices like pellets crashing against my ears.

I've eased myself away from the lights and the action, staying close to our table, or wandering the room, watching the dancers, smiling at people, talking little. Fredrik, of course, loves a party, and after checking to see that I don't mind, he's taken over the dance floor. Now I'm standing by the kitchen, no one looking my way. Fredrik knows me well enough to know that if he can't find me, I've simply escaped.

And that's what I do. Guinevere makes a run for it. Through the kitchen, where Mrs. Clouthier is preparing the lunch for the ten o'clock break. (She smiles, nods at me. She knows.) Out the back door into the hallway that leads to the residence wing. The boom-boom-boom of the dance floor sound system is muffled now, with two doors and a kitchen between it and me. Already I can breathe the air again. Down the hallway, open the door to the Lounge that separates the boys wing from the girls.

Nathan McCormick is watching hockey, sprawled on one of the couches in gray sweatpants and an Ottawa Senators long-sleeved T-shirt. He looks up in surprise as I come in, then recognition dawns.

"Hey, it's Guinevere," he says.

I want to say something smart and funny, but my head is too full, too tired. As I open my mouth to reply (Ha ha. So bright, so clever), I glance at the TV.

White ice. Red, blue, black swirls of jerseys and helmets and skates. Sticks crashing. Habs and Senators.

That stops me. Père will be watching the game, tucked up in his big chair under Grandmère Geneviève's afghan, tissue box and tea mug at hand. Alone at home because Papa is in Ottawa and I am here, dressed up in these foreign clothes for Hallowe'en.

"My grandfather will be watching this game." *Stupid thing*

to say. But I suddenly long to be at home with him, watching the swirling colors crisscross the ice, looking after him, sharing a pot of tea and the afghan. Cheering for his Habs.

"Habs or Senators?" asks Nathan. "Habs, I bet."

I nod, wonder why I feel like crying.

"Your grandfather'll be happy then. The Habs are kicking the Sens' asses," he says, and his hockey-boy talk makes me smile. I imagine a ghostly Papa and Père on the other couch, cheering for the *bleu, blanc, et rouge*, exchanging comments about kicking asses.

"Well, goodnight." I want my room. I want darkness. I want to be alone.

"Hey," says Nathan, twisting on the couch to look over at me. "The skating thing. How's it going?"

You know how it's going, I want to say to him. *It's hideous.* Instead, I just shrug. Turn to go.

"You'll get it, don't worry," he says. "It's hard to start when you're older."

I've never thought of myself as "older." Always as young, younger, youngest. But it's true. Little Abigail and her friends are kids and I'm the same age as Polly, our teacher.

"How old were you when you learned to skate?"

"Still learning," he says. I tilt my head, showing that I sincerely doubt that. "But, yeah, okay, the first time I really skated on the ice, I was two, or a bit under that."

When I was two, I was picking out tunes on the piano, kneeling on the bench so I could reach the keys. *Still learning.*

A flurry of action on the TV screen draws his attention back to the game. I'm gone.

CHAPTER 29

SKATING LESSON NO. 2

Little Abigail is my new best friend. We toddle along at the end of the line, keeping each other's spirits up as the other girls in our class surge ahead, both literally and otherwise. Abigail and Imogen, bringing up the rear.

"Did you want to take skating lessons?" Abigail asks me as we move sideways across the blue line, getting the feel of our edges (according to zookeeper Polly). Abigail is wearing her cage helmet again so it's a bit like talking to a bird.

"Yes, I did."

"I didn't." She says it without any tinge of complaint, catches me looking at her, questioning. "My mom said it was skating lessons or swimming lessons," she says. "And I'm afraid of drowning."

I know exactly what she means.

"I'm glad you're here," she says, then looks at my chunky gloves. "Are you going to be a hockey player?"

We've reached the end of the sideways line and are supposed to skate forward toward the next line and do it all again in the other direction. We're both doing it right, but we're slow. Polly skates back to check on us.

"All right here, ladies? Looking good! Remember to keep those knees soft." No sign that she still thinks I'm useless as she flits away toward the front of the line again, where the over-achievers are already finishing.

"No, I don't want to be a hockey player," I say to Abigail. "I just want to skate like one."

She nods. Looks over her shoulder at the far end of the ice where Nathan and his little minions are weaving around pylons again. "Like that guy," she says.

Yes, I want to skate like Nathan McCormick.

I've been back on YouTube, feeling like a stalker but, oh, well. Type in the terms "Nathan McCormick" and "skating" and another slew of videos stacks up on the screen.

McCormick skating through Sudbury defense. Nathan McCormick skating highlight reel. Nathan McCormick outskating Seagram. (Who is "Seagram"? I watch that one first. Seagram is the Oshawa Generals player expected to go first in the NHL draft. Thank you, Google.) *McCormick skating leaves Russian defense in the dust. Nathan McCormick, figure skating.* (That's a good one. Someone has taken video highlights and arranged them in time to Strauss's "Blue Danube." It's sort of our media project done badly. The skating is magnificent, though, complete with a perfect twist as he leaps over the blue line to avoid a hit and reconnects with the puck on the other side.) *McCormick best skater in junior hockey.* And on and on.

Our second class is going better than the first. My legs don't feel as tired, maybe because I've had my tumble to the ice; it's done so I'm more relaxed now. Abigail chatters and stumbles and approaches every activity with good-natured effort, so I suppose having me there helps her, too. No more trembling lip for her. No more trembling knees for me. Polly even gives us high-fives.

At the end of class, Polly has us all join hands and we follow in a line behind her, like a skating centipede, round the end of the ice in a big circle. The little girls are hooting, giggling, breathless with joy. Me, too. Polly smiles at us all—at me on the end of the line (still wearing one big glove)—and joins in with the laughter. No one falls as she takes us around one more time and then gently deposits us against the boards to giggle some more and catch our breath.

"Oh, that was awesome!" says Abigail, her huge smile bursting from behind the cage.

"You're all pro skaters now," says Polly, and she smiles at all of us, even me.

Being nice.

CHAPTER 30

CLAPPERTON, AGAIN

An email arrives on Monday morning:

Hi Genny,

I heard from Richard that you were able to connect at your concert at Redpath Hall. Glad you had a chat about joining L'Avenir next season. We've had some interest from the Winchester Chamber Music Festival for next year, and they're very familiar with your work, of course. Let me know if you want to talk about some other possible gigs we're looking into (Elora Festival, Chalmers Chamber, some small concerts at the Royal Conservatory in Toronto, for example).

How's the Quartet coming? Sounded great the last time we rehearsed at your place in Montreal. Looking forward to seeing you in December. We can chat some more about L'Avenir then.

Cheers,

Tony

Read once. Read twice.

Delete.

CHAPTER 31

GUY WITH A CAMERA, PART 2

Two big things happen on Tuesday morning.

First, we wake up to the first snow of the year. Not just a light, wet, experimental autumn try-out, either. It's a full-on, mid-winter dump, requiring mad scrambling in closets to find appropriate footwear.

I know it's there as soon as I roll over to check the time (6:10 AM). The light in my room, even with the curtains pulled, is completely different today. There's not much light, of course, now that it's November, but the shadows are gray, everything washed out. Snow does that. Snow sucks the color out of everything early in the morning. Later, maybe, if the sun's out and there are no clouds, we'll all be deafened by a full orchestra of lights and colors. But at 6:10 AM, rolling out of bed for my morning journey to the piano in the chapel, I feel as if I'm moving through a monochrome landscape of dullness. Tempered by cold.

(Snow means winter. Winter means Christmas. Christmas means London. And my mother. And Clapperton. And all that.)

Something else happens on Tuesday morning.

Our gym class is outside today. It's the tradition on the first snowfall of the year for a co-ed game of snow soccer. I'm a defender (I volunteer for that position so I don't have to run as much), and by now, the sun has cleared off the clouds and it's one of those brilliant days that actually hurts my eyes. Fredrik is our goalkeeper, so I just hover near him down in the defensive zone and try to stay warm. When the ball comes near me, I let Melanie (who is on my team and much more enthusiastic about the game and the conditions) take over. It's a good system.

The action is ragged and often hilarious, since snow has a way of interfering with passing and kicking and running. People fall frequently. The ball sails out of bounds over lines no one can see. Miss Bucher is reffing on one side, Mr. McLachlan on the other, and there are lots of complaints from the players about the officiating.

"But, sir! She was out!"

"Play on."

I just let the action swirl around me and enjoy the sun on my face. The air is heavy with joy. Everyone is happy, even the complainers. The first snow and sunshine, and pretending to be fierce when really we're all just soaking up the freedom of a November morning, running wild on a snowy field. Like ponies. Like kindergartners.

"Hey, who's that?" asks William.

There's a break in the action and the teams are lining up for a throw-in. ("Ah! Sir! It should be ours! It went off Melanie's foot!" "No way, sir!" "Blue ball!" yells Mr. McLachlan, unshakeable.)

We all look where William is looking, across the pond to the Stevenson farm field. Someone in a heavy parka is pointing a huge camera lens at our game. He lowers the camera as we all fix on him, takes a few unsteady steps backward in the snowy cornfield. Raises the camera again and is clearly clicking off a series of shots. Of us.

Yes, but which one of us?

Victoria's father has been in the news lately for a questionable policy decision he is part of in the Prime Minister's office. William's mother—well, we're not sure what she does, but everyone knows it's highly top secret and she travels with two Mounties at all times. Fredrik's father is an ambassador, a diplomat. So is Berit's. Then there's Melanie, and Braedon, whose parents don't even work in Canada. A boy named Philip Barras, whose mother is a Spanish film star, and Andrew Carter, the son of that drummer in a well-known rock band.

Nathan McCormick, famous for all sorts of reasons.

And me. That girl who plays the piano.

"Everyone back to the gym, please," says Mr. McLachlan in his I-mean-business voice, and everyone obeys immediately. He faces the photographer, as if memorizing him while Miss Bucher herds us back to the school. The man with the camera is making his way back across the field toward the road, probably to his car.

"Could have been a gun," mutters Andrew.

Braedon laughs it off. "Right." He snorts the word.

"No need for that kind of talk," says Miss Bucher, who is still herding. No sign of Mr. McLachlan.

Gym class is nearly over anyway, so we head to the change rooms to get out of our snow-soggy outdoor clothes and get ready for the lunch break. The chatter is somewhat subdued. Most of us have had our moments with photographers or press, and stories are now being shared. Victoria and the woman who followed her into the washroom at the Chateau Laurier to ask questions about her father. Braedon's mother pushing him and his brother down to the floor of the limousine after a particularly unpleasant episode at a public square in Turkey. Someone else remembers her parents calling the police to chase away a television crew who wanted answers about some corporate missing-money scandal.

Fredrik has been followed by reporters eager to talk to him about being gay, although he thinks they actually just wanted to invite him to a club. (He didn't go, of course, although he did speak to them and they published an upbeat story with some excellent photos. Fredrik's father, the ambassador, is very supportive.)

I'm pretty sure no one would be standing in a snowy field taking pictures of me during a game of snow soccer, so I distance myself from the chatter, put in my earbuds, and take my lunch to my table by the window. The drama is unsettling, distracting, like the pecking of birds. I would rather think about my skating lesson this afternoon. Fredrik is coming to watch Nathan (and I suppose me, too) on the ice and scout out the arena. Prepping for shooting, he says. Just getting a sense of what's possible.

But Nathan isn't in the lunch room. He's not in class on Tuesday afternoon, and he's not at skating, either. One of the parent helpers has taken over the minions.

Polly sidles up and holds me back when my skating twin, Abigail, leaves my side to start working her way through one of the new activities.

"Victoria saw Mr. Colville take Nathan into his office, and that Hockey Canada guy showed up again this afternoon," she reports, eyes wide with meaning.

Clearly Victoria needs to sign up with William's mother. She's always on the intelligence beat, apparently.

"I bet that photographer was getting pictures of him," says Polly. "Did he say anything to you?"

She must think I have the inside line to Nathan's movements, his thoughts. (That's what walking through St. Laurent Centre with someone will do for your reputation, I guess.)

But she's wrong. Nathan has a giant *go away* sign wrapped around him. I recognize it because I have one most of the time, too. Although Polly is oblivious to it, apparently.

"No. I haven't seen him since gym class," I say.

Polly is disappointed. Or she doesn't believe me. I don't wait around to figure out the difference.

Later, at the arena, Fredrik is sitting up in the seats near the mothers, under the heaters. He has his little red book out and is making notes. When I skate close to that side of the rink, he calls out to me as if I'm performing in a show.

"Great job, Genny!" Like a proud dad. At first, the mothers aren't sure how to take him, but soon enough they're all chatting together, laughing.

Fredrik has a gift.

After my lesson, he stays in the stands and waits for me to join him.

"This place is soulless," he says. "There's no way we can film in here."

I look at the huge oval of white ice and try to see what Fredrik sees. In my mind, there's movement and color. I picture a single skater (Nathan) maybe in blue, or black, a dark shape creating lines and circles against the painted lines and circles.

And then I see the advertising on some of the boards. And the dark scuff marks left by pucks and sticks and hockey players. And the metal stands, the half-open gate to the penalty bench. The institutional gray brick walls with pipes running here and there, and red-light exit signs. And above it all, the struts holding up the roof, with bands of fluorescent lighting hanging between them.

Fredrik is right.

"Maybe when you see Nathan skating," I suggest. "When you get right down on the ice."

"The magic of film, you mean?" he laughs, then shakes his head. "No. This won't do."

We sit, watching the humming Zamboni flooding the ice in its precise pattern, round and round, oval upon oval.

"I have to think about this," he says.

CHAPTER 32

EMAIL

On Wednesday, Victoria emails our entire class a link to the *Ottawa Sun* sports section, which includes a story on the upcoming Hockey Canada and International Ice Hockey Federation hearing for Nathan McCormick.

Banned or Back? shouts the headline, with a smaller heading underneath: *Future of junior star McCormick to be decided on Friday.*

The story includes a photo of Nathan in full Ottawa 67s uniform, wheeling on one skate with the puck on his stick, eyes already looking up-ice for the goal, or maybe for one of his teammates. He's tipped so far over on the edges of his skate blades (see? I know about edges now), I don't understand how he can still be upright.

There's another shorter story, too, with a photo obviously taken from our gym class, although Nathan is the only figure in it. He's caught mid-kick, eyes intent on the target (zeroing in on Fredrik in goal, maybe?), arms outstretched for balance, or, more likely, holding off a charge from one of the players on our team, just outside the frame. He looks exactly the same as he does in the other photo, without the hockey gear, without the helmet and visor. He looks as if he's enjoying himself.

Out of sight, out of mind reads the headline of the accompanying story. I don't read either of them, other than looking at the photos, which are wonderful.

Discussion during the day focuses on the likelihood of Nathan being banned for life from playing hockey.

"That'll never happen," says Braedon at lunch. The rugby boys nod. Chew and nod.

"Biggest junior star next to Seagram," says Jeff. "The NHL isn't going to let him slip away. Not a chance."

"Too much money at stake," says Braedon. More knowing nods.

I'm over by the window, re-reading the email Papa sent last night, but I'm listening, too. I'm not sure what the boys mean about the NHL and money. But I can guess. I also suspect that if Alain were here, he would know exactly what it all means and would be able to explain it to me in that marketing language he loves: *ticket sales, revenue, sponsors, endorsements, brand.* I know enough to know that Nathan McCormick, junior hockey star, has a value.

Mr. Colville sent us a message today (writes Papa), *explaining that a photographer was seen near the school taking photos during your gym class. He says the police were called, and the man was found to be a newspaper reporter from Ottawa. Nothing grave or threatening, although the reporter was interested in one of your classmates, specifically.*

I already know all this because Mr. Colville called our class into the chapel on Tuesday afternoon for a brief assembly. Security concerns. Parents contacted. No danger. Etc., etc.

If you are worried about this, we can talk or Skype on Wednesday evening. I'm tied up with classes and auditions most of the day. Pity me! Not a single decent cellist in this group of first-year students! Woe to Dr. Moritz and the junior chamber orchestra!

Lucky Papa only has to audition the first-years. He directs the upper-year ensemble, so the newbies fall under the guidance of one of his colleagues. Père sometimes reminds him that we were all first-years once, but Papa only responds: "Yes, and we all grew out of it, didn't we?"

Chin up, my love! I will retrieve you on Friday afternoon and we can talk more about this intrusive and annoying photographer, if you feel the need. Otherwise, it will be an all-Korngold weekend. Père sends his love. Papa

And then the post-script:

By the way, I received an email from Anthony today. He wanted to make sure he had your email address correct (which he did). If he has written to you, perhaps it would be polite to reply? Or perhaps I'm interfering. (Père tells me to mind my own business!) Something to talk about, if you wish, between bouts of Korngold this weekend ... Love, Papa.

CHAPTER 33

CONVERSATION OVERHEARD IN LIBRARY

"It's no wonder he's the way he is," says Victoria. "If you believe this stuff about his family. I mean, wow."

"Brutal, I know!" That's Polly.

They're talking about Nathan, of course. He's been the focus of everyone's attention since Tuesday, when he disappeared with the Hockey Canada guy (according to Victoria) shortly after our gym class. The stories appear in the papers and online on Wednesday. He's an item in the TSN sports roundup every day this week. People are talking. Most of the senior year at Hillside is talking.

"I wonder where they dig this stuff up?" she says. "I mean, it's not as if he would tell them anything in an interview. He doesn't seem to talk much, does he?"

"Nope. You should see him at skating." That's Polly, of course. "All business."

"Coaches might talk about him, maybe?" says Melanie. "Other guys he played with?"

"Maybe old friends from his neighborhood?" suggests Polly.

Old friends. I picture the boys at St. Laurent and that awkward, crude, brief encounter that took place on our way from the sports store to the food court. I'm not sure those boys were friends, though.

The girls are at the next table, talking quietly (it is the library, after all), but they may as well be shouting. It's strange how the more secretive the conversation, the easier it is to zero in and decode. My eyes are on *Hamlet* and the homework questions, but my ears are always, sometimes painfully, open and receiving.

"You can't believe everything you hear, though, right?" Victoria says.

"Twitter," says Polly. "Brutal."

"Look what happened with that video from the World Juniors."

"Viral. Within hours."

They're quiet for a moment, maybe seeing Nathan's pounding fist and blood on the ice. Which is exactly what I'm seeing.

"Did you see that one story about him and his father ...?"

"Girls, quiet, please!" Mrs. Amers, the librarian, ends it and quiet descends.

I open my eyes (I didn't actually know that I had closed them) and focus on my *Hamlet* homework again.

Write a paragraph that connects the following quotation to an incident in your own life: "There is nothing either good or bad, but thinking makes it so."

CHAPTER 34

CONCERT

Dominion–Chalmers United Church always makes me feel a bit seasick at first, with its arches swelling around us like waves. But today I'm safely inside my piano—they've brought in the baby Steinway, an old friend—and Papa and Père are steering us, and it's as close to heaven as ever could exist, I think.

Père. He's perfect today, better than perfect.

The last long Korngold chord slips off our strings, but I'm still away—until we crash into the wall of applause and it all shatters.

Right. Père catches my eye, winks. We rise and bow. Bow again. The audience is on its feet, calling out for more. *Encore! Encore!*

Haydn, of course. The "Presto" from the G Major, the one that sounds like a sailors' hornpipe and rips along at such a crazy tempo that the three minutes go by like that. A crowd-pleaser, Père calls it. He nails every note and the crowd is clearly, loudly, boisterously pleased.

We bow again, me in the middle, doing my best to look at the audience and climb out of my piano and back into the world, although it usually takes me some time off stage to do that. (And then the inevitable crash, as the fatigue sets in. I'm not thinking about that yet.) Faces are smudges over the blurry, clapping hands, but I smile, look at Papa, who gives me a squeeze. We both look at Père, smiling his thanks to the audience and to us. He winks at me and I turn my smile back to the crowd, too.

And then ...

Are you kidding me? Richard Bezic is standing over on the right-hand side. Looking straight at me.

Papa's hand is on my arm and Père leads us off the stage, so maybe no one notices my change in expression. I'm not in my piano anymore. Lifted out—no, wrenched out—by the sight of pale, determined Bezic, Clapperton's little sidekick.

"Bravo," Papa says to Père as soon as we enter the green room, and they embrace, pull me in for a celebratory hug with them. "Well done to all of us."

"Now the fun part," Père grins at me.

"Magnificent performance." Alain breezes in the door, trailing two of the concert organizers, and it's down to business with congratulations and instructions on where to find the reception upstairs, and who is waiting to meet us, and all those post-concert details that send me in search of a few moments' peace in the Ladies.

It's a one-person Ladies, so I lock the door and turn to the mirror. Stare at myself and undertake a brief, one-sided practice conversation. *(Thank you. I'm glad you enjoyed it. Very nice to meet you. I've been playing since I was about two, I think. Thank you. Thank you. No, I haven't decided about joining your stupid freaking ensemble.)*

That last one directed at Richard Bezic and the invisible Anthony Clapperton, who is apparently stalking me.

The hall is crowded and humming with voices and excited post-concert energy. Papa, Père, and I are quickly towed in different directions—a kind lady from the organizing committee takes me in hand, and I'm grateful because she stays with me, makes introductions, starts and ends conversations, asks a helper to bring me some cold lemonade (how did she know?), and, best of all, keeps me so engaged that Bezic can't worm his way in.

"So delightful to see a young woman making such an impact on the classical music scene," says someone.

"Thank you." Impact?

"You must have to practice all day to play like that," says another.

"No, not all day." Polite laughter, smiles. "But I do practice a lot."

"Do you have time for anything else?" asks the first lady.

Should I tell them about skating lessons? Maybe not.

"Well, I do have school and homework," I say.

They ask about Hillside, about finding time to practice

(I tell them about my early-morning chapel time), about the fun of performing with my father and grandfather, about traveling. The groups change as my handler leads me around the room, and the questions are repeated. At one point, Alain joins us, checking to make sure I'm following the script, which I am, of course. No crazy photo ideas today, so it's smooth sailing.

And then Bezic, who appears out of nowhere when my nice guide is momentarily distracted. He's probably been following us around the room, like a shark, and found a moment to strike.

"Hello, again," he says, smile plastered to his face. (Which makes it sound as if it's a mask, but I'm being unkind. He's just smiling, that's all.) "Congratulations. Excellent performance."

"Thank you."

Awkward moment as the ladies I was just talking to move away to give him room. They're smiling at us indulgently and I can read the speech bubbles over their heads: *Romance!*

Deep breath, Imogen. He's harmless.

"That Haydn always makes me laugh," he says, and we spend a few moments talking about the tempo, and how it doesn't work if you don't ramp it up.

"My grandfather calls it a crowd-pleaser," I say and he laughs.

I look around and see Papa across the room, in conversation with a small group, but he catches my eye, notices Bezic, nods, smiles, all without taking a break. No rescue there. Père is deep in lively conversation with a gentleman his own age, both of them laughing and using their hands to discuss something that looks to have more to do with gardening than music.

"So I was just wondering," says Bezic, bringing me back to our corner of the noisy room. "Have you thought any more about L'Avenir? The ensemble?"

This is what I really want to say: "Why are you pestering me?"

I don't, of course, because that would be rude, and Alain has drilled into me the necessity of being nice to people who have bought tickets. Even the Bezics of the world.

Besides, I know why they're pestering me. They need a pianist that people have heard of—people like the audience, and organizers, and critics. *It's Imogen St. Pierre, you know, Trio St. Pierre, that girl who's been playing with her father and grandfather since she was five or six—or was it seven? How interesting. Let's buy a ticket.*

And just like that, in that exact moment, the post-concert exhaustion sets in.

Across the room, Père is now busy charming three ladies who have fluttered up to talk to him. He leans toward each one as he speaks, always smiling. A handsome, respected, older musician who played his violin today as if he were twenty again, instead of eighty. No tired fingers, no missing notes. Today.

I turn back to Bezic with an effort. "Still thinking about it," I manage to say.

"Great, great." He nods, pauses, appears to be chewing the

inside of one cheek. "So, Tony and I were wondering, in the meantime, if you'd consider just playing one concert with a small group of us in the spring, in April."

April. I can hardly see past the Christmas tour right now.

"Here, at Dominion–Chalmers," he continues when I don't reply. "We'd like to play the Poulenc sextet as part of the pre-Festival series." I still don't say anything so he carries on. "Of course it would be a big change for you—winds instead of the piano trio you're used to."

"What are you two conspiring about?" asks Alain, who appears out of nowhere.

(Ha! Alain does not appear out of nowhere. Think magic wand, black hat, rabbit. It's all an illusion.)

"Just asking Imogen if she'd be interested in performing with Tony and me and a few others at the pre-Festival in April," says Bezic, in a voice that sounds bright, hearty, unnatural. "The Poulenc sextet. Winds and piano."

"What a brilliant idea," Alain says. For a moment, I'm sure he's going to clap his hands. He doesn't.

The fatigue continues to creep over me and I start to feel inches shorter, as if I'm melting a little into the floor. My drink is long gone, and a glance around the room shows me Papa and Père still deep in their own post-concert socializing. I've been abandoned.

Stranded with Bezic and Alain and the invisible presence of Clapperton.

"Just this one concert," says Bezic to Alain. "I know you probably have Trio St. Pierre booked through the spring and, of course, we'd work with you. We know Imogen's your responsibility."

"What do you think, Genny? Could be a fun diversion for you," Alain is saying in his marketing-guy voice. There's something here for him, too, I see. Everyone wins.

"No commitment or anything, Genny. Just one concert. See how it goes," says Bezic.

I just want them to go away, and I'm too tired to think of any appropriate response. If I could just go and talk to Papa and Père—but even then, I have a feeling I know what they would each say. *Options. New experiences. These are good things.*

If I say yes, maybe they'll leave me alone. One concert.

"Okay," I say. "I'll have to check with Papa, though."

Alain and Bezic are gushing with excitement and pleasure. It occurs to me that they're on the same team, that maybe this was all planned, that I've been tricked.

Maybe. I'm just so tired right now, I don't really care.

From across the room, Père sees me. Nods at me and smiles. Politely extricates himself from the group he's talking to and comes toward us, to my rescue.

But he's too late.

CHAPTER 35
CHAPEL

I run into Nathan on my way into the chapel on Monday morning. No, I mean literally run into him. I go through the doorway just as he's approaching from the other side and I bounce off him.

The evening before, Papa and Père deliver me to Hillside, after dinner with Alain and two of the concert organizers in Ottawa. A full meal and the warm car, added to the usual post-performance fatigue (not to mention dealing with Bezic), and I'm asleep before Orleans. I wake up at the doors of the school with Papa gently laying a hand on my shoulder and saying my name.

The lounge is unusually crowded and buzzing as I sleepwalk through on my way to the Girls side and my room. Fredrik's the only face that comes into focus. He waves at me and I manage to wave back, but all I can think about is being alone and horizontal. I leave the buzz behind.

Now it's Monday morning, early, gray inside and outside.

I navigate the sleeping hallways on my way to the chapel. As I pass each window, I catch sight of a light net of snow lying on the grass and trees.

A perfect backdrop, I think, because this morning is all about Messiaen and the *Quartet*.

In fact, the next two weeks are about the *Quartet*. We took a step back in preparation for the Ottawa concert, but Papa says it's time to dig in again. That's where I am as, head down, I walk, searching my musical mind, trying to find my way back into Messiaen's deep place. I can't wait to get back to work on it, to submerge myself again. Dig the darkness and the light out of my piano keys.

The chapel door is propped open, so I go through the opening and ... slam into something hard, chin first.

"Shit! Sorry!" Nathan McCormick. I stagger backward.

No breath. I think I just ran into a wall with my face. My watering eyes close automatically, head ringing.

"I'm so sorry," he says again, sounding a little panicky, actually. "I didn't see you coming. I'm really sorry—are you okay?"

I open my eyes now and see him right there, leaning toward me, one hand out as if to hold me up.

"I'm fine." I smile at him, try to laugh. "I bounced off."

He drops his hand and straightens up.

"I'm so, so sorry. Honestly, I didn't hear you coming."

"It's okay, really. Nothing broken." I wiggle my fingers.

Now he looks at my hands. A vision of hockey gloves flashes across his face, I'm certain.

"Really." I smile my reassurance at him, try to look as if I'm breathing normally. "I'm fine. Don't worry about me."

"Oh, okay. Good," he says, but he's still standing there, and it occurs to me to wonder why he's here, in the chapel, early on a Monday morning, anyway.

Why does anyone come to a chapel, idiot? To practice on the piano, of course. But also those other things: *to pray, to meditate, to talk to God (if you believe in that stuff).*

"Sorry, you probably want to get to work," he says, nodding toward the piano at the front.

I nod. Observant boy.

"I was just, you know, hanging out here for a while," he says, looking around. "Nice place to be alone. But you'd know about that." And he suddenly and surprisingly grins at me. No question, he's remembering the day I fainted. The day he was here, sitting in the shadows. Alone and thinking about ...

Beating the crap out of that guy. And his upcoming hearing ... which was, of course, on Saturday.

"Have a good practice. See you in English class," he says, going around me, heading for the door. "Sorry about the body check."

The buzz in the crowded lounge last night. Everyone hanging out. I only noticed Fredrik, but was Nathan there, too? Was it a celebration?

He's released the door from its hook on his way out and it closes slowly behind him.

"But how did it go? The hearing on Saturday?"

I'm too late. He's already gone; the door is closing and he doesn't hear me.

CHAPTER 36

AT BREAKFAST

It went well, apparently.

I arrive in the dining hall for breakfast, still feeling jagged from an hour of wrestling with the "Liturgie," the first part of the *Quartet*. It's under my fingers, but the whole movement feels like an irregular heartbeat and leaves me trembling. All I want is toast and tea—the kind of breakfast I eat when I'm sick. I'm not sick, of course.

But I'm aware of only my own air, my own space, at the moment. I assemble my breakfast, head for a table by the window, and hear ... no, see Fredrik waving to attract my attention. (Yes, I would actually like to sit all alone, but yes, that would be rude.) I make myself go toward his waving hand and hope he doesn't want to talk much. When I get closer and look again, I see that Berit and William are there, too.

Tray down, sit down. Breathe. My hand trembles as I reach for my tea.

"You're not really here, are you?" asks Fredrik.

"No, not really."

"Korngold again?" he asks. "No, that concert was yesterday, wasn't it? You must have been with the *Quartet* this morning."

I'm sipping tea—sweet, hot tea. It's helping. So is Fredrik, and I want him to know that, so I force myself to reply.

"Yes, the *Quartet*."

"What's the *Quartet*?" asks Berit.

I don't have to answer because Fredrik takes over, explains everything—the prison camp, the the German officer helping Messiaen and the other musicians find instruments, allowing him a place to work. The performance in 1941 in the cold prisoner-of-war camp barracks, German officers in the front row. The music, God and angels, light in a dark place.

By the time he's finished, I'm eating my toast and beginning to feel almost present again, as if I can actually go to class and focus on what's going on around me.

"I'd love to hear your performance," says Berit. "When is it?"

"Over Christmas, but it's in London," I say. "St. Martin-in-the-Fields."

"A bit of a trip from Oslo," she laughs. "But you never know."

William says he'll be home in London for the holidays. Says he'll check the dates. Maybe Berit could fly over for a visit? Fredrik, too?

I sip, eat, listen to them talk. It's okay again. The air is starting to settle around me.

"Maybe you could ..." Berit stops mid-sentence and the air changes. Someone is standing just behind me and she looks up in surprise.

"Sorry to interrupt," says Nathan McCormick. "Freddie, I just wanted to let you guys know that I'm going to be in class, but I have to go do this phone interview thing right at nine, so I'll be a bit late. I'll be there, though, in case we have time to work on the project."

"Sure, no problem," says Fredrik, nodding his okay as he turns in his seat beside me to look up at him. "Thanks."

Sip my tea. Put two and two together. Phone interview means good news, surely?

"See you later." Nathan is walking away but Fredrik isn't finished.

"*Lycka till,*" he calls after him.

"Thanks," Nathan calls back.

Everyone's listening by now.

"I knew he could understand Swedish," Fredrik says to us, *sotto voce*.

I turn around, finally, just in time to see Nathan walking out and completely unaware that everyone in the dining hall is watching him go.

CHAPTER 37

SPORTSTALK RADIO

Fredrik sends me the audio link on Monday night, late. I'm already in bed, tucked up under the duvet (taking one last look to see if there are any messages from Papa) and, even though I know it will probably mean I won't be able to fall asleep right away afterward, I listen anyway ...

SportsRadio Guy: *And we're back. Ottawa's own Nathan McCormick had everything going for him: as an all-star on the 67s, he led all OHL defensemen in points. He's been on three World Junior teams and had a possible gold medal within his grasp. NHL scouts were already saying his name alongside Kyle Seagram and Jonathan LeMay, not to mention labeling him as a franchise player like Crosby and McDavid. Big, strong, tough—yup, a few fights in there—but smart and the best skater in the league, they said. A team player, they said.*

And then the World Juniors in Russia, and a vicious hit from Swedish forward Lars Andersson on Canadian captain and McCormick's lifelong friend, Luc Charette. McCormick goes in to defend his teammate and, well, folks, the rest is history. Thrown out of the game after a pretty ugly fight. Suspended from the tournament. Suspended indefinitely by Hockey Canada and the International Ice Hockey Federation. His hockey career in jeopardy.

But no one was happier than Ottawa hockey fans when it was announced this weekend that Hockey Canada and the IIHF have decided to lift the suspension, after meeting with McCormick and John Raeside, who also coaches the 67s. That means Number 92 is headed back to the OHL. But there are still some questions. When will Nathan McCormick be back on the ice? What does it all mean for his hockey career? Let's find out.

Nathan McCormick is on the phone from his school—that's right, he's at school, skipping class to talk to us right now—and his coach, John Raeside, joins us from Ottawa. Let's start with you, Nathan. How are you feeling about the decision by Hockey Canada and the IIHF?

(I note the announcer doesn't mention the name of Nathan's school or where he's calling from. But everyone must know, thanks to the little story in the paper, the photo of Nathan playing snow soccer ...)

Nathan: *Yeah, it feels really good to know I'm going to be able to play hockey with my team again.*

(Excellent radio voice. Lots of bass.)

SportsRadio Guy: *Did you miss it?*

Nathan: *Yeah. Yeah, I did.*

SportsRadio Guy: *Were you ever worried that your career might be finished?*

Nathan: *I just never let myself think that way. I tried to stay positive.*

SportsRadio Guy: *You haven't played for ... what? ... almost a year now. Have you been on the ice at all? Keeping in shape? When will you back in uniform for the 67s?*

Nathan: *Yeah, well, that's something I have to talk about with the* OHL *and the 67s. I mean, I haven't been playing hockey. I've been skating a bit, though.*

(Helping his minion army weave in super slow motion around orange pylons on the ice at the Brick Hill Memorial Arena on Tuesday afternoons ...)

But I've been working out pretty steadily. There's a good gym, a good weight room at my school, and I spend a lot of time there.

(I did not know that. But I suppose it's not surprising. I'm in class, or in my room, or practicing, or eating, or at home. I'm not exactly hanging out in the gym to see who's lifting weights and running on the treadmills ...)

But I have a lot of work to do before I can suit up. Coach Raeside and I are still talking about that.

SportRadio Guy: *And then there's the* NHL *draft coming up in June. Are you going to be ready for that?*

Nathan: *Yeah, I think so.*

SportsRadio Guy: *Can I ask you about your last game against Sweden? What happened? I mean, we all know what happened. You got into a fight with Lars Andersson, broke his nose, and were escorted off the ice and suspended. Can you tell us what really happened?*

(There's a pause here. My hands curl around the edges of the duvet. I picture Nathan's crazed fighting-boy face from YouTube and wonder if that's what he is seeing, too, the blood on the ice, the sound of his fist pounding into that guy's face. The pause goes on a beat too long and I'm sure he's not going to reply ...)

Nathan: *Actually, it's exactly what everybody saw on* TV. *I mean, really, that's all I can say.*

(I love this answer. Classic "Go away.")

SportsRadio Guy: *Oh. Yeah, but what ...?*

Coach Raeside: *Uh, Brad?* (Brad? The announcer's name is Brad?) *If I could just interject here ...*

SportsRadio Guy: *Oh, great. Sure ... John Raeside. Coach of the 67s and also the coach of last year's gold-medal World Junior Men's hockey team.*

Coach Raeside: *Thanks, Brad. And thanks a lot for having Nathan and me on the show, too. Great to talk to you and let fans know what's going on. But actually, if I could just help*

Nathan out here for a minute, the hearing was just this past weekend, as you know, and both Hockey Canada and the IIHF *have issued formal statements and have asked us to respect the official announcements and not get into the ... uh ... nitty gritty, if you will, of the incident during the World Juniors last year. We had an* in camera *session, cleared up a lot of things that maybe weren't so clear ...*

(Hmmm. That sounds interesting).

... and both our national and international hockey bodies are happy to see Nathan get back on the ice, where he belongs. And Nathan and I, and the Ottawa 67s organization, couldn't be happier, either, I have to say.

SportsRadio Guy: *Great, thanks for that, John. But you know people are going to want to know what was going on, what was said, right? I mean, that fight was pretty spectacular and the* IIHF*'s position was surprisingly harsh—at least that's what most Canadian fans felt. People want to know—about the fight, about the decision. All that stuff.*

Coach Raeside: *Yup. I understand that. I do. But that's where we are.*

(End of comment. I'm going to hire John Raeside as my marketing guy. He's perfect. No one will ever ask me to do stupid photo-shoot stuff ever again.)

But I can say that Nathan is doing a great job of staying in shape ...

(Ultimate Frisbee, beginner CanSkate, Hillside weight room ...)

... and has worked hard on staying positive and focusing on getting his Grade 12 this year. Because you know as well as I do, Brad, even if he gets to play less than half a season, Nathan McCormick is going to go very high in the draft in June, and he'll be playing somewhere in the NHL next year.

SportsRadio Guy: *You sound sure of that.*

Coach Raeside: *Oh, I am, Brad. Absolutely sure.*

SportsRadio Guy: *How about you, Nathan? Are you looking ahead to the draft?*

Nathan: *Yeah, the draft will be great. I'm really looking forward to it. I have a lot of work to do before that, though.*

SportsRadio Guy: *And ... any teams on your radar?*

Nathan: *I guess, well, every team is on my radar. I'd be honored to play anywhere in the NHL.*

("I'm not telling you a thing, Brad." That's what he really said. Alain would love this guy.)

SportsRadio Guy: *The Sens would be awesome, though, eh? So, Nathan, we all know the story—your family ... uh ... was moving away, and you went to live with your aunt, and then with the Raeside family so you could stay in Ottawa and keep playing hockey. That must have been difficult for you.*

(I did not know this. I never really thought about Nathan's family, about parents, siblings. That's what the girls were talking about in the library. Everyone—but me—must know this stuff.

So, where is his family now? This aunt? Is she the one sending him to Hillside?)

(Look at me! So many questions!)

Nathan: *Actually, it was great living with the Raesides. John's two kids are like a little brother and sister to me. I got to stay at my school, play hockey. It was great. I owe a lot to the Raesides.*

SportsRadio Guy: *John? That must have been a bit of an adjustment.*

Coach Raeside: *Not really. Nathan fit right in. We loved having him as part of the family. He's off at a different school now, living in residence there, and to tell you the truth, Claudette and I kind of miss him. We notice our grocery bills are down, though—just saying.*

SportsRadio Guy: *Ha! I bet! Well, best of luck with the 67s this year, John. And Nathan, we'll be watching for your return to the 67s and the lead-up to the draft. Great news about the suspension, and good luck, both of you.*

Nathan and Coach Raeside: *Thanks. Thanks, Brad.*

SportsRadio Guy: *Nathan McCormick and coach John Raeside. Hockey Canada and the International Ice Hockey Federation have lifted the suspension on Nathan McCormick and he'll be returning to the 67s sometime this season. We'll take a break, then when we come back, I'll be talking to ...*

(... some hockey person with the Ottawa Senators....)

Click. Off. Ear buds out.

It's dark, quiet, and getting late—after midnight now. I lie in bed, knowing I have to get up early to practice, knowing I need sleep. But I have to let the voices find their way out of my head because, right now, they're still echoing and nudging too many thoughts to the surface.

Thoughts like this: his family moved away and he was left behind; he's going to be playing hockey in Ottawa again, which means he's probably going to be leaving Hillside Academy at some point during the school year, which means ...

We really need to get our media project finished soon.

CHAPTER 38

FILM SHOOT NO. 1

Fredrik stands on the ice holding up his phone camera. He's revolving, filming Nathan, who's skating wide circles around him. Literally.

"This good?" asks Nathan.

"Great—maybe a bit slower. Wider circles. Good."

I'm sitting in the stands after my skating lesson, legs still a bit shaky. Thanks to Fredrik, who has worked his magic on the manager of the Brick Hill Community Arena, we have ten minutes of ice time before the Zamboni comes out.

Well, actually, the boys have ice time. I have think-about-the-soundtrack time.

Nathan swoops in and out, wider and narrower circles. Skating forward, then like magic, he's suddenly skating backward. They're talking but I tune out the voices and listen.

Listen to the blades on the ice. Listen to the air. Close my eyes.

Listen for the music.

Open my eyes again.

Nope. I've got nothing.

CHAPTER 39

SICK

Weeks pass.

I catch a cold and go home for three days. Or is it four? The days run together as I lie on the couch, watching movies. It's late in November and so many assignments are due. School continues without me, and I expect that other than Fredrik, no one misses me. (No get-well emails from Victoria. Ha!)

I don't think about the media assignment because there's nothing I can do. Fredrik is in charge and texts me his progress.

Haven't found the magic yet. You?

No. Nothing

Feeling better?

No

Coming back when?

Don't know

Turn off my phone. That was two days ago.

Père brings me regular doses of tea and soup and potato chips. (Chips are like ambrosia when I have a cold. Why? I don't know. Maybe it's the salt, or the scratchiness of the chips on my scratchy throat. Maybe it's because they're bad for me and I'm already feeling bad. Whatever. Papa has stocked up on chips and Père brings me offerings in my special cereal bowl.)

No practicing, either, but I do spend hours listening—to the *Quartet*, to the Poulenc sextet.

Clapperton sends me "the dots"—that's what he calls the score—and a handwritten letter saying how much everyone is looking forward to performing with me in the concert planned for Ottawa. I listen, follow the dots, let the piece soak in. Lots of dots, or maybe more like pinpricks. Actually playing the notes won't be a stretch, but finding a way into the music might be. Maybe once the *Quartet* has been performed and tucked away out of sight?

On the fourth day of my cold, Père brings me my hundredth mug of hot tea and waves at me to shift around a bit so he can take over the end of the couch. I pull my feet up and curl into myself, noting that my back is enjoying the stretch, my bones don't ache anymore.

"Feeling better?"

Yes, maybe, but I don't respond right away, keep my eyes on the TV. This temporary free pass from the world—from Hillside, from practicing, from thinking about Hillside and practicing, and all those other things that hover just on the edge of my thinking brain—is habit-forming. It's bewitching. I could stay here on the couch forever, which is probably why Père is asking.

I glance at him and he's watching me, smiling, because he understands. He knows me.

"Good girl," he says. "Tomorrow, back to the keyboard."

I turn my eyes back to the movie—something ridiculous and fantastical and not like real life at all—and don't let him see that I'm filling up with tears.

"What a silly movie," he chuckles, and I feel one of his strong, elegant hands settle on my curled-up feet, warm and heavy through the afghan, holding me safely in place.

CHAPTER 40

MORE

"I think we need to do something," says Fredrik on my first Monday morning back at school.

We are, actually, doing something, Fredrik, Nathan, and I. We're sitting in English class, talking about our media project.

Well, that's not strictly true. I'm not talking. Talking makes me cough, and I'm so very tired of coughing. Mr. Norton has given me permission to sip on a tall thermos of hot tea during class in an effort to keep my throat soothed, and it's working, but only if I stay quiet and still. I'm wearing my warmest fleece jacket over a hoodie over two more layers. It's almost like being wrapped up in a blanket, and I suppose I should be hot, but I'm not. All I can think of is how much I would like to be back on the couch at home, watching stupid movies with Père. Away from this classroom. Away from this media project. Away from school and these people.

What's wrong with me?

Last night, Papa drove me back to Brick Hill with a supply of tissues and Hall's cough drops, and instructions to stay warm and take things slowly. The girls on my floor were watching some crazy dating show in Victoria's room as I went by, and Victoria called out to me, asked me to join them.

Nice of them, but no. I thanked her and took my cough and my tissues to my room, got ready for bed, climbed under my duvet, and looked up videos on YouTube. Wished I were still at home.

"We need to do something like what?" asks Nathan, and I'm back in English class again.

Fredrik is not happy. His vision for our media assignment—our short film—is being elusive.

Just as elusive as my vision for the film's soundtrack. My ears—inner and outer, it seems—hear only Messiaen and Poulenc, over and over and over, and nothing else seems to be able to make its way past the gates.

Messiaen and Poulenc and a lot of coughing.

"Something like a team road trip," says Fredrik, his eyes focused somewhere far away—maybe on the rocky expanses of his Swedish home and native land.

"Road trip." Nathan does not sound convinced.

"Yes," Fredrik nods, thinking. "A road trip. Or a retreat or something." He directs his bright blue headlights toward Nathan. "We need ... more."

Nathan has his chair tipped back, relaxed, his arms crossed.

"More what?" he asks.

"More everything. More from Genny. More from you," says Fredrik.

The front legs of Nathan's chair clunk back to the floor. Long pause in which the air starts to twitch. The two boys are watching each other. I'm watching them, trying not to cough.

"Okay," says Nathan slowly. A pause, then, "What do you want?"

Fredrik nods, smiles a little, and I realize I've been holding my breath. I hear other voices—"... and then we could have Brian say something about cars," Victoria is saying on the other side of the classroom—and I cough, finally. It hurts.

"Well, I'm just trying to understand where you come from, and your hockey background. I hear that your family moved away and you moved in with your coach. So what happened there?" asks Fredrik.

Nathan shrugs.

"My family moved away and I moved in with my coach," he says.

"But why?"

"Because I needed a place to live in Ottawa so I could stay with the team."

"No." Fredrik shakes his head. "I mean, why did your family move away?"

And then Nathan looks at me. I just catch the swift movement of his eyes, toward me, then away. He's looking down at his desk now, but I think what he's really seeing is us walking through St. Laurent and those boys speaking to him, those rough boys and their crude comment about me.

"It's not a secret," he says finally. "My dad moved out. My mother took my little sister and went to live in Calgary. I wanted to stay in Ottawa, so the Raesides let me live with them. That's it." He shrugs again.

Fredrik absorbs this, nods. Says, "There was something about living with a relative. Do you have relatives in Ottawa?"

"My aunt, Aunt Liz. I stayed with her for a while before the Raesides."

"But you didn't want to stay with her?"

Fredrik is like a lawyer, or one of those dogs that bites into something soft and doesn't let go, relentless. I'm amazed that Nathan isn't resisting more. I also have a feeling that Nathan isn't telling us everything.

"Stop, Fredrik. Why do you need to know all this?" I ask, and they both look at me in surprise (maybe because of my new deep, sexy voice, thanks to my coughing-damaged throat, but I don't think so).

"It's okay," Nathan says. "I'm used to people asking me questions."

And I know how to avoid answering them, too, says the speech bubble over his head, which I see and I'm sure Fredrik sees as well.

He leans back, crosses his (very big) arms across his (very wide) chest again, and talks while looking down at his desk.

"My family ... moved away. I stayed. I was already playing with the 67s. I just wanted to play hockey. My aunt knows that, so she and the Raesides made this arrangement. I stayed at my same school, stayed with the 67s."

He shrugs and looks up at Fredrik. End of story.

And then he glances at me again. *Shhhh.*

"Okay, but then there's the fight with Andersson. I mean, where did that come from?" Fredrik, still on the trail ... of something.

A moment, in which the air around me shivers and shifts.

"Making progress on your project?" asks Mr. Norton, who has appeared beside us, out of thin air, apparently.

Fredrik smiles up at him.

"Oh, yes, sir. We're making excellent progress."

Even though Nathan hasn't answered his question.

CHAPTER 41

UNIVERSITIES

University acceptances arrive all in the same week. McGill, Western, Laurier, UBC. Much money offered. I text Papa to let him know. He says musical colleagues of his and Père's across the country are checking in with him to see if that Imogen St. Pierre on their university's candidate list is who they think she (I) is (am). The musician pipeline must be gushing, because Papa mentions calls from friends at Julliard and the Curtis and the Peabody, schools I didn't even apply to.

Alain calls.

"Your father tells me that you can go anywhere, any university music program in the country or beyond," he also gushes. "If that's what you want to do, of course. How's the Poulenc coming?"

Père emails his congratulations in a brief message:

What a big decision for you! Let me know if you want

background information on any of these big university music departments. The stories I could tell ...!

So, long story short: I can go anywhere to study and play my piano. Or I can just stay home and play my piano with Papa and Père. Forever.

Wednesday afternoon, and I'm re-reading Père's email by the window at the end of the hall in our residence, when Victoria, Polly, and Melanie appear (well, actually their bubbling voices appear first, then the three of them in uniform: body-hugging yoga gear from top to toe). They've been in the gym, obviously, and glow even more than usual.

"Hey, Genny." Polly waves. "How's it going?"

Yesterday afternoon at skating, I actually got the hang of pushing and gliding, actually got up some speed and was able to cruise in a circle and stop without crashing into the boards. Polly is taking all the credit, of course, but I don't care. It was magic.

"Hi, Genny." The other girls pause, smile.

"Hi." Phone down. Apparently conversation will be required.

"Did I hear you telling Fredrik that you've had some early acceptances already?" Victoria asks. "Congratulations! I haven't heard anything." She makes a pouty baby face that actually looks really good on her. She's just one of those people who never, ever, looks bad.

I nod. Is early acceptance unusual?

"Hey, we're just dropping our stuff and going to the lounge

before supper to watch an episode of *Marry Me*. Join us!" Victoria says, while her ladies-in-waiting nod.

Sometimes I think too much and this is one of those times. Why are they asking me? What will we talk about? What is *Marry Me*?

But I force myself to shrug, smile, say "okay" with something resembling enthusiasm, and join them on the stairs back to the lounge. Braedon and Jeff are there, crashed on the couches, watching some sports news show, but the girls cajole them out of it—"Oh, you guys! You can watch that stuff any time!"—and commandeer the prime seating. It's fascinating. It's magic. How do they do that? Melanie gets the show started and I try to grasp the concept, while the girls analyze the action (what she said, what he said, what she did, what he did) in a running commentary.

Braedon and Jeff also provide a running commentary, uncomplimentary and disruptive. Everyone is laughing, including me (okay, just a little). Maybe this is what university would be like. This hanging out together and then going to play my piano.

"He said he loved me," a beautiful, heavily made-up, teary young woman on the screen is whispering to another beautiful, heavily made-up, teary young woman. They embrace and sob.

Victoria, Polly, and Melanie shake their heads, silent, enthralled. The boys are laughing outright. Braedon throws a pillow at the TV and the girls rise up like disturbed gulls, flapping their wings.

My phone buzzes with a text and I pull it out. Papa, probably. But no, it's Fredrik.

Road trip Friday. Thing @ my parents. You me Nathan. Permission form required.

No, because I'm going home to rehearse this weekend. But before I can respond, Fredrik has added.

Can your dad pick u up at my place Friday night? 11pm-ish?

I suppose Papa *could* come to Ottawa. He seems to be having a lot of meetings there lately. I still want to respond "NO."

Maybe

I'll need something to wear. How will we get to Ottawa? The silliness going on around me in the lounge and the weight of Fredrik's text starts to suck the air out of the room and I stand, suddenly, drawing eyes from the others.

"Sorry—a message I have to get ..." I say, which sounds lame, but the gulls and their pillow-armed attackers understand that kind of thing, carry on, don't even watch me leave.

In the corridor that leads to the dining hall, I find the nearest exit (when did it get so cold?) and hurry across the quadrangle to the chapel.

Supper starts in thirty minutes. I'll play until then.

Phone off.

CHAPTER 42

ROAD TRIP

Papa is in Ottawa on Friday and meets us at the Rideau Centre, bringing one of my concert dresses to wear tonight at Fredrik's house.

But before that can happen ...

The logistics of this exercise have been fraught and complex, but Fredrik has managed everything to perfection.

First, permission forms, processed under the watchful eye of Mr. Colville on Thursday evening just after supper. I fill out the details *(Friday, December 3; to Ottawa for social event at home of Fredrik Floren; transportation provided by Ambassador Floren; meeting with father afterward to spend weekend in Montreal; return to Hillside Academy Sunday night).* I then attach it to an email message, details provided by Fredrik, to Papa, who signs, scans, and returns, with a message for me: *What a nice outing for you! Yes, of course I can bring your shorter dress (yes, I know the one. You wore it in Edinburgh, at the Usher,* oui*?) And yes, meeting at the bookstore in the Rideau Centre at 6 PM is fine. I will be in Ottawa anyway ...*

Papa is spending a lot of time in Ottawa, which is convenient for me tonight. On this occasion, he will have to wait until late evening to pick me up from Fredrik's for the drive home as well. But this doesn't seem to bother him.

I will spend the evening with some colleagues. Don't worry about me, my love. Père will keep the home fires burning ...

Nathan's permission form is processed without any noticeable enthusiasm on his part. He doesn't share the details with Fredrik and me, except to ask if we can make a detour on the way to Fredrik's house. He needs to pick up something appropriate to wear.

"My coach's house," he says. That would be John Raeside, of course. I'm very well-informed after listening to that radio interview.

"No problem," Fredrik says. "First we'll have Johan take us to the Rideau to meet up with Monsieur St. Pierre, then to—where in the city do we need to go?"

Nathan gives an address in a neighborhood near St. Laurent, and Fredrik reconsiders.

"Your place first, then the Rideau. Then on to my place."

Which is in Rockcliffe Park, of course. I can imagine the home of Ambassador and Madame Floren will be stone-façaded and landscaped to perfection. Polished floors, antique furniture—or maybe angular and broad-colored, like a small and intimate IKEA store.

I leave the boys in the office with Mr. Colville, awaiting the return of Nathan's permission form (which is coming from—where? His coach? His Aunt Liz? Some other guardian?), and return to my room to finish up two assignments and listen to the last section of the *Quartet.* Typing words about *Hamlet* on my keyboard is like trying to run in sand tonight. I wish I could go to the chapel and spend a half-hour on that other keyboard, the black and white one.

(Do I really even *want* to go to school next year?)

On Friday, Victoria and her entourage slide in behind me as I'm standing at the lunch counter, trying to decide if I'm hungry enough for soup.

I'm not. I'm rarely hungry. I crave tea and toast, maybe an apple. "Eat!" Père is always urging me, hands out, as if offering an invisible platter of *something.* "It takes power to drive those hammers and you are like a sparrow when you should be a hawk."

"Did I hear you're going to some party in Ottawa with Nathan and Fredrik tonight?" asks Victoria, the unspoken words *You? Really?* hang in the speech bubble over the heads of all three girls. I think maybe *Can we come with you?* is in there somewhere, too.

I nod: "A party at his parents' house, yes." It's a *thing*, but I'm not sure they would know what that means.

The three girls are all eyes, nodding. Shiny, undulating hair. The impression they create is of a row of magazine-cover bobble heads.

"I have a feeling Nathan isn't really party-at-the-ambassador's-house material," says Victoria, turning to the other girls. The nodding continues.

"Why not?" I ask, and the nodding suddenly stops. Maybe they hear in my voice what I am surprised to hear: something fierce and battle-ready.

"Well, you know where he comes from, don't you? Where he grew up?" Victoria has lowered her voice for once. She's using her telling-secrets voice. "The other side of Montreal Road?"

They've merged, these three Sirens. Shoulder to shoulder to shoulder, eyes with little pinpricks of fire, trying to scorch me. I think they want to share the dark stuff with me, show how unprepared and unworthy I am to accompany the godlike Nathan McCormick anywhere.

That stuff doesn't work on me, though. I've already seen where Nathan comes from. *Shhhhh.*

"No, I don't really know much about him," I say, reaching for a bowl and the soup ladle. Soup it is. Soup to drown them out.

Later, after classes, Fredrik, Nathan, and I meet up in the front hallway outside the office to wait for the car. We are on the same journey, but disconnected—Fredrik is texting furiously. Nathan is in *Go away* mode, Sens cap pulled down low, eyes on his phone, and ear buds in place.

My overnight bag feels heavy and awkward as I stand a little apart, waiting, wishing I were going home to Père. Fredrik's big plan, this road trip, this nudge he thinks we need to get our project started ...

I don't care. Maybe I haven't recovered from my cold yet. Maybe it's Clapperton and the dreaded Poulenc. I could happily curl up under the duvet in my room and sleep for two days.

"He's just a few minutes away," says Fredrik and I force myself to be polite, to turn and nod in acknowledgment.

Nathan doesn't react, hasn't heard a thing.

"Are you hungry?" Fredrik asks me. "Let's stop at the *patisserie* and get something for the road."

Nathan, still with his head down, still away. Fredrik observes him but says nothing, smiles at me.

"My parents are looking forward to seeing you again," he says. "I think my mother had the piano tuned, just in case."

The car, when it arrives, isn't a car. Well, yes, it is. But it's also a lavish transportation vehicle. A super van. Leather seats. Tinted windows. Cup holders and places to plug in devices. WiFi.

"*Hej*, Johan," says Fredrik, shaking the gloved hand of the uniformed driver, an older man who answers him in Swedish and then welcomes Nathan and me aboard in perfect English. My bag is lifted gently from my hand and placed in the back.

"This is cool," says Nathan, looking around at the interior, testing a few controls on the arm of his seat.

Fredrik is in the back row on what looks like a cushy leather sofa. My seat could pass for a luxury armchair.

"You can actually swivel," he says, and we spend the next few minutes experimenting, finally swinging around so that Nathan and I are facing backward, a cozy little circle. All we need is a drinks table. Or a fire pit, maybe.

"This is how your father drives around Ottawa?" Nathan asks and Fredrik nods.

I have both hands around a tall cup of tea. The boys went with hot chocolate, and Fredrik insisted on picking up some muffins, more like cupcakes really, to hold us until we get to Ottawa. Nathan has polished off three, but I'm only halfway through one and probably won't finish it.

"He likes being able to have meetings while he's on the road with his staff, and this way, people can see each other," Fredrik explains. "A real limousine would be just too much, so this is his choice."

Nathan looks around. Nods. Chews. Shows no sign of wanting to reach for his ear buds and raise the *Go away* sign.

Our road trip—our *thing*—begins.

CHAPTER 43

FIRST STOP

Fredrik has taken advantage of a long red light to climb into the front seat to help Johan navigate to the address Nathan gives him.

We're in the neighborhood of Coach Raeside's house where, apparently, Nathan keeps part of his wardrobe—in this case, his suit, or whatever he's planning to wear to this party tonight.

Nathan has swiveled around and offers directions. "Next lights. Turn right. Third street on the left." Nathan talks. Fredrik points. Johan drives until Nathan says: "This is it."

"Come on." Fredrik is already reaching for the door, while I'm peering through the late-afternoon murk at the brick house, a white front door perched on a porch framed by two sentinel pines. A bare-branched maple fills much of the front yard.

Nathan turns to open his side door and catches my eye. Shrugs. It's okay.

Our team of three emerges.

CHAPTER 44

LATER

"I can play this, too," says Alicia Raeside.

She puts her little thumbs on Middle C and plays the next keys in each direction with both hands. C, B, A, G, G with her left. C, D, E, F, G with her right. Pauses to enjoy the resolution and then climbs them back toward Middle C, where she finishes by lifting both hands off the keyboard as if some invisible puppet master is tweaking her strings. Silent applause thunders throughout the concert hall (family room).

She looks up at me, waiting for me to say something.

"I like that one. Does it have a name?"

Vigorous nod. "My teacher calls it 'Steps.' Do you want me to teach it to you?"

I learn "Steps" and play it for her approval. I suggest we try playing it at the same time, which confounds her ("But we can't *both* be on Middle C ..." Furrowed brow.) I place my thumbs on a c two octaves higher and away we go. Then she wants to try a different octave, too, so now we're stepping all over the keyboard while she starts giggling, pressed against my side, and I don't even mind. It's lovely.

"Listen to you!" says Claudette Raeside from the doorway.

From behind her, across the front hallway, I can hear the rumble of Nathan's voice in the living room with John Raeside and Aunt Liz. The French doors are closed.

The aunt is a surprise. As we come in through the door from the street—Nathan, then me, then Fredrik—she is standing in the front hallway. I'm still turned, bent over and taking off my boots as they embrace, long and hard. Little woman, very big boy.

"I didn't know you were going to be here!" Nathan's voice is different. This is what a happy Nathan sounds like.

"John called and said you were doing a fly-by to collect your gear for a party," she says. "Thought it was a nice chance for a little visit."

Two little Raesides, a boy and a girl, are popping with excitement, and as soon as Nathan lets go of his aunt, they leap at him. Evidently he's used to this.

Fredrik and I have been standing back, but now Nathan introduces us, the kids still clinging to him. Handshakes all round.

I thought this was going to be a quick stop, but apparently we are having a proper visit. We're ushered into the living room, the kids chattering at Nathan while he juggles them and continues a conversation with his aunt. Fredrik leads me to the loveseat and we sit. He leans forward a little, as if he's driving and I'm the passenger. (Of course, Fredrik does this on purpose, and I love him for it.)

Conversation, and tea, and soft drinks, and homemade chocolate chip cookies, none of which I need, thanks to our stop at the *patisserie* back in Brick Hill. I sip and nibble and observe, not required to do anything more. This isn't my show.

Conversation. Hockey, news about the 67s, some player named Broderick who was late for practice (not the first time, apparently). Aunt Liz asks about school, so Fredrik joins in and is his charming self. I smile and nod.

"Imogen plays the piano, Ali." Mrs. Raeside—Claudette—smiles over at me after a few minutes, and says to her little daughter, who has her hands wrapped around Nathan's arm, "You should play something for her."

"Okay." Alicia lets go of Nathan and bounces off the couch. "The piano's over there, in the family room."

"You're not going yet, are you?" She turns back to Nathan and he shakes his head.

"Nope. I'll say goodbye, don't worry."

Alicia, satisfied, leads the way. Command performance, and I follow. Behind me, I can hear Claudette telling Fredrik that Lucas is a gaming whiz and would love to show him the set-up in his room. Fredrik, as I do, knows an exit line when he hears it.

Ten minutes later: "Listen to you!" says Claudette.

"Mommy! Imogen taught me a new way to play 'Steps'! Listen! We'll play it for you." Alicia says all this without turning around, hands finding their position over the keyboard.

Her mother stands beside us as we perform several variations. Much giggling from Alicia. I keep it classy and adopt my best performance face. Alicia is in stitches now and misses a note. So I miss a note, too, and we descend into atonal chord thumping. Claudette applauds.

"Best concert I've heard in years," she says. "Imogen plays the piano in concerts, you know, Alicia. Maybe she would play something just for us?"

Alicia sits beside me on the bench as I play *Wachet Auf*. Her mother had asked her to move but I say no, it's fine. She can watch my fingers. I remember this, sitting with Papa, with Père, and marveling at the way the movement of fingers on ivory creates the music, and then doing this with my mother and hearing only the sound of the hammers striking the strings. My poor mother.

The French doors open across the hallway and Nathan is speaking: "Yeah, I can't wait."

I've moved on to a Brahms waltz and when I'm finished, it's time to go.

CHAPTER 45

RENDEZVOUS AT RIDEAU

The Rideau Centre is packed on a Friday night. I suggest to the boys that they can wait down in the posh, warm, comfortable car while I navigate the crowds for my rendezvous with Papa at the book store, but Fredrik insists.

"We all go. All for one, etc., etc."

The journey from the Raesides' house to the Rideau is quiet. Nathan's suit bag hangs on a hook over one of the rear windows, and he spends the short trip gazing out the window, silent. I do the same on my side, with echoes of the Raesides' family room in my head. The sweetness of *Wachet Auf* cancels out the mad parade of lights and traffic outside.

Fredrik, when I glance at him, is texting. Possibly letting his parents know our ETA. Or maybe letting William and Berit know what a bore his traveling companions are. He catches me watching him and grins. Goes back to texting.

Late November means it's Christmas at the Rideau, complete with carols playing over the tinny PA system and eye-smashing decorations everywhere. The bookstore is already advertising seasonal specials with pop-up Grinches pointing to the holiday movie display. I find Papa in the magazine section, leafing through the latest classical music magazine, with my dress (also in a suit bag) draped over his arm.

"My love." He kisses me with a one-armed hug as I drift in close beside him and he hands over his cargo. "The dress. And I hope I have picked the right one. Shoes in the bottom."

"Hello, Fredrik." He turns his attention to the rest of the team while I unzip slightly to see whether he really did pick the right dress. (He did. Relief.)

"Monsieur St. Pierre," says Fredrik, shaking his hand. "Always a pleasure, sir." Fredrik can say things like this and still sound like a well-brought-up Swedish boy, not some old guy playing a duke in a black-and-white movie. "And may I introduce our friend, Nathan McCormick."

"*Enchanté,*" says Papa, his elegant, long-fingered hand disappears in Nathan's paw for a moment as they shake, and he looks hard at Nathan before releasing him. "Ah, Monsieur McCormick, you are a hockey player, I believe? Your name is familiar to me."

I'm astonished. So is Nathan, but then, he's also used to people recognizing him.

"Yes, sir." That's it. Nathan doesn't offer any details, his voice and face in neutral.

Papa nods, looks at me, smiles. *A hockey-playing boy*. I'm quite sure he's picturing me on the ice, learning how to skate, wearing the hockey-boy-recommended hockey gloves.

"And you're off to a party ... how lovely." He includes the three of us in his beam of approval.

"Yes, my parents are having a few people over to celebrate my mother's birthday, so we are going to join the festivities," says Fredrik, and I am immediately filled with horror.

"You didn't tell me it was a birthday party," I accuse him. "I don't have a gift."

"Me neither," says Nathan.

"No gifts required." Fredrik waves us off. "Just our company. Really, that's all she wants."

I'm rattled now. Fredrik has told us nothing about this event, except for the need to dress up a bit. What else hasn't he told us?

"I'm sure it will be a lovely evening," Papa says. "And if you give me the address, Fredrik, I will be waiting outside in the car at eleven o'clock to bring Cinderella home from the ball."

"Oh, please come in, sir. I know my parents would love to say hello. They're huge fans."

Papa smiles, nods, and shrugs in one graceful movement and then turns to me. "And before I forget." He lifts a shiny magazine off the shelf in front of us.

Maclean's. There's an unflattering photo of a politician on the front with an incendiary headline plastered across the top. Papa points to a section on the bottom: "On the shoulders of giants: Ten young Canadians on the rise."

A photo from that hideous photo shoot. My face, serious and pale and, frankly, not very appealing, looking into Ebenezer's camera. And in the background, my classmates' eyes peering over copies of *Hamlet*, held open and covering most of their faces.

"Ha!" Fredrik is leaning in on the other side. "Look who's front and center behind you!"

Of course, the Sirens. Victoria, Polly, and Melanie have bagged the front row of the chorus. I hadn't paid any attention to what was going on behind me that day, but this doesn't come as a surprise. Obviously the permission forms for publishing photographs of my classmates made their way through the system.

"Open to the story," Fredrik urges me. "Let's see the full photo."

"It's actually quite a nice piece," Papa says, close to my ear, reassuring.

I finally find it and open the magazine to the right page. The first spread includes three photos: two small ones on the left-hand page and a larger one on the right: me out front, and my English class behind me, with their faces obscured by their open copies of *Hamlet*. I flip quickly to the next spread and see seven more photos, smaller. I suppose I should be thrilled. *Maclean's* has given me the spotlight.

"You look lovely," Papa hugs me. "And I see Fredrik right there."

Sure enough, there he is, just off to the left, his tufted Viking hair and blue eyes and *Hamlet*.

"Montreal's Imogen St. Pierre brings a lifetime of musical virtuosity to the concert stage," Fredrik reads out loud. *"As a member of the Grammy- and Juno-award-winning Trio St. Pierre with her father and grandfather—celebrated cellist Maxim St. Pierre and national treasure of the violin, Félix St. Pierre—this eighteen-year-old piano whiz has been wowing international audiences with her ability to raise the most difficult scores to ethereal heights—and she's been doing it professionally since age six. Look out Jamie Parker, Angela Hewitt, and Marc-André Hamelin! The future of this country's ensemble piano performance just might be found in the hands of this exquisite young prodigy.*

"Wow, Genny!"

The flattering and exaggerated words don't register with me, however. What does register is that Nathan is not in the accompanying photo. I know he was there, of course. Maybe he stood just far enough off to one side that he knew he'd be cropped out. Or he positioned himself behind Braedon or Jeff, hidden.

Or maybe he just moved away from the camera's bullying

lens and waited—until that moment when he stepped in and it all came to an abrupt halt (without a single punch thrown). In any case, he's not there in the photo.

Which might explain why he has drifted away from us and is now flipping through a hockey magazine in the sports section.

CHAPTER 46

PARTY

"I adore your music," gushes Madame Alvarez. She is the wife of someone from the Spanish embassy.

We're standing in the Florens' main living room (they have several) where the party is underway. Food has been consumed, drinks drunk. We're sipping tea and coffee now. I suspect the mask of polite interest on my face is starting to slip. Fredrik didn't tell me I would be on my feet for most of the evening.

Nathan in a dark suit, shirt, and tie is ... well ... impressive. Fredrik embodies the sleek European fashionista (can men be fashionistas?) in shades of blue. Judging from the looks on their faces earlier, when I join them in the upstairs sitting room after changing into my black concert dress, I also hit the mark. Standing there, we all laugh, mostly at ourselves.

"Selfie before we go downstairs and act like grown-ups," says Fredrik and, when Nathan hesitates, he adds, "I'm not going to post it all over Facebook, don't worry. It's for us, that's all."

I am squished between them in the middle, Fredrik—phone extended, to my left—and Nathan on my right, carefully leaning in at my shoulder, barely making any contact. Fredrik orders us to "Say cheese!" and I hear—no, not "cheese"—the rumble of Nathan's low laugh. Then we do a serious one, smiles forbidden. Photo session over, we move apart and wait as Fredrik texts both images to us.

The smiling one is silly, unflattering in the worst way, but the serious one—the serious one works. Three pairs of eyes, different eyes, but it's as if we were all thinking the same thing as the camera captured us. No idea what that thing is. Whatever. It's a good shot. I will look at this one again.

"Ready?" Fredrik looks at me, grins, elfin. Looks at Nathan. Yes, we're ready. We follow Fredrik downstairs to the party.

Later ...

"Thank you," I nod and smile at Mme Alvarez.

She continues the conversation and I recognize the words of someonc who actually knows something about our music, about Père in particular. I'm happy to talk about Père all night, so I answer her questions about his past performances, and his quirky sense of humor, and his mentoring of young musicians. Nothing about his tired fingers.

As we chat, I glance briefly around the room. Fredrik is

completely at home, of course, and has been eddying among the guests for most of the evening. Nathan was taken over by Mr. Floren as soon as we appeared (Instructions from Fredrik? An intuitively good host? A Dad move?), and I've heard snatches of hockey talk, but since many of the guests are not Swedish, the beaten and bloodied ghost of Lars Andersson doesn't hover accusingly in any corners. Also, there has been lots of food. Nathan has coped just fine.

"Excuse me, Sofia, and I'm so sorry to interrupt, but Elsa has to leave soon, and we have been meaning to ask you about your trip to New York last month." Mrs. Floren appears out of nowhere with a short blonde woman. Elsa with a forgotten last name. (I met her at some point earlier. We nod and smile. Greek? No, maybe also Swedish?)

The conversation turns to hotels and airports and art galleries, and I feel a touch on my arm.

"Will you excuse us, please?" says Fredrik's mother and draws me away from the chatting women, who smile and continue without us. A seamless exit. Mrs. Floren is a pro.

"Come, my dear," she says to me in French, her hand still on my arm. "I hope you don't mind, but I'm sure you need a break from all this babbling."

"Not at all," I protest but she just continues to smile and lead me away, out of the room, down a long hallway to an open door. I follow her into a gently lit room with heavy drapes and several low squishy couches and chairs. A table with flowers. A Persian carpet. A fireplace. Exquisite paintings on the walls.

A piano.

"I had it tuned this week," says Mrs. Floren. "Please, feel free to relax in here. I'm sure you need a break."

Fredrik has obviously briefed his mother well.

"You're too kind," I say, feeling guilty. Papa would be disappointed in me, in my bad manners. Escaping from a party to hide away in the piano room.

But my head, my fingers, are already reaching, even if my feet are not. She is kind. She pushes me, smiles.

"Go. I'll sit here and listen for a moment, then I will leave you in peace," she says. "My own private concert. How lovely."

So I do that. I play for her, Stenhammer's *Late Summer Nights*, dredged up from my memories of a concert series we did at the university in Uppsala when I was thirteen. I hope she doesn't notice that I make far too many mistakes, but I'm so happy to be here, away from the party, I just improvise. I improvise way past Stenhammer and into some other place.

At one point, I hear the door gently open and close—the air changes briefly—and I play on until the long day of school and travel and having to be around people I don't know catches up to me, and I bring it all to a close with a single long note. Lift my hands off the keyboard and rest them in my lap, eyes still closed. Breathe. Wish Père were here to massage my shoulders as only Père can.

"That was good," says Nathan. "I could have fallen asleep."

Quick recovery from a moment of terror. I thought I was alone in this room.

"What every musician wants to hear," I say over my shoulder.

"What was that you were playing?"

I shrug. I suppose he wants to know who the composer is, but of course there isn't a composer. I'm the composer, but I couldn't notate what I just played if I tried all night. It comes out of somewhere, it exists for as long as I play it, and then it just floats away as the strings and wood stop vibrating.

"Just making it up as I go along," I say.

I turn around on the piano bench and look at him. He's in one of the chairs, jacket off, tie loosened, legs stretched out long in front of him, with his hands laced together on his chest. The poster boy for relaxation.

"So, what do you think of our road trip?" he asks me.

I shrug, half-turn back to the keyboard, rest my hand on the keys.

"I don't know. I enjoyed meeting the Raesides. Alicia is sweet." He makes a noise that (I think) indicates agreement. "And Fredrik's parents have been very kind." I run my right hand up the ivory keys and feel the edges slide under my fingertips in a pattering like running footsteps. "This piano is lovely."

"I can play the piano, too, you know."

"Really?" I turn to look at him.

He heaves himself out of the chair. "Shove over."

He sits beside me and starts playing—oh, God, no—the bass part of "Heart and Soul."

He's awful, but I will give him credit for playing with energy, at least. I do my part, keep it simple at first, then add some extra notes, Baroque-ify it. His grasp of tempo is non-existent, but he makes up for it with his enthusiasm. I start to giggle and bail on him after five repetitions.

"See?" he says. "Not a complete fail."

"No." I'm still giggling. "Not a *complete* fail."

He doesn't rise from the bench, though. "Play something," he says, and shifts a little further down to give me room.

"What do you want to hear?"

"I don't know. Anything. I'm not really up on classical music."

I start with a Chopin Etude (the "Tristesse," my favorite), then the same Brahms waltz I played for Alicia, then segue into the new-agey "Lightning's Theme" from *Final Fantasy III*. Maybe he's a gamer. He sits quiet and still until the end.

"I can see why you want to protect those hands," he says.

Then he asks, "What's it like? Getting up on stage in front of all those people to play? Do you get nervous?"

Do I get nervous about playing? I haven't thought about that for a very long time.

"In the beginning, when I was younger," I say, remembering the reassuring warmth of Père's hand holding mine in the wings, pre-performance, at the National Arts Centre. "I used to be nervous before going on stage, but now, as soon as I sit at the piano, no. I'm fine."

He's beside me so I don't actually look at him, but I see out of the corner of my eye that he's nodding.

I feel brave. I mean, it's just the two of us here. No audience, no listeners, no Radio Guys or TV commentators. So I ask.

"Do you get nervous before your games?"

What I really mean is, *Are you afraid? Are you afraid you'll get hurt, or someone else will get hurt? Are you afraid of fighting? Of all that violence out on the ice?* I don't think the word "nervous" covers this, but it's his word, and that's as far as I'm willing to go.

He shrugs. "No. Not nervous. Fired up. Ready."

Long pause in which I consider the YouTube image of his face after beating the crap out of Andersson. *Fired up.*

"But sometimes," he adds, "in the middle of something, like a really close-in scoring chance, or a big hit or something, you get this rush of ... I don't know ... I guess it's adrenalin. And it can be good, if you're the one about to score or hit some guy. But it can be bad, too, if you're on the receiving end. Or if someone gets hurt. Like watching a car crash happening in front of you and you're driving right into it or something."

Another pause.

"I guess that can be pretty bad. Scary. Yeah. But then it's over and you just keep going."

He slides off the piano bench and returns to the chair. Flops down, stretches out, looks over at me. Shrugs.

"I love hockey so much, I just take that stuff as part of the game."

Now, *that* I understand. No matter how difficult or boring the piece is, or how much the audience coughs, or how horrible the hall's acoustics are, or how unsure I am of the other players (Clapperton!)—or how often Père's fingers fail—I still need to play my piano.

Fredrik appears at the door.

"Ahhh. The time-out room."

CHAPTER 47

IN TRANSIT

Somewhere out there in the dark are cows and farmers' fields, barns, silos, probably deer and coyotes. Rocks and stones. This part of Ontario is full of stones that shimmy up to the surface with the frost and require picking in the spring. We're somewhere past Casselman and there's no moon tonight, so no street lights or reflection off the snowy expanse that stretches away on each side of the highway, sometimes hidden behind curtains of pine bush and scrub.

Marc-André Hamelin plays Percy Grainger (Papa selected the playlist, probably this one because of the comment in that *Maclean's* article). Sweet English piano music and a humming car engine. A smooth road, not too much traffic, and easy driving for Papa. We don't talk, so I drift in and out of this moment and find myself, occasionally, back in Fredrik's piano room.

The boys talk while I turn back to the keyboard. They talk

about hockey, Nathan's hockey mostly. About his progression up the sports ladder and what it's like to be selected by a team, groomed, trained, coached, discouraged and encouraged, keeping at it hard, because you hope that you might one day make it to the NHL. How hard it is. How much work is required. Fredrik is genuinely interested—this world is far removed from his own—and he asks good questions that Nathan answers without holding back. They laugh sometimes. Male bonding in progress.

I just play. After a while, I lose myself and stop listening to them, and it's only when Fredrik's mother taps on the door to tell us that Papa has arrived to take me home, that I lift my hands off the keys and realize that the boys had stopped talking quite some time ago. Our *thing* is over.

"You had a nice time?" Papa asks early on in our drive along the 417 toward Montreal.

I tell him about the amount of food and the Spanish woman who wanted to know all about Père. Mrs. Floren's freshly-tuned piano. He asks about the drive to Ottawa, so I tell him about Fredrik's father's amazingly luxurious van, and stopping at the Raesides' house and playing "Steps" with Alicia. ("Ha!" Papa loves this. "Memories of another little girl!")

"It was nice to meet your friends," Papa says, nodding. What he means is that it's nice that I have friends. Fredrik—well, of course. Nathan? After five repetitions of "Heart and Soul," I suppose we could be considered friends, too.

"I think you had fun tonight."

"I did have fun," I admit. "But I'm tired now. I'm looking forward to getting home and not having to make conversation with people I don't know. I just want to sleep in my own bed with no noisy girls down the hall. And practice on my own piano." And see Père.

"The *Quartet* tomorrow," Papa reminds me.

Yes, back to work. Christmas is coming.

CHAPTER 48

WALKING

Papa has asked Vianne Courtemanche to join us for rehearsal on Saturday.

"You're more beautiful every time I see you," she says to me as we hug and kiss at the front door. A whiff of perfume. Wild, wavy silvery hair that tickles my face.

Vianne is like an aunt to me. She is obligated to say things like that.

"Thank you for joining us." Père also embraces her. "Brave woman!"

Vianne is a woodwinds specialist at McGill and plays in several ensembles, although less and less now. She's involved in some sort of administrative role in the Schulich School of Music and works with the National Arts Centre orchestra. She and Papa have collaborated many times, rehearsed in our living room, always with laughter, often with wine.

I know that my mother hated Vianne, which makes me like her even more. (There, the dark side of Imogen rises to the surface ...)

"Delighted to assist," she says. "I'm no Tony Clapperton, but I can count a measure and hit a few notes on this thing."

"This thing" is a Buffet Crampon, an exquisite instrument like Clapperton's, but hers, inherited from some former teacher, is cherished and old and magnificent.

"Oh, well, I guess that will do," says Papa.

Later, much later, when I'm down deep and having difficulty climbing back to the surface, Vianne says to me, "Bundle up, we're going out to get some air."

It's cold now, December cold. There's snow on the yards and trees, and just enough frost on the sidewalk that our boots crunch a little as we walk slowly, arm in arm, from one pool of light to the next. Vianne is swathed in a full-length black felt coat with a hat of fur and a bright red knitted scarf (knitted by tiny elves using some kind of silken, shimmery yarn) wrapped several times around her long neck. She is, as always, elegant, stylish, ready for some designer's runway.

I'm wearing my long black puffy parka, my favorite hat crocheted by my long-dead grandmother, Papa's tartan scarf.

We don't match, Vianne and I, but I love her anyway, and I know she loves me, too. She holds my arm close to her side, her other hand holding my mittened hand. We're attached.

It's lovely and cozy. Our steps match, slow and measured and soothing. The cold air, the even tempo of our walking, the emergence of a few Christmas lights in the gloom. I take a deep breath and feel myself coming back to myself.

"It's a difficult piece in many ways, isn't it?" says Vianne. Squeezes my arm. Of course, she knows me.

"Yes. But I love it," I say.

"Yes, me, too."

"I wish you were performing it with us, Vianne. I wish you were coming with us to London."

She laughs at that. We walk past the stop sign and on to the next block.

"A tour together. What fun!" she says. "I miss you, Imogen. I don't see you nearly enough."

"I'm usually away at school. On weekends we're usually rehearsing. Then back to school."

"What about next year? Do you have plans?"

The big question. My shrug transmits through our joined arms. "I don't know. I've been accepted at all the universities I applied to, but ... well ... I just don't know."

"You don't know which one to pick? Or you don't know if you want to go to university?"

"Both."

We walk some more.

"You could stay home and come to McGill," she says. "Just

think—your papa would be your teacher for Theory and Analysis. I could audition you for the chamber music ensemble."

And Père would be there, too, and when I came home we could talk about our day, play duets, watch hockey on TV. Maybe watch Nathan on the ice against the Habs.

"Yes, I've thought of that," I say. "Staying home, I mean."

We've come to another stop sign and pause, together. There's a park across from us, a dark expanse of snow and trees, dotted with lights along its path. We turn and start back toward my house.

"Or you could make the big leap," says Vianne. "Julliard, although there's that whole American big city thing. Western, not sure that's a good fit for you. Did you apply to UBC? Such a marvelous city, Vancouver! Gorgeous university campus, of course, and the Chan Centre is excellent."

I don't say anything.

"Far away, though, isn't it?" she says. "Not such a bad thing, getting away."

"Do you think so, Vianne?"

She doesn't answer right away. We walk for a few minutes, past houses, from light post to light post.

"I think perhaps things are changing," she says finally, squeezing my hand.

Père. She means Père, of course.

We don't speak again until we come through the front door of my house.

"Change can be a very good thing," she says, just loud enough for me to hear as we peel off our coats and scarves, reach for tissues.

And then she's saying something to Papa, who greets us with offers of beef stew, freshly baked bread, and wine. Laughter from Père and candles on the table in the dining room. Enough for now.

CHAPTER 49

FROZEN

Père and I are working through the final movement of the *Quartet* on Sunday morning. Piano and violin only, so Papa is sitting in the armchair, listening, assessing, sometimes nodding.

It's an odd piece that way and in performance, it will be even stranger. While Père and I bring it to a close, Papa and Clapperton will be sitting, still and silent, on stage with us.

Actually, I'm glad I'm not the one who has to sit on stage without playing for seven or eight long minutes, more or less. Once this piece is done, I want to stand, bow, and leave the stage. Go to a dark corner and shake for a few minutes, alone. Well, maybe with Père beside me.

We've played it through four times now. Those last high chords, Père's angel voice on a barely vibrating string, then the silence.

"Your phone is buzzing," Papa says.

Sure enough, there it is, over on the couch with my school bag and books. I can see the tiny words lighting up the screen as a text comes in.

"Go," smiles Père, laying down his instrument and stretching. "We are done. I know I'm done. Lunch, Maxim?"

It's Fredrik, texting both me and Nathan.

Pond frozen. Will talk to Norton. Filming this week

I read the words and wonder exactly what he's expecting from me. Another text arrives.

Bring warmest clothes. Night shoot. Under the lights

There are no lights around the pond. On the path toward it, and on the school building, some distance away, yes. Lights—supplied by video-wiz Fredrik? Maybe the moon and stars? No matter. Apparently I will be sitting in the dark/light, watching Nathan skate and Fredrik film while I try to hear the perfect soundtrack. And yes, that will be cold.

But I trust Fredrik. I know he has a plan, so I respond:

K

From Nathan, nothing.

And then, much later, after supper, as I'm getting my things together for the drive back to school, Nathan texts me. Me alone.

Bring skates

CHAPTER 50

CHRISTMAS CONCERT, PART 1

I'm practicing on Monday morning in the chapel when Monsieur Manuel shows up.

"Sorry to disturb you, Imogen, but we have a situation and I wonder if you can help."

M. Manuel is from some tiny town in the Gatineau, a jazz trumpeter with regular gigs in Toronto and Montreal—and even the States sometimes throughout the summer. How he ended up teaching the music program at Hillside is a mystery to me, although I know most musicians have to teach or work in a store or something. Teaching here can't be easy, especially since there's a string program as well as a band. Actually, I think it must be hell for him.

"It's the Christmas concert," he says, shakes the papers in his hand. A score.

The concert. The annual musical free-for-all that marks the

end of December's classes. The night the school puts on a show. Parents are invited to attend before whisking their sons and daughters away for the holidays. (For everyone else, it's a bus to either Ottawa or Montreal the next day, and connections to airports and train stations.) The choir sings, the band and string orchestra play separately and together. A few soloists do their thing (there's a boy in Grade 10, Tomas Oliveri, who has the voice of an angel. No doubt he'll be on the program.) And then, to keep things from getting too tame, some of the students organize themselves into acts and perform their own arrangements of popular seasonal songs. It's supposed to be fun and good-natured, even the less successful performances. Everyone applauds enthusiastically. There's a little reception afterward with snacks and drinks. The Season of Good Cheer is officially kicked off.

From the look on M. Manuel's face, it appears this year might be different, however.

"It's the Finzi 'Eclogue,'" M. Manuel says. "The Grade 10 strings have been working on it all term, with Maya Chang on the piano. You know Maya?"

I nod. Maya is a talented flautist. Piano, not so much.

"Well, she got called home a week early and won't be here for the concert." M. Manuel runs one hand through his messy (charming but messy) black hair and shakes the score in his other. "I could probably fake my way through it but I'm also conducting.

I need a pianist. Do you know it? Do you think you could drag us through it for the concert?"

I do know the "Eclogue for Piano and Strings," although I've never performed it. It's for string orchestra, not a trio.

"Probably," I say. "Could I take a look?"

It's not the full score—more of an "Easy Piano" version intended for high school musicians, the bare bones of Finzi's sweet little piece. Shorter, too. It won't be difficult to pull this together.

"We'll need to rehearse you with the orchestra," he says. "Would you be free during the lunch break today for a first pass, maybe?"

I set the score on the piano's music stand and look for the trouble spots, the tempo changes. My fingers find their place on the keys and I try out the first few bars. No, this won't be difficult.

"Yes, lunchtime I could come. In the music room?"

He nods, looking like a man who has been pardoned from hanging. "You're a lifesaver, Imogen. I can't thank you enough."

But there's more.

Before English class starts, Victoria, Melanie, and Polly surround me at my desk, twittering with excitement.

"Genny! We really, really need a favor."

Ominous.

"It's a music thing, so pretty easy for you, I'm sure," says Polly, my skating buddy.

They're going to perform "All I Want for Christmas Is You"

at the concert, and they want it to be "classy," so could I please play the piano for them? Maybe come up with a "classy" arrangement? Would I be able to rehearse it with them this afternoon before supper?

"I'm not sure I know that song," I say and they're struck dumb.

"Of course you do," Victoria assures me. Of course I don't. "Melanie—open YouTube and show her that scene from *Love, Actually.*"

"I know it," Fredrik says, and he starts singing something vaguely familiar until Melanie finds the clip on YouTube and swings her laptop across the desk in front of me, turning up the volume to drown him out.

Okay, yes, I know it. And they want it "classy."

"Please, Genny! We don't want it to be just another karaoke version, you know? We want to change it up a bit, and you're so good on the piano." Victoria is excited about collaborating.

Why not? A little Finzi. A little classy pop Christmas cheer.

"Sure, okay."

Victoria actually hugs me for the first time ever. "Thank you *so much!*" she gushes. "This is going to be awesome!"

This is what I'm thinking:

Papa and Père always attend the Christmas concert. I'll have to warn them.

CHAPTER 51

FILM SET

"Oh, come on, Mr. Norton! Can't we stay and watch?"

Victoria is whining, pouting, trying to look adorable. Mr. Norton is oblivious, of course. He's shaking his head, pointing up the lawn—the expanse of dark, snowy lawn—toward the school, in full herding mode.

"Go. This is a film set and no extras or spectators are required. Everyone back to the school building, please."

Skaters are straggling off the ice, clumping awkwardly over to the three benches available for skate changing. Some of them ignore the benches and stomp up the snowy yard to the school doors where their warm shoes wait inside. Lots of talking and laughing, red faces, dripping noses.

"Not fair," Victoria says, looking back at Nathan who is still out on the pond skating slow circles around the perimeter, swooping a bit as he changes edges, hands in the pockets of his jacket, hoodie hood up over his Sens cap. He doesn't seem to feel the cold the way we all do.

"Special dispensation," Fredrik says to Victoria. "Sorry. It's a closed film set."

"Why? What are you going to be doing?" she asks.

Fredrik shrugs. "I'm going to be filming a guy skating around on the pond in the dark."

I'm standing apart, shivering in my puffy parka. While I was skating (slowly, carefully, hockey-gloveless among my ice-friendly fellow students), I was fine, but now, standing still and waiting for Fredrik to give me instructions, with the darkness well set-in and the temperature definitely dropping, I'm starting to shiver.

"Do you have everything you need, Fredrik?" asks Mr. Norton after he's shooed Victoria and her posse back up the path to the school.

They talk technical stuff for a moment. The video equipment we will use, including the school's drone-mounted camera. The lighting—Mr. Jamieson is currently checking power cords and light stands and giving Fredrik instructions on placement and adjustment of what look like stage spotlights.

I look over at Nathan skating in and out of shadows on the ice, oblivious. Perhaps this pond is his version of a piano in the chapel.

"Well, break a leg," says Mr. Norton to Fredrik and me, finally. "Let's leave them to it, Andy."

We hear the snowy crunch, crunch of their footsteps recede as Mr. Norton and Mr. Jamieson merge with the darkness beyond our lighted film set, and then Fredrik catches my eye. Rubs his hands together like some mad professor.

"This is going to be great," he says. Grins.

All I can think about is getting warm, but I can't help smiling back at him, Techno-Wiz Boy, ready to roll.

"Nathan?" he calls. "Ready?"

Nathan looks up, carves a slow corner and heads toward us. "Ready."

"Genny?" Fredrik looks at me and I nod. Try not to shiver.

"Right. Let's go."

CHAPTER 52
BENCH

I'm finally warm. That's because I'm squished between Nathan, who gives off heat like a 100-watt light bulb, on my right, and Fredrik, squeezed in on my left, as well as a heavy blanket tucked around my legs. Clever Fredrik has brought a whole duffel bag full of warm gear, including a thermos of hot chocolate. "I forgot the Baileys, though," he says.

The boys don't appear to feel the cold: Fredrik, the hardy Viking, and Nathan, who is used to spending his time in cold places, surrounded by ice and perpetually in motion. As a lifelong Montrealer, I'm letting the side down.

We're sipping hot chocolate from cups Fredrik borrowed from Mrs. Clouthier in the cafeteria, and we're taking a break. Well, the boys are taking a break. I've been sitting on this bench, shivering, or else walking slowly along the edge of the pond (still in my skates), well out of camera range, watching Nathan skate while Fredrik flies the drone or looks through the lens of the camera and creates his magic. We've been here for an hour now and I'm freezing.

When Fredrik lands the drone after its fifth run, Nathan skates over and says, "You're cold, aren't you. We should take a break and warm up."

Fredrik had been intent on his toys and now he looks over at me.

"Oh, Genny, I'm sorry. Hot chocolate break on the bench. Come on."

He puts an arm around me and leads me to the bench, pulls out the blanket. I would protest that they shouldn't worry about me, they can keep on filming, I'm fine, but in fact, I'm so cold, I'm not sure I can get the words out.

"Here." Fredrik deposits me in the middle of the bench, tucks the blanket around me, and Nathan immediately sits beside me. Crowds me, actually, and when I make a move to shift over and give him more space, he puts his arm around my shoulders and pulls me in close to his side. Like a dad, protective.

"Jesus, your teeth are chattering. Why didn't you say something?"

It's odd to be so close to him like this, perhaps even awkward, but blissfully warm, so I just sit still, looking out at the pond with its odd shadows, cast by the spotlights arranged around the perimeter. If Victoria were here right now, she would die of envy.

"Here, this will help," says Fredrik and places a cup of hot chocolate between my trembling, mittened hands. He offers Nathan an empty cup and comes back to the bench with the thermos and a cup of his own. Fills them up.

"Skål!" He and Nathan clink cups. I'm too busy holding mine with two hands and sipping to join in.

Heaven. This is heaven. It's like when I was younger and Papa would tuck me into bed and pull the duvet tight, gather it around me so I was swaddled and cozy warm. Only, here on this bench, it's not goose down surrounding me, but Nathan and Fredrik. And hot chocolate.

"Thank you, Fredrik, the chocolate is helping." I drink it slowly. Close my eyes. Yes, this is a lot like being tucked into bed. Actually, I think I might be ready to go to sleep now.

The boys are talking about the shoot. When Nathan speaks, his chest rumbles near my ear. They talk about the filming they just did, technical things like where the light is best, and what Nathan did on that section at the far side of the pond, how fast he was going, whether they need to do that part again. Fredrik is excited about the drone camera and explains what special effect he was looking for with the lighting.

Me, I drift in and out to the sound of their voices. The hot chocolate is gone, there's no reason to move or speak or even look at anything. I open my eyes but they just want to close again.

Fredrik: "It's like you're disappearing every time you go into those shadows on the far side ..."

Nathan: "The ice is crap over there, so it's just as well you don't need much from that part ...."

Fredrik: "The overhead is going to be spectacular ..."

Nathan: "They did something like that with a camera at training camp for the Worlds last year ..."

Père: *"Fais dodo, Colas mon p'tit frère ..."*

(Why is Père here, singing that old lullaby?)

I open my eyes, shake myself awake, and Nathan shifts a bit but stays glued to my side. I'm fine with this because I'm warm, finally, thanks to him.

Fredrik: "My parents enjoyed meeting you the other night."

Nathan: "It was a good night. I didn't know what to expect but it was good."

Fredrik: "Nice meeting the Raesides, too, and your aunt ..."

Out on the pond, the shadows of trees lie like fingers spread across the ice, with the marks left by Nathan's skate blades. If I were to get up from this bench and step out on the ice, I think I would hear sounds every time I move from light to dark to light. As if the air is different inside and outside the shadows. If I were more awake, maybe I could try ...

"Fais dodo, Colas mon p'tit frère, Fais dodo, t'auras du lolo ..."

Père's voice in my ear as I sit with him in the rocking chair in my bedroom. He's rocking us a little. From somewhere—the kitchen?—I can hear Papa's voice, my mother's voice, raised and angry.

"Yeah, it was pretty bad," Nathan is saying. "When he hit my little sister, that was it. I beat the shit out of him."

"Wow, that's terrible. Your sister—was she okay?"

"Yeah, she was okay. Eventually ..."

I'm awake. Did I really just hear Nathan say that?

"So that's when you went to live with your aunt?"

"My mother took my sister and headed to Calgary to live with a cousin, so, yeah. That's when Aunt Liz stepped in. And the Raesides."

I try to imagine Papa hitting someone. Hitting anything.

"Where's your father now? Do you ever see him?"

There's a pause, in which I hear the unmistakable call of an owl.

"He used to show up at school. Sometimes at the rink. He'd try to talk to me. He was usually drunk, though."

"I'm sorry," says Fredrik. Perhaps he's imagining his own beautiful, sophisticated, kind parents in battle—and failing, as I do.

"Yeah, well. Then that thing at the Worlds happened, and the media stuff, and everyone figured I should just get out of town for a while. Get away from the attention."

We're silent for a few more minutes, then the owl hoots again—*Whooo, whoo-hoo, who, who.*

"What the hell is that?"

"A Great Horned Owl," says Fredrik. "They're all over the woods here. Haven't you ever heard them at night?"

"No, I don't spend a lot of time outside at night, I guess." Then I feel him turn his head toward me. "You awake?"

I nod. I'm incapable of speaking yet.

"Warm?"

Nod.

"Ready to skate?"

Now I look up at him. "Me?"

"Yes, you."

Nathan stands up and takes the empty cup from my hands. Places it on the bench. Hauls me to my feet.

"Come on."

CHAPTER 53

SKATING

If I could fly, I'm sure this is what it would feel like. Skating around the pond in wide, swooping circles with Nathan McCormick holding my hand.

Holding me up, more like.

He's doing all the skating, of course. I'm mostly just being dragged along for the ride, a bit like Polly leading Abigail and me and our friends at CanSkate Level One.

But not like that at all, either.

We leave the bench, and clomp over the snow to the pond, where I push off for a few hesitant glides.

"You got it," he says. "But let's really move here. It's too cold to go slow. Come on."

He reaches for my hand and brings my arm in close to his side. "Okay?"

Am I okay? I guess so. Yes, I nod.

We start slowly. Nathan pushes off, left, right, and gets into a rhythm with his strides (the cutting sound of his blades in the ice!).

"See? Just like you do at the arena," he says. "Just match my strides. Right, left, right ..."

I'm doing it. Well, I'm doing it feebly, anyway. And then I realize it's all about tempo, and now I'm matching the tempo of his strides, and that makes us swoop a little, side to side, as we circle the pond. In and out of the shadows, round and round. And then we're going so fast, pushing aside the curtain of cold and wheeling through. It leaves frosty tears on my cheeks, tears in the corners of my eyes. The inevitable runny nose. Clouds of our breath—my breath as I laugh out loud. It's magic. Falling would be impossible, skating like this.

I lose count of how many circuits we do, then Nathan draws away and—suddenly he's skating backward, facing me. He reaches for my other hand so that he's pulling me along.

"Hey, don't stop skating," he laughs. "This isn't a free ride, you know."

Stride left, stride right, match his backward motion, and around we go again and again. And then he lets go and I'm skating on my own. He's beside me, laughing at me.

"See? You've got this."

I'm skating, pushing off and gliding and pushing off and gliding. Slowing down on the corners (he takes my hand then to keep me from stumbling on the crossover, then lets go again on the straight part). I'm the lines of color on the white ice. I'm skating like the Habs. (Well, not like the Habs, of course, but skating well enough. If only Papa and Père could see me ...)

And then he's beside me again, takes my hand and pulls my arm in so that we're once again circling the pond together.

In and out of the shadows, the ice ringing under our skate blades, the owl hooting again. I think to myself: I'm *happy*. If I died right now, I would die happy.

He drops my hand again and takes off over the ice, carving out a pattern of his own around my careful right, left, right, left. Like a fly buzzing around the head of a horse. Or better, like some crazy Bach variation: me, the plodding chorale; him, all the wild counterpoint. We're both laughing now.

"Too bad Polly can't see you out here," he says.

"Maybe she'd bump me up to Level Two."

My legs are getting tired. A little stumble, a recovery, a wobble.

Nathan swoops over, takes my hand again. "Had enough?"

I nod. "I don't want to fall."

I'm not wearing my hockey gloves, after all.

Back to the bench, where we thump down, still laughing out clouds of breathlessness.

And then I see Fredrik landing the drone.

"You filmed us?" Nathan calls to him.

"Oh, yes," he grins at us. "I filmed you."

Oh, dear.

"Good one," laughs Nathan.

"I thought my role was to come up with the music," I say. "I didn't think I would actually be in the movie."

Fredrik joins us at the bench with the thermos and we refill our cups. I'm warm now, after all that skating, but the hot chocolate still tastes wonderful.

"I may have the music already," he says, and I turn to look at him in surprise.

"You do? I thought I ..."

"You did. In my parents' piano room on Friday night," he says.

"I warned you that you should have told her," Nathan says.

"Is that okay with you, Genny?"

"Oh, yes. That's okay with me."

Yes, that's more than okay. That's perfect. Now I don't have to think about it anymore. Granted, the soundtrack will be a surprise. I have no idea what I played that night, of course, while the boys were talking about hockey and then later, when I didn't even notice that they had stopped talking, just before Fredrik's mother came to tell me Papa had arrived. But if Fredrik thinks it will work, I will trust him.

The three of us sit there for a few minutes, looking out at the pond and sipping.

"I guess we're done, then," says Nathan. "Film shoot in the bag. Music recorded. Over to you, Freddie. Work your magic, but remember, Genny and I are expecting an A on this assignment. Just saying."

Another sip, another call from the sentinel owl, and then the cold starts to creep over me again and I shiver.

"Time to pack up," says Fredrik. "Before Genny freezes to death."

Nathan puts his arm around me again, a brief hug, then moves away, taking the warmth with him.

CHAPTER 54

VISITOR

I'm packing.

Tonight, after the Christmas concert, Papa and Père and I will drive home, have one day to rehearse, and pack before flying to London on Sunday, where six concerts and Clapperton and my mother await.

Clapperton: five (five!) emails have arrived in the past two weeks, friendly "check-ins" he calls them, full of enthusiastic discussion of our upcoming concerts together, both in London and in Ottawa. And (he's dreaming) beyond.

Looking forward to seeing you again and collaborating on some new musical projects, he writes.

Shudder.

My mother: one short email announcing a reservation for Afternoon Tea at the Winter Garden in the atrium of our hotel, The Landmark, on December 18 at three o'clock.

I look forward to seeing you then, she writes.

Everyone is looking forward to seeing me, apparently. Truthfully? I'm not so looking forward to it as they are.

A knock, and Victoria's smiling face appears around the door.

"Hey, Genny, can I come in for a sec?"

Of course she doesn't wait for an answer. Instead, she floats in, looking around at my sparsely decorated (as in, no decorations whatsoever) bedroom. She's already dressed in her concert attire: form-fitting green-red-white ugly Christmas sweater and black leggings. Hair sleek, shiny, and beautiful.

"Packing, eh? Wow, you're so tidy!"

I smile, friendly face in place, as I continue folding clothes and placing them in my suitcase.

"I don't have much in the wardrobe department, so it's actually kind of easy," I offer by way of conversation.

I picture her packing: piles of every kind of apparel imaginable, a total mess of colors and clothing all over her bed and being stuffed into suitcases and duffel bags. Cosmetics and beauty products. Shoes, don't forget the shoes.

"You're smart." She sighs and plops down on the end of my bed. "So, are you ready for tonight?"

"I am. Are you?"

"I think so. Thanks again for helping us with the piano part and all that. It really sounds fantastic."

"You're welcome. No problem."

Why are you here? That's what I'm thinking.

"I know it's kind of beneath what you're used to playing," she says, and I look up at her then.

I sense a reply is required.

"It's all music," I say, thinking of Père and Monsieur Duval and "Pays de Haut." "And the concert is all about fun. I think people will like it, and you sound really good."

Suitable response? Yes, apparently. Victoria flashes her cover-girl smile.

"Yeah, we do sound good, don't we?"

I nod and keep packing. No ugly Christmas sweaters and leggings for me. No, it's my long black turtleneck and black jeans and boots, exactly what I wore for the photo shoot, with the festive addition of a red silk scarf—a long-ago gift from Vianne—draped around my neck. My hair is down and will shortly be gathered into a knot with a clip. My standard look: not formal, like it would be for the concert stage, but just perfect for blending into the background and letting the girls, and Tomas Oliveri (yes, I'm accompanying his "O Holy Night"), and the Grade 10 string orchestra take the spotlight.

"How did your filming go the other night?" Victoria asks.

Ah. Now we're getting to it.

"Good, I think. Cold."

"We could see you guys, you know," she says. "From the third-floor stairwell, we could just see through the trees to parts of the pond."

Voyeurs. I can't imagine they saw anything interesting. Other than Nathan skating. And maybe the drone flying around.

"What's he really like? Nathan, I mean."

What is this? When I look at her, she's smoothing her long, perfectly manicured fingers over my quilt, as if feeling for the edges of the diamond-shaped fabric my grandmother stitched there so long ago. She's not looking at me.

"He's nice. I don't really know him very well."

That makes her look up. "Oh, come on! You spend so much time with him. That day at the mall and at skating. And all this media project stuff. The trip to Ottawa on Friday. Does he, you know, talk much? He just seems so into himself most of the time."

I have a feeling that Victoria's and my definition of "into himself" are somewhat different.

"He's all about hockey," I say. True.

She makes that "Hmmm" noise, as if she doesn't believe me.

"Really. I think that's all that matters to him."

Hockey and his little sister. And his aunt, who saved him. And the kind Raesides and their children. And defending a friend from a Swedish bully.

And maybe me, a little. *Be nice. Jesus, your teeth are chattering.*

But I don't say any of that. Instead, I ask, "Why?"

She sighs, then: "I'm really, really into him, but he doesn't even notice me."

Romance. Of course. I knew that, didn't I?

"Does he have a girlfriend?" she asks.

Nathan? No. Not a chance. I shake my head.

"You and he aren't ... you know?" She makes it sound as if she's joking, but she's not. I can tell.

"No."

"I just wondered, because we could see you skating together and everything."

"No," I say again. "We're just friends."

The classic line—*just friends*. Five repetitions of "Heart and Soul." Skating around the frozen pond, hands linked. Keeping me warm on that frigid bench. Asking me about feeling nervous. Friends.

She bounces off the bed with renewed energy. That was obviously the answer she was looking for.

"Well, after tonight he'll be going back to Ottawa for good, so I just wanted to check. I might try to talk to him after the concert."

She flashes me a smile, heads for the door.

"Thanks, Genny! You know, you should wear your hair down more often. It suits you. See you at supper!"

Exit, stage right.

Nathan and Victoria. Ultimate Frisbee teammates. I try to picture them skating around the pond together. Yes, I can see it quite easily, although I'm not sure what they'd talk about afterward as they sat on the bench. They'd look fantastic, though.

And then I come face to face with something Victoria said.

Tonight I go home to Montreal, pack my suitcase again, head to the airport with Papa and Père and Alain. Soon I'll be on a concert stage, buried inside the *Quartet*. And I'll be enduring tea with my mother and negotiating the onslaught from Clapperton & Co. and sending powerful thoughts of strength to Père's hands.

And when I come back in January, Nathan will be gone.

CHAPTER 55

CHRISTMAS CONCERT, PART 2

The basement of the chapel is a pre-concert maelstrom of nervous and excited students.

Earbuds in (a track called "Rain on Tent." Very soothing). I find a corner, close my eyes, and run through the "Eclogue." I love it, so sweet and yearning. I don't even care that the Grade 10 string orchestra ignores M. Manuel's emphatic conducting and drowns me out. I just play it and think of Mr. Finzi up there in heaven, listening to this piece that he never finished, never heard performed while he was alive.

Someone touches my arm. Tomas Oliveri, looking a bit pale.

"I'm sorry, Genny. Do you mind running through it just one more time with me? Would that be okay?"

"Of course." I recognize the look of pre-performance terror on his face.

"My parents are going to be here from Toronto and I always

feel more nervous when they're in the audience," he says as we make our way to the piano through skittering groups of performers, some clutching instruments.

(Funny. I know that Père and Papa will be sitting somewhere near the back of the chapel, and that calms me. The reverse.)

Tomas's voice is a sweet, pure tenor. Even though he holds it back a few notches for our run-through, I can hear the perfect intonation. Breath control. Beautiful round vowels. Miss Therrien, the choral leader, joins us as we near the end, nodding approval.

"I think you're ready, Tomas. Don't you agree, Imogen?" She smiles and pats his arm in reassurance.

"Agree completely." I smile at him and he moves off with Miss Therrien (throws a hurried "thanks!" over his shoulder at me) toward the junior choir, assembling in the far corner.

And now I see three ugly Christmas sweaters coming my way.

"Oh, Genny, we were looking for you," says a breathless Victoria, with excited Polly and Melanie in tow.

At our first rehearsal, they asked if I could do "a sort of different" piano sound for "All I Want for Christmas Is You," slower than the original. Less bouncy. Less pop, more ...

"Hot," insists Victoria. "You know, kind of sexy."

I'm drawing a blank. Sexy. Sexy piano accompaniment for a Christmas pop song. All I can think of is "Bolero," so I try to imprint some Ravel on our arrangement—lots of rhythmic bass—

and they seem to like it. It's a bit odd, but it gives them a chance to choreograph some slinky moves, like a girl band. Thank goodness all I have to do is sit at the piano. Miss Therrien, who has to okay the homemade vocal performances, has given them the thumbs-up, but I can't help wondering what the reaction will be from the audience.

As it turns out, the audience loves it. The girls look fantastic, of course—the not-so-ugly ugly Christmas sweaters, tight black leggings, hair cascading around their shoulders as they sway, step, swirl through their performance.

Papa and Père—yes, there at the back of the chapel—catch my eye as I acknowledge the applause from the piano bench. They're clapping like everyone else. They're also laughing—at me, a bit, I imagine, looking so out of place next to the Sirens.

"Brava! Bravi!" calls Père as the girls bow again and sweep off to the exit, stage left.

I remain at the piano bench, waiting for one more vocal performance. After this, the "Eclogue." Then Tomas and his "O Holy Night." And finally, a rousing chorus of "We Wish You a Merry Christmas," played by the string orchestra, with me on piano, and sung by all performers squished together at the front of the chapel. I expect to be hidden by that point, which is perfectly fine with me.

Two Grade 11 students with guitars are working their way through a decent version of Gordon Lightfoot's "Song for a

Winter's Night," a perfect opportunity for me to blend into the background (I'm all in black, after all, and the chapel isn't all that well lit), and check out the audience.

Papa and Père sit at the back, smiling. They each catch my eye, nod. Père winks.

Mr. Colville is in the front row, of course. Mr. Norton and a group of my teachers are halfway back on the other side. Students who aren't performing are dotted throughout the audience with their parents. Fredrick. William, and Berit. My eyes drift over a little girl, a little girl who is looking at me.

Pause. Moment of recognition. Alicia Raeside gives a tiny wave. I smile back.

I look next to her and see that all four Raesides are in attendance, with Nathan at the end of the row. He doesn't appear to be paying attention, however. Either he's napping or on his phone or reading the program.

The song ends and I refocus, turn to the keyboard, adjust the score and find an empty, quiet, pre-performance space in my head. It's the ritual that Papa, Père, and I always follow before we play the first note of anything. *Set it in silence*, Père says.

But at this moment there are distractions—such as the clunking, chair-scraping arrival of the string orchestra, and M. Manuel explaining that the "Eclogue" isn't really a Christmas piece, but that the orchestra has been working on it all term. He explains the reason for my participation. (Imogen St. Pierre, to the rescue, etc. Everyone applauds and I haven't even started playing yet ...) Then there's the ritual of tuning. And finally the expectant silence on both sides of the conductor's podium.

I gather myself and breathe. Yes, ready. Look at M. Manuel who nods at me, raises his baton—and I begin the sweet, floating opening theme.

Later, when Papa finds me at the reception, I'm still a little woozy. He kisses me on both cheeks and pulls me in for an embrace.

"Imogen, my love! The 'Eclogue' was sublime. A perfect performance. I'm so very proud of you."

"Very special," says Père, taking his turn to kiss and embrace me. "We are so rarely sitting in the audience when you perform, so what a treat that was for us."

It wasn't a perfect performance, of course. I added a few notes here and there, left some out, but the string orchestra in all its glory drowned me out just enough that it didn't really matter anyway.

"You saved the day." M. Manuel is shaking my hand. "She's wonderful, isn't she?" He turns to Papa and Père and the musician conversation begins. Tonight's performance, challenges of teaching and conducting youth musicians, acoustics of the hall, upcoming performances ...

I stand next to Papa but, really, I'm drifting away. They talk and I keep my polite in-public smile in place. All I want to do is find a quiet place (in the back seat of the car on the way back to

Montreal would be perfect) to come back to earth on my own time. Which would be much later and, ideally, at home.

It doesn't work that way, of course.

Victoria and her mother approach and the social rituals are observed.

"What a lovely evening," says Mrs. Hanson-Massey, who is glamorous. Spectacular, actually. "The girls did a wonderful job, didn't they?"

M. Manuel slips away (wise!) but Papa and Père gallantly take her on.

"Delightful," Père smiles at her and turns to Victoria and me. "Your arrangement was very original." (He doesn't mention "hot" or "sexy.")

"Thank you," says Victoria. "We wanted to do something a bit different." (She doesn't mention "hot" or "sexy," either). "Genny was great with the piano part."

The parents and grandparent start talking about other parts of the evening, about Hillside in general, and Victoria turns to me.

"Thanks again, Genny. Have a great holiday. I'll see you in January."

"Thanks—you, too."

She narrows her eyes a little, assessing me. "Your hair really does look good down like that. I'd pay lots of money to have those waves."

I put a hand to my hair—horrors! I was so focused on tonight's performance, I completely forgot to braid it back before going to sit at the piano at the start of the evening.

She and her mother are moving off amid farewells, seasonal good wishes.

Mr. Colville comes by. Mr. Norton. Mrs. Folkard. Tomas Oliveri and his parents, gracious with praise for my accompaniment (Tomas looks relieved and also embarrassed by his mother's fangirl enthusiasm). Fredrik and his parents. Then, for a moment, we're alone, just we three.

Can we go now? I turn to Papa, hoping he'll read my mind, but he's looking at something else, someone approaching.

"Hello," says Claudette Raeside, who appears in front of us with little Alicia by the hand.

"Oh, hello." Introductions, explanations. Alicia and "Steps." Papa laughs and tells them about little Imogen at the piano, makes Alicia laugh.

"We loved your playing, Imogen," says Claudette. "I think you've inspired Alicia to practice a bit more."

"Maybe you can come back and play with me again," Alicia suggests.

"I'd like that." I mean it, too. She's all dressed up for this evening's outing, looking adorable. I wonder why they're here, actually, since there's no rule about attending the concert. John could have picked up Nathan this afternoon and disappeared. Maybe Nathan wanted to stay? Hard to believe, judging from how attentive he wasn't during the performance.

"We'd love to see you, anytime," Claudette says to me. "Come and visit Nathan, if you can find him at home. He tends to live at the rink, though. Or the gym."

Papa asks her something about the hockey life, the demands on a young player with school and practice and games and traveling, how that compares to the life of a young musician. I try hard to stay focused. Alicia moves closer.

"Please come and visit," she says. "Maybe you could come to my recital."

"That would be fun. I would be the one clapping the loudest."

"And you could come home with us after and have cake. Mom always does cake when Lucas and I have recitals or important stuff at school."

"That's so nice. I wish my papa would do that."

"You don't have a mom?"

Ah, the big question.

"Well, I do have a mom, yes. But she doesn't live with us. She lives in England and has a new family now."

Alicia nods. "Divorced."

"Yes."

She takes my hand. What a sweet girl.

"Ah, there they are," says Claudette.

John and Lucas join our circle and Nathan is suddenly there beside me.

Handshakes, greetings, compliments, and best wishes all round. Everyone being social and festive. I'm losing focus rapidly.

"I liked that one you did with the orchestra," Nathan says to me, while the others are onto something about the Christmas concert at Alicia's school.

"Thank you."

"How did you get roped into the thing with Victoria and the girls?"

"She can be very persuasive. She said she wanted something classy. I guess that means ask the weird girl who plays the piano." That makes him laugh.

But I remember that Victoria and her starry eyes will probably be making an appearance soon, before he leaves for good ...

Leaves for good.

Maybe I should warn him.

But there's no time. Goodbyes are in progress as the Raesides make their move toward the exit and, within a moment, two moments—"Merry Christmas. All the best. Good luck"—they're gone, taking Nathan with them.

I see Victoria extricate herself from a group that includes her mother and Mr. Colville, Polly, Melanie, various parents. She slips out the door.

Papa looks at his watch, says, "Time to go, I think?" and Père asks, "Shall we get your things?"

The car is warm and my corner of the back seat, as I hoped,

is cozy, soothing. James Ehnes plays the Barber violin concerto. We don't talk. I don't feel like talking.

My phone buzzes in the pocket of my parka.

Have a good xmas

Ah. Okay.

Thanks. You too

Nothing for a few moments, and I consider asking about his conversation with Victoria. Then, I can see he's typing something:

Let me know how our media project turns out

K. Good luck with your hockey team

Thnx

Another long pause, so I put my phone away, but it buzzes again a few minutes later.

You're a good skater i'm a crap piano player you win

And immediately, he adds:

Thnx 4 everything

He's thanking me?

You're welcome

I watch the screen of my phone for a few minutes but, after that, nothing more.

CHAPTER 56

FLYING

Père and I sit together on the flight to London and it's perfect.

Of course, the airport was madness as always, and by the time we've cleared security (questions from stern people in uniform, the management of our bags, a violin and cello, and all those papers), and spent an hour in the lounge before boarding, I'm ready to get on the plane and be *away*. Get *started*.

Get it over with, actually.

Clapperton and his expectations loom. Yes, even more emails.

The *Quartet*, too. I feel ill with the *Quartet,* as if it's a virus that's invaded my blood, taken over my body. It's all I hear and feel. My fingers are twitching and urgent, as if my piano keyboard has sprung out of my hands and head and needs attention, now.

And, of course, there's my mother. And the whole Christmas thing. Hotels. Concert halls. People I don't know asking me questions. Nice people. Strange people. Important people, with Alain hovering and managing.

Sitting with Père at the front of the plane (we're in Business Class, thanks to Alain and his excellent relationship with Air Canada) is bliss. Papa is across the aisle with his cello as a seatmate, Alain a row back beside a frowning woman whose eyes are fixed on her computer screen. If anyone can distract her, Alain can. There's room to stretch our legs, and the servers bring food and drinks, and we have little screens at our seats for watching television and films if we want. We don't want.

It's dark now. All I can see outside my window are occasional concentrations of lights where the towns lie, often obscured by wispy clouds reflected in the lights of the plane. Then long expanses of nothingness. The trees and rocks and rivers of Quebec and Labrador and, after that, the dark mass of the Atlantic.

Père and I sit and sip ("Imogen, have a glass of wine with me, please. I insist."). We don't talk much. And that's perfect, too.

Soon, soon enough, we'll arrive in a very probably gray, damp London morning. But soon isn't now. Right now, we're between here and there and we're flying.

I sip my wine and stare out the window. *Flying*. Over the dull hum of the plane engines and the emerging chirps of conversation from Alain and the frowning lady, I try to remember the sound of skate blades cutting into the ice of the pond at Hillside. Yes, just.

And the cold, and the firmness of Nathan's arm under my hand as we flew around the dark-light ice ...

Beside me, Père sips, sighs, contented.

I could do this forever.

CHAPTER 57

REHEARSAL

"What do you think about tightening up the dynamics and tempo in the fifth movement," says Clapperton at one point.

Since it's a movement for only cello and piano—as in, Papa and me—his suggestion isn't all that helpful.

Papa sits forward and stands his cello up, holding it by the neck and letting his bow rest on his knee. He's thinking about it. Nods his acknowledgement, although not his agreement. Then he looks at me.

"What do you think, Imogen? Should we be more rhythmic here, as Anthony suggests?"

Immediate response?

No. He doesn't know what he's talking about.

But we are an ensemble. There are rules in ensemble playing, so I take a moment to consider. This section is rich, built on long, slow phrases by the cello, supported by throbbing chords from the piano underneath. Papa and I have developed a language of our own throughout this part. It's hard to explain but we both feel it when we play, and it works. Clapperton, I realize, can't hear it.

No, I was right. His suggestion is crap.

"I like the long notes on the cello, the slow tempo, how unforced it is. I like the way you draw that part out," I say after a moment, keeping my eyes on the score so that I don't have to look at Clapperton. "I feel it's like a voice. Like the voice of an angel, maybe, telling the story. There's nothing rhythmic about it. It's just free."

Taken out of context, that sounds like crazy talk, of course. But we're deep inside the *Quartet* now, and for me it's angels and God and voices from heaven and other dark places, voices all over the place. It's a very unsettling conversation we're sharing in this piece, but I'm sure of my role in it now. And Clapperton is wrong.

Silence. I lift my eyes from the score and look at Père, who is watching me, a smile lifting one corner of his mouth. He nods, almost imperceptibly, but enough to crash over me in a wave.

"Well, I suppose if Imogen sees it that way, and you do too, Maxim." Clapperton backs down.

"I do," says Papa, but his voice is kind, like a teacher giving a hard-working student a disappointing grade. "I couldn't have said it better."

Rehearsal continues. Clapperton doesn't make any further suggestions.

CHAPTER 58

"The poor boy," Père says. "He's trying very hard."

Too hard, I want to say.

We're eating supper in the dining room of our hotel, and it's formal and posh (a wonderful English word) and delicious. Just we three tonight. Alain is meeting with another publicist over drinks and dinner, the nice lady who works with an Australian brass quintet that has come to play in the same concert series we're doing. The series is some Commonwealth thing, some commemoration of the Empire and Empire-building. Soldiers, sacrifices, important people, history. Something like that, anyway. I have chosen not to pay attention. It's an English thing, so it's surprising that our Montreal-based trio is part of the program. There's also a chamber orchestra from Vancouver, ethnically mixed and very young. The program is all over the place, basically.

"Yes, he's very earnest and certainly determined to make the piece work," Papa agrees. "But perhaps a little too determined. Thank goodness he backed down on the fifth movement, though. Imogen, you were brilliant."

Mouth full of Yorkshire pudding—exquisite!—so talking is impossible. I grin, though, and nod. Enjoy being referred to as "brilliant" by my brilliant maestro father.

"His playing is superb," Papa continues. "Absolutely outstanding in the third movement."

The third is a clarinet solo with huge, long notes and great swells of volume. And a tricky ending, all in the clarinet's lowest register. He is brilliant.

Which is why I'm willing to tolerate him.

It was raining tonight. We were soaked by the time we climbed into the cab for the trip back to the hotel from our rehearsal with Clapperton at the Royal Academy of Music. Père and our jolly cab driver talk about map reading and roundabouts while Papa and I snuggle together for warmth.

I shiver and dream of how perfect it would be if I could just change into pajamas and order room service, but of course Papa won't let me.

"We're in this together, my love," agrees Père as we separate at our rooms. "Half an hour, Maxim? I will see you both downstairs. I hear the roast beef is simply *délicieux!*"

He's right. It is. Dinner is especially sweet without Alain here, talking shop. Just we three, being treated like celebrities by the Landmark's attentive staff.

Afterward, we move to the Mirror Bar so Papa and Père can have a nightcap. For me, tea.

"Tomorrow, royalty," says Papa. "Have you been practicing your curtsy, Imogen?"

"My curtsy is perfect. Don't worry. I won't embarrass you."

"No, I think we should be more worried about Père."

"I promise to behave myself."

My grandfather smiles as he says it. Sips. I can picture him cooking up ways to rock the boat as some Royal bestows royal attention on him. He's met royalty before, of course. He and the Duke always share a moment.

My china cup is delicate, white and gold, with a perfectly shaped handle that I can actually wrap my long fingers around. No pinching required. My tea is rich, pungent, and soothing.

Alain has texted Papa, saying he will meet us here shortly for a "What's happening over the next week" conversation, but for now, it's just the three of us. Lounging in our soft armchairs in this posh hotel bar. Full of roast beef and Yorkshire pudding.

Content.

CHAPTER 59

ANTHONY

Clapperton is nervous. He has wiped his hands with a handkerchief twice now. (Who carries a handkerchief anymore? Maybe it's an English thing.)

I glance at him and he catches my eye as he jams the cloth back into his jacket pocket. Shrugs. Looks a lot like a teenager caught misbehaving.

"Sorry, I haven't got used to this kind of thing," he says. "Especially with the Royals. Sorry."

He's apologizing to me?

We're standing with Papa and Père, who are actually turned away and talking to the wind players from Australia next to us. It's a receiving line, I suppose, waiting for The Royal Personages to arrive. The hall we're standing in at the Royal Academy of Music seems to be stories high, with massive windows and columns. It's a cavern, really, and the sound of our voices fills it with a dull thrum of resonance.

"It's okay. I'm not used to it, either."

I'm not. Shaking hands with important people, making small talk, all that play-acting that gets tacked onto performing—all I want is my piano, Papa and Père, the music, the audience. And once the last note finds its home, I am ready to go home, too.

"You don't look like you're not used to it." He sounds as if he's accusing me of something. "You always look completely composed."

Do I? My astonishment must show on my face because he laughs then. Nods.

"You do. Always in control and always so calm. I envy you."

"Don't envy me. I'm not so calm as you may think."

He should have seen me before my first session of CanSkate Level One. My shaking fingers trying to tie up those skates, until that mother knelt down in front of me to help. Or the time Papa had to take my hands in his, and look sternly into my eyes so that I would stop giggling about the Schubert 99, Schubert 100 mix-up. (Although I still think that was really, really comical. And terrifying ...)

"It's just that coming from the background I do, this whole 'meeting the Royals' thing is somewhat important," he says. "My father, if he were alive, would be so proud, and my mum ... well ... she can't stop talking about it to the other ladies in the All Souls Women's Auxiliary."

Clapperton, transformed before my eyes.

A grown-up boy with a dead dad and a mom who does good works and brags about *our Tony*, the clarinet player, meeting royalty.

"I'm from this little town in the north, you see." He isn't trying to impress me for once. A new experience. He's not even looking at me. I think he's embarrassed. "Nobody from my year at school went to uni. Most of them went into farming. Or a trade. Or the military. I was ... unusual."

Little Tony Clapperton, the weird music boy.

"It was hard," he says. "So, this is quite a big deal."

I suppose I should be saying something but I'm not sure what. Instead, I just nod, agree. It's a big deal. I understand that. Oh, wait ...

"I understand."

"But you're still not nervous." The old Clapperton reappears.

I shake my head. "No. Not nervous. But I would prefer not to be here."

That makes him laugh.

"Of course, you're Canadian. And French-Canadian at that, so I suppose the Royal Family doesn't have the same significance for you and your father and grandfather."

"No, I suppose not."

"Well," he says—and I see the nervous boy from the north again. "It's an important moment for me. My mother will never forgive me if I have sweaty palms or otherwise disgrace myself."

"Are we ready?" asks Papa, suddenly there beside me again.

"Yes, of course." Clapperton is Clapperton again.

The edge of his crumpled handkerchief still peeks from his jacket pocket, so I reach over—he is momentarily startled—and tuck it out of sight.

"Thank you, Imogen," he says.

A stir near the doorway. Showtime.

"You're welcome, Anthony," I say as I turn back to Papa and see Père, just beside him, smiling to himself.

CHAPTER 60

QUARTET FOR THE END OF TIME

I am gone somewhere in the music. Not lost, just gone.

Of course, Papa and Père and Clapperton are there, too, just as gone as I am.

We're in the open space at the front of the church, on a low stage constructed in the sanctuary, or chancel, or transept. Whatever. But once we walked out and acknowledged the applause (and oh, my God, the sound created by clapping hands in that space is like being tumbled around inside the ocean), the walls and chandeliers and enormous windows behind us—they disappear. The shifting-in-their-pews, pre-concert *ahem*-ing audience disappears, too. I look over at Père and his eyes are closed, preparing. Papa is watching Clapperton.

Clapperton is watching me. I raise my eyes to him, once I've found my place on the bench, once I've rested my hands on my lap for a moment and prepared them to hover over the keys and reveal that first chord, quick on the shadow of his opening clarinet declaration—I look over at him and he's waiting for me. I nod. He looks at Papa, at Père. They nod. We're ready.

For someone who was so nervous about meeting The Royal Person just two days ago, Clapperton is remarkably calm now. But of course, this is his place. Music boy. Weird boy. Like me.

As I watch him, he closes his eyes, breathes, puts the clarinet to his mouth ...

And about forty-seven minutes later I come back.

Even without the applause, which surges over us immediately, I know our performance has been everything we wanted it to be. Perfect? Well, no. That never happens. But good. Very good.

I float through the bows, feel Père's hand on my arm as we move to and through the reception room, smile at faces, hear voices, shake hands. Alain is there, too, embraces me and whispers, "Well done, Imogen. Well done." Papa kisses my cheek, hugs me, is pulled away by someone. Clapperton is suddenly there and hugs me, too—so odd and uncomfortable, but I let him because I'm still floating and hearing the voices, as if Père's violin is still singing that last note.

And then, "Hi, Genny."

William.

It takes me a moment to process that William is standing in front of Clapperton and me, here in this crowded reception hall after our concert. William, from Hillside. William, who lives in the UK when he's not at school. William, the dragon to Berit's King George.

He's laughing at me. "You look like you're seeing a ghost. It's me, really."

"I'm sorry. It's just such a nice surprise," I manage.

Clapperton clears his throat and William turns to him, hand out.

"Oh, sorry. William Cowling," he introduces himself. "Genny and I are classmates in Ontario. I'm home for the holidays. Managed to cadge a ticket. Great performance," he says to both of us.

"Ah, thank you. How do you do." Clapperton is formal, tense, as he shakes William's hand. Suddenly I can't wait to get away from him. The room is loud with voices, wallpaper music turned up a little too high, Clapperton's dislike of William (Why? He doesn't know William) loudest of all. He and William are talking about English schools, Canadian schools; I don't know what they're talking about ...

"Excuse me," I interrupt, and they both turn to me in surprise. "Sorry, I just have to—to step away for a moment. You're not leaving yet, are you?" I say to William (does my voice sound a bit desperate?) and he shakes his head, smiles. Clapperton glowers.

A helpful woman by the refreshment table directs me to the Ladies loo and I slip into a cubicle without making eye contact. Yes, even pianists have to pee sometimes, and the two or three (or four, or five, I don't really look) women in the washroom smile but don't speak to me.

Breathe, breathe, swim back to the surface, Imogen. Behind the locked door I flounder. It's always like this and I should have been prepared, but I never am. The voices of angels and God are still ringing in my head, my ears, and I'm still trying to find my way back. And usually Père is there close by, or Papa, or Alain, or some familiar face or ritual or word to lead the way.

William.

I find him still talking to Clapperton, but people are hovering now and Clapperton is being pulled away. William sees me and comes quickly in my direction, a man on a mission.

"Come on. You look like you need a cup of tea," he says, ever the Brit, and leads me through the throng toward the refreshments—a sort of Starbucks à la wine bar.

I can't manage a saucer—too shaky—but I clutch tea in a white cup while he stocks up on cream biscuits and his own tea, leads me out the door—I don't even glance back, but I'm sure Alain is frowning somewhere—and down the hallway to an alcove, a corner, where there's a bench and no other people, and the air isn't moving so much.

"You looked like you needed to escape," he says.

I sip, nod, sip. Smile at him in gratitude.

"It must be terribly daunting to get up there in front of people and do what you do." A pause. "Anthony is rather good, isn't he?"

"Yes, he's exceptionally good," I agree. He's also a complicated and not very appealing collaborator but, whatever.

William grins, sips, looks at me. "I think he likes you."

I think William is right.

"You didn't get my email, I take it?"

"No, sorry. I haven't been checking my mail. I don't have a roaming package on my phone, so I don't turn it on very often. And we've been rehearsing and doing other stuff ..."—other stuff like meeting members of the Royal Family—"... so I didn't see your message. I'm sorry."

He waves away my apology and brings me up to date on messages that have been circulating from the Hillside tribe on social media. Polly and Victoria's skiing photos, and Berit, stuck in Ottawa for the holidays after all and reading every dark Scandinavian crime novel she can find, and Fredrik at some special charity dinner in Stockholm where he got to meet Erik Karlsson, the hockey star from the Senators, and, speaking of hockey players, a selfie of Victoria and Nathan ...

"What?"

"Oh, yes. Victoria posted it on Facebook."

So. She did it. She got to him before he left.

"Here, I'll show you."

Before I can say, "No, it's okay, I really don't want to see it," William has his phone out and is scrolling through his Facebook app, looking for the photo. Finds it, holds it out for me.

It's from the night of the Christmas concert, taken in the front foyer of the chapel (I can see the painting of a former Head in the background). He's looking into the camera and she's leaning into him, almost in front of him. He's not smiling, just looking. She's beaming.

There are 83 comments. The first one says, "Wow, Vix!" (Vix?) "What a hottie!" I don't read any more. Hand the phone back to William without saying anything.

"Of course she's delusional," William is grinning at me. "Nathan McCormick would no more hook up with Victoria than he would take up figure skating."

I almost spit out my tea, but instead snort my amusement. Yes, very funny, the idea of Victoria and Nathan as a couple. Very funny.

"Imogen, here you are." Alain appears around the corner and greets us, the picture of good-natured bonhomie. I know better. "People are asking for you. May I steal her, please?" he asks William with a charming bow. "Now that you've had a little respite?"

"Of course." William is all politeness and good manners. "I must go anyway, Genny. Lovely to see you, and your performance was beautiful." He puts down his tea cup and comes over to give me a hug. "Happy Christmas, and I'll see you back at school in January, right?"

"Thank you," I say (I also consider for a moment whispering *Rescue me, please!* into his ear and decide against it). "It's been lovely to see you, and thanks for this tea break, too."

And then it's back to work until Alain releases us, and Père and Papa and I can return to the hotel for a quiet dinner in our suite, ordered from room service.

CHAPTER 61

TEA WITH MY MOTHER

"The review in *The Telegraph* was positive," she says, spreading Devonshire clotted cream on her scone and not looking at me.

She hasn't looked at me once since we sat down under the giant palm trees—yes, palm trees—and the seven-story-high glass ceiling in the Winter Garden. She looks at her food or tea cup, or just past me. Sometimes her eyes flit over me, rest on my hands, or the rolled collar of my black sweater, or my hair, which I'm wearing down. (Thank you, Victoria, I will.)

Our brief, awkward hug in greeting at our table—she is already here when I arrive, early—is like hugging a broom. She's skinny and unbending.

She hasn't changed. I can feel the tension, the resentment, resonating in every word she says or doesn't say, every action. Slicing open her scone, dipping into the clotted cream, and spreading the strawberry preserves. Her hands shake.

Maybe she's nervous?

I certainly am.

"Yes, it was a good concert, I think," I say, focusing on my own scone, which is so delicious I could eat a dozen.

"The reviewer had good things to say about you in particular. He said something like you were the net holding all the players safe. Very complimentary, especially considering your age." It doesn't actually sound all that complimentary when she says it.

But then, a long time ago, she was the one creating the net for Trio St. Pierre. She was the pianist, the wife, the daughter-in-law. The musician.

Until Imogen, the freaky musical child, came along.

We eat a little in silence and I try to think of something acceptable to say.

"How are Gavin and Annabel? Are they having a good Christmas holiday?"

Talking about her other children should work, shouldn't it?

Yes, she tells me about their school concert. A choral solo by Gavin, recorder ensemble for Annabel, and their piano duet. The air around her grows softer as she talks.

Proud mother. She pulls out her phone and scrolls through her photos, finds one, and passes the phone to me.

Two round pink-cheeked faces, teeth missing, blue eyes alight, gaze at me from the screen. My mother is blonde, an English rose. Another thing we don't share. The kids are sweet and I tell her so.

"If you scroll in either direction, you'll see more," she says, moving on to the sweets now that the little sandwiches and scones on the lower levels of the tea plates have been dealt with.

So I scroll through images of my half-brother and -sister in school uniforms and tennis gear. (Of course. Tennis.) In bathing suits on a beach with their father, my mother's second husband, a round-faced, round-bodied man with flopping blond hair, who appears always to be smiling. (I'm sure my mother loves that.) She appears in a few selfies, a few photos taken by someone else, and she's smiling, too, in her beach wear and her tennis whites, with her beautiful little children encircled within her arms.

"They look so happy," I say as I pass the phone back to her.

"Yes, they're very happy children, I think."

Unspoken: *And I tried to make you happy, too, you ungrateful, weird, unlovable freak.*

I don't think I can eat any of the sweets so I pour more tea. The silence lengthens.

"Are you enjoying your school?" she asks finally. "Do you like living away from home?"

"School is fine, I suppose. I have friends there." Fredrik, Berit, and William would impress her, I'm sure.

"Any pictures?"

Do I really want to show her my pictures? I only have a few, but maybe it will satisfy her and she'll talk about something else. Or better yet, wrap this meeting up and let me escape back to my room.

I turn on my phone and go to my photos. There, Imogen as Guinevere, with Fredrik holding my arm and looking manly as my King Arthur.

"Halloween," I say, handing it to her.

"Ahh." She starts to scroll through my few photos, pausing to examine them closely. "He looks nice."

"Fredrik is a good friend. He's from Sweden. He talked me into being Guinevere because he was King Arthur."

"And I see King George and the Dragon, too. Very English." She actually smiles as she holds up the phone so I can see the photo of Berit and William. Scrolls through a few more.

"He's cute." She looks up.

"I'm not sure anyone has ever described Fredrik as cute before."

"No, this other one. Who's this?" She holds up the screen so I can see the selfie Fredrik took at his mother's birthday party, our *thing*. Fredrik, me, and Nathan, not smiling. I hadn't thought about him for days, and then the conversation with William, and now there he is, looking right at me.

And just like that—I don't want to tell her about Nathan. I don't want to even say his name to her. Nathan doesn't belong anywhere near my mother.

"One of my classmates." Even to my own ears it sounds choked and unnatural.

"Has your father met him?"

"Yes."

"And what does he think? Your father?"

What, like, to give his *approval*? Like we're *together*? Is that what she's getting at?

"I have no idea."

My mother takes another look at the phone, then pushes the button to turn it off and hands it back to me. The expression on her face—well, it's not a smile, exactly. It's tight and strained and makes her look older.

"So you're seeing this boy on the sly, then," she says.

"No. I'm not 'seeing' anybody." *Nathan and Victoria on Facebook and 83 comments*. For the first time since we sat down at this table, our eyes meet and hold. I can't believe how quickly this wave of fury is breaking over me.

She looks away first. Shrugs.

"My mistake. Sorry. I just thought maybe you were finally breaking the spell your father and grandfather have woven around you. That's all. Broken free."

This is what I want to do: I want to slap her. Hard.

"It's time, Imogen. You have to do it soon," she continues as she pours herself more tea. Her hand is shaking and the china pot clatters a little as she sets it down. When I stay silent (because, honestly, I'm afraid of what might come out of my mouth), she adds, "You need to get away, Imogen. You need to escape them. It's not healthy."

Still I don't say anything. I now know what the expression "seeing red" means, because the short distance between us and around us is a seething, bloody mess of my anger.

"Get out while you can. Go to university. Move away and get a real job." She stirs in sugar, milk. Lifts the cup with a shaking hand and takes a sip. "Or they'll ruin you for any kind of normal life. You don't know the damage those two men can do."

A beat while I try to catch my breath, then:

"Excuse me, I have to go now." I've pushed my chair back and am standing, looking anywhere but at her. "Please give my best to Gavin and Annabel."

I lay my linen napkin beside my plate, turn, and walk away.

She doesn't say a word or try to stop me.

CHAPTER 62

LATER

Père and I are walking, arm in arm, along the rainy twilit sidewalk of Marylebone. We don't talk, we just walk, the way we've done forever, for as long as I can remember. When I was little, with my hand in his, and now that I'm as tall as he is—almost taller, really—my hand tucked into the crook of his arm.

His arm seems thin to me. I think I can feel his bones through the layers of raincoat and wool sweater, but still the hard muscles and tendons of the violinist.

We have a concert tomorrow. We are part of a larger ensemble—all the Commonwealth musicians are on display, so we're performing a trio by Canadian Marjan Mozetich, *Scales of Joy and Sorrow*. At rehearsal yesterday the other musicians applauded us, which was unexpected.

Père and I have a rhythm when we walk, soothing and hypnotic.

After twenty minutes, we turn and walk back. No turning

corners for us ("That's how to get lost," Père always says about walking in a strange city). No. We go straight out one way, then turn and come straight back.

He was reading the newspaper in our suite when I returned from tea.

"I need some air," he says, stretching. "Some exercise, I think, Imogen, my love. Will you come and hold me up?"

And so we walk.

"Lovely," says Père as the hotel comes into view. I'm not sure if he means the classic façade of the Landmark or our walk, but it doesn't matter. They're both lovely.

The swishing of vehicles on the wet road and the steady rhythm of our footsteps have erased the worst of my mother's voice.

"Good now?" asks Père as we approach the door and an attendant reaches to open it for us.

"Good," I nod.

He nods, squeezes my arm.

CHAPTER 63

AND THIS IS THE END

On Christmas Eve, we stay up late and have our Réveillon.

"A hybrid affair," says Père, because it starts with a very English carol service back at St. Martin-in-the-Fields.

"Church of England. Anglicans," Papa says under his breath. "They might as well be Catholics, really."

"Easier on the knees," Père reminds him.

I tell them to *Shhh*.

The swell of the organ and choir fills the entire vault of the church, and we three join in the singing of the English carols. We're anonymous in the congregation of Londoners doing the same.

Back in our suite, Alain joins us for oysters and champagne and meat pie—"Do you mean *tourtière*?" asks the young man from the hotel kitchen that Papa negotiates with to prepare our Réveillon meal. "That's French, right?"

"No, no—well, perhaps that's what you call it." Papa shrugs.

Père joins in and they reach some sort of agreement.

I'm not complaining. The result is a wonderful mixture of light pastry and steaming ground pork. A little too much gravy, maybe, but delicious.

And beans baked with maple syrup. ("Can you find maple syrup in London?" Papa asks the young chef. "Oh, have no fear, Monsieur!" he assures us.) And onion soup and potatoes, and apple cake.

After midnight, instead of attending mass, the four of us go for a walk, which is much needed.

Père and I bring up the rear and enjoy the sight of Papa and Alain strolling in their long trench coats, hands waving as they discuss—well, I'm not sure what, but something important, certainly, based on how animated they are.

We're much more sedate, my grandfather and I, our arms linked. Yes, there is some giggling, thanks to the champagne and the simple joy of being here with Père, celebrating Christmas together. We have a few small gifts waiting back at the hotel, and we'll exchange them when get back. But for now, we breathe in the chilly air of London and walk.

"Two more concerts and we are done," says Père. "Will you be happy to go home?"

Home means school, and exams, and decisions. I shrug.

"Yes, there's much to think about, isn't there?" he says.

"I don't want to think about that now. Not on Christmas."

"No, of course. Tonight is about peace on earth and goodwill toward men."

We walk on. Papa and Alain are far ahead and I see Papa turn to look back at us, maybe making sure we're still in tow. He waves at us and turns back to Alain.

Peace on earth and goodwill toward men is an excellent concept, but somehow that's not where I am right now. Not peaceful and not feeling much goodwill—except toward my father and grandfather and, yes, even Alain.

You need to escape them. It's not healthy.

I think my mother is the damaged one.

"You are thinking," says Père. "I can always tell when you have something on your mind because your hands tense and relax, over and over."

"Really?" I had no idea, but he must be able to feel this through the sleeve of his warm coat.

He nods and makes a noise that isn't quite a laugh. A breath of a smile, maybe.

"Yes, even as a baby you would open and close your fists, staring out at us as if you needed to tell us something, until your father or I would reach out a finger and you would hold on and make noises like a fish," he says. "It was quite delightful."

A fish. Perfect. Underwater and trying to swim to the surface—that's a feeling I know.

We walk, and I think about what it must have been like at our house when I was a baby. Apparently my mother didn't reach out her finger to give me something to hold on to while I made fish noises. Why, then, am I so hooked on her words now?

"My love, let it go for now," Père says, putting his hand over mine and squeezing, as if wringing the drops of tension out of it. "It's Christmas Eve and we're together. Your father and Alain behaving like children, and us, decorous and mature, bringing up the rear."

"You're right. I'm just thinking too much."

There's much to think about, isn't there? He said it himself.

After the concert—*Quartet for the End of Time*—I saw him with Papa. They embraced for a long, long moment with their arms tight around each other, and when they drew apart, while Père smiled at his son, I'm sure my father's eyes were full of tears.

I know what this means, even though they haven't said anything to me yet. They will, soon.

This is the end of time for us, us three. This tour is our last. There are no concerts lined up next year. That's what the past few months have been about—Père's tired hands, and Papa's meetings in Ottawa with his musician colleagues about opportunities there, and Alain pushing me toward Clapperton and Bezic and l'Avenir. All their talk about university choices. Vianne taking me for a walk and easing me toward a future of change.

Fine. I get it.

And Père knows that I get it. So we just walk on, arm in arm, neither of us speaking because there's nothing more to say.

CHAPTER 64
JANUARY

I'm enjoying my work on the Poulenc sextet, despite myself.

The thought of sitting at the piano at Chalmers with Clapperton and Bezik and their friends doesn't fill me with much of a glow, of course, but the music is so interesting and physical, I find myself slipping through the dark hallways to the chapel earlier and earlier each morning to submerge myself in its throbbing rhythms. I find myself attacking the piano and pounding away as if I'm driving a stake into the ground. Chopping wood. Hammering.

Also, I'm awake a lot. Through the night and early in the morning. Sleep is elusive, so I escape to the piano instead.

Our return to school coincides with a January thaw and strict instructions to stay off the pond. I don't mind because I know my skating days are numbered. I've actually passed a few CanSkate "stages," approved by Polly, on the ice at the arena. It seems those few moments of flying across the frozen pond with Nathan revved up my skill level just enough. My cautious turns around the well-lit, echoing ice surface at the Brick Hill Community Arena aren't as much fun. My skating adventure is coming to a close. I'm fairly certain Polly will be relieved. Maybe Abigail will miss me.

"You look tired," Fredrik says to me at breakfast on Monday morning, three weeks after our return to school.

"I've been getting up early, practicing a lot."

"This is for that spring concert you were telling me about? With those other musicians?"

I nod, look down at my toast, and focus on spreading the strawberry jam evenly. Fredrik knows not to ask about Trio St. Pierre.

It was in the news, or on the CBC or something. Much singing of praises and lamenting the loss of a world-renowned Canadian musical institution. Père did interviews and had his photo taken. Papa announced his move to the newly formed Ottawa-based Chalmers Chamber Ensemble. More interviews, more photos.

Alain wanted to announce my plunge into the brave new world of l'Avenir, but I said no, not yet. He backed off for once, and I'm sure I could see Papa's invisible hand on Alain's arm. I will do this concert, this one performance.

Then, who knows? I don't.

"Is this one as weird as that piece you played in London?" William asks. He and Berit sit across from us. Our formation.

Weird? Is the *Quartet for the End of Time* considered weird?

William must see the look on my face as I consider and he quickly backtracks.

"I didn't mean weird, exactly." He is trying to hard not to offend, which I find endearing.

"Oh, yes, the Quartet is pretty weird. The voices of God and the angels," I agree. "I'm not sure what it sounds like to the audience."

"It sounded brilliant," he says. "You were brilliant. She was brilliant." He turns to Berit, who sighs.

"I would have loved to have been there. Instead, I was stuck here, reading yet another Henning Mankell." I don't think she's complaining, really.

The dining hall buzzes these mornings, or maybe it's just that my ears are ratcheted up. I hear Victoria say: "My dad says he can get us tickets."

"Well, I would have loved to be either going to Genny's concert or reading mysteries," Fredrik says. "Three old aunts, two sets of grandparents, crappy wet weather, and all my friends off skiing in Switzerland. Or playing concerts in London."

"What about Erik Karlsson?" William reminds him.

"Well, yes, that was fun," he nods.

Today is the "reveal" of our media project film and Fredrik is excited. Apparently he told Erik Karlsson about it and there was a suggestion that something similar would be interesting for the Ottawa Senators. Something to do with social media. Websites. *Jumbotron vignettes ...*

The film, our project, is still an unknown. I haven't seen it yet because Fredrik won't let me have a preview. No one has had a preview, he says. It's the premiere, he says. It's going to happen right there in Mr. Norton's English class, with our classmates doing their duty as peer evaluators and the two of us—director/cinematographer/editor (him) and soundtrack provider, and, I suppose, actor (moi)—taking bows.

I hope, I hope we're taking bows. I imagine Victoria baring her claws and sharpening her pencil.

Once we got home from London, I turned on my phone again and went through my emails, mostly spam, but also messages from Fredrik, and Vianne, and William (who had asked for details about the London concert and where to get tickets). Ten texts from Fredrik, with photos, about his boring Stockholm holidays.

One from Nathan.

Merry Xmas how's London?

I think about replying now, but what would I say?

London was good. My father and grandfather are disbanding our trio. My mother hates me and thinks I should get away from them. (Be warned: she thinks you're cute.) Anthony Clapperton is human. Also creepy. The highlight of London was when William came to our concert. How's Victoria?

I don't reply.

"Come on," says Fredrik. "Showtime."

CHAPTER 65

IN SKATING OVER THIN ICE, OUR SAFETY IS IN OUR SPEED, PART 1

The title comes from the American writer, Ralph Waldo Emerson. Fredrik found that all by himself, but I love it.

And I love the film, seven minutes of movement, light and shadows (mostly shadows), the sound of blades on ice and muffled words exchanged by the two skaters, and my piano (as if he pulled the music from inside my head).

First Nathan alone but never in full view. His skates carrying him, everything moving without ever showing the full Nathan.

And then the other skater (me, of course, but mostly a dark shape). Feet moving across the ice, hands linked, shadows all over the place. The swooping drone captures us from above and lets us disappear into the shadows. And then back we come across the ice again, into the light. (I don't know how Fredrik does it, how he makes the drone fly like that and film us.)

And the music, looping around the images the way the skaters loop around the shadows on the ice. And then we're gone, but the music and sound of blades—and one brief outburst of laughter. Me. I had no idea I laughed like that.

In skating over thin ice, our safety is in our speed. Nathan, skating over thin ice. Me, too. How did Fredrik know that?

The words cross the screen as Nathan's blades cut into the ice and disappear into the shadows. One last flight of notes from my piano and then darkness—and the sound of Nathan skating away.

The classroom is completely silent as the credits roll briefly under the spare notes of my piano and the film fades out.

Mr. Norton watches the black screen for a moment and turns to look at Fredrik and me with an expression that tells me we are going to get a very good mark on this project.

"Is Nathan McCormick an amazing skater or what?" says Victoria, breaking the spell.

CHAPTER 66

THE SEE HEAR MEDIA FESTIVAL, PART 1

We're in English class a week later. Yes, we got a good mark on our film project, and Mr. Norton has just been huddling with us, encouraging us to enter it in a film festival with a category for high school students, held in Toronto. The See Hear Media Festival, it's called. But the film would need some "retooling" to meet the entry requirements, says Mr. Norton.

Fredrik is all over this.

"Imogen and skating. And Nathan, the hockey bad-boy, now the teacher. And how he leads her around the ice and it gets easier." Fredrik is thinking out loud as Mr. Norton nods, makes suggestions.

Yes, Fredrik has more film he can edit in to make it a bit longer. Yes, we can add a soundtrack of me talking, Nathan talking. Yes, there's lots of musical soundtrack available, too, lots to work with. (Who knew, that while I was meandering around the keyboard that night at Fredrik's house, he was collecting me? How long did I play, anyway? How long did the boys sit there, listening?)

Really? I look at Fredrik when he suggests Nathan talking on the soundtrack. *How?*

Nathan is gone. Living with the Raesides in Ottawa now and doing his semester exams under supervision there (according to Victoria). He's going to do his last few Grade 12 credits online through the Independent Learning Center because he's back training and playing with the Ottawa 67s now, and, after two weeks, he's already scored four goals.

"Don't worry. Magic," says Fredrik. I believe him. Mr. Norton is just walking away toward the front of the classroom, and Fredrik already has his phone out and is texting, contrary to school rules. Texting Nathan, I presume.

I haven't heard from Nathan since he sent that text during the holidays, the one I didn't answer.

Merry Xmas how's London?

Victoria may be receiving texts, or she may just be checking websites, because she keeps us informed about his scoring accomplishments and what the media is saying about him.

"No one can believe how fit he is," she says.

"They're saying he's going to go very high in the draft, even though he's missed most of the season."

"He has amazing hands," she gushes, but I'm pretty sure she's quoting the hockey media on this one. She wants us to think she's speaking from experience, of course, but I think they're talking about how he moves the puck with his stick, how effortless he makes it look. (Thank you, Ottawa 67s website and YouTube. I, too, know how to surf online).

He looks so happy, too.

"I'll work on a script," Fredrik is saying. He's off his phone now and scribbling in his red notebook. "All you have to do is read it, or—" he stops, thinking about another approach. "Or I could just ask you questions and I'll record you answering them."

"Or you could tell me what you want and I'll write my own script," I say. If we're going to do this, I don't want him inventing me.

Fredrik stops scribbling, looks up at me with a huge smile.

"Genny! It's the new you!"

I am new, he's right. I have abandoned the version of the girl who started this school year with a purpose and a place—safely between my father and grandfather, safely far away and oblivious to my mother's anger and judgment. Safe is gone. So why not write my own words, even if I have to fake them? Who would know? Who cares?

"We'll talk later," Fredrik says. Class is about to start. Mr. Norton is opening his notes, ready to offer prep advice for the exam coming up in a couple of weeks.

"Oh! Mr. Norton, can I make an announcement?"

Victoria. He looks at her over his glasses, still organizing some papers and making sure the computer is projecting the correct screen for his review lecture. Nods.

"You have one minute, Miss Hanson-Massey."

Tickets. She has a block of tickets to the Ottawa 67s game next Friday night after our exams are done. Who wants to go?

"Two, please," says Fredrik right away.

I look at him and he looks at me.

"Research," he says.

CHAPTER 67

FROM AFAR

Hey Genny,

("Hey"?)

I hope your trip back to Canada was pleasant and that you're now enjoying some down time with your father and grandfather.

(I'm writing exams, you idiot. We are not even in the same city.)

I can't tell you how much I enjoyed our performances together during the Christmas season. I really think we have a special musical connection ...

Okay, the hairs on the back of my neck just stood up. Not fear. More like horror.

... and I look forward to our next collaboration, in April, with L'Avenir at the Dominion–Chalmers pre-Festival concert.

My hanky will be safely stowed out of sight.

Anthony

Oh, God. I knew this was a mistake.

CHAPTER 68

HOCKEY NIGHT IN OTTAWA

It's so loud, even before the game starts. Loud and bright. The ice is white, blinding. So many hockey-jersey-clad people milling around and trying to make themselves heard over the pounding music being blasted from the sound system. It's a rink. All those hard surfaces—all that ice!—with nothing soft, no curtains or carpets to absorb the waves of cranked-up, in-your-face, canned music.

I'm not sure how long I'll be able to stand this. Maybe it will be more bearable once the game starts?

Most of our Grade 12 class has made the trip to TD Place in Ottawa. The bus ride was as expected: the humming diesel engine, the tires thrumming on the road, my ear buds tight in my ears, and my eyes turned out the window to the dark expanse of snowy farmers' fields and patches of bush along the 417. Fredrik sits beside me, but turned into the aisle, talking to

William and Berit behind us. They don't disturb me and Glenn and the *Goldberg Variations*.

The Hillside Academy contingent's seats (courtesy of Mr. Hanson-Massey, as we are reminded several times by Victoria) are in one of the corners. When the players appear from the walkway and Nathan steps on the ice, my classmates—well, some of my classmates, the female classmates, led by Victoria—cheer loudly. The boys mostly just clap. A few hoots or something equally beast-like. The boys don't care if Nathan sees them, but Victoria, Melanie, and Polly stand and remain standing, clapping and cheering.

He looks up. Doesn't wave. I could swear he looks right at Fredrik and me, but it's hard to tell with the glare of the lights on his gladiator helmet and visor, and his attention to the puck he's stickhandling as he circles the ice inside the blue line. With his friend, Luc Charette, there beside him.

He looks huge in his hockey equipment, actually. Especially when he skates beside Charette, his captain.

(Blood on the ice, Charette lying there, unmoving. McCormick beating the crap out of Andersson. Do images like that ever go away, I wonder? Does he still hear the crunch of bone on bone and feel the cartilage of Andersson's nose giving way under his pistoning fist?)

The game is—spectacular. Fast, loud, exciting. Number 92, McCormick, skates through the other team, puck attached to his stick, making passes and taking passes, shooting. He scores two goals, gets three assists, and is the game's first star. Little kids line up along the railing over the corridor to fist bump his enormous glove.

Victoria is jumping up and down, calling out his name. We're all cheering as he comes out to acknowledge the crowd, waves his stick in the air and actually makes a point of waving at us, his fans. Of course Victoria believes he's waving at her.

"My dad says if we go down near the dressing rooms, the players come out around Section 19," she tells us all. Tour guide. Proprietress of the hockey star.

Fredrik and I don't tell her about the text we both received a few minutes ago, probably typed by his still-sweaty fingers on his phone.

Come down to hallway section 19

So we're all there when he emerges from the players dressing rooms into the hallway where fans are waiting, hoping for autographs, selfies. Little kids looking adorable and adoring. Nathan wears a suit and tie, like all the other players, hair still wet from the shower. He meets his star hockey player obligations while we wait. Victoria is practically hopping from foot to foot with excitement, as if she can't wait to get her hands on him.

But when he's finally able to break free, it's not Victoria he looks at, aims for. It's Fredrik and me.

"Hi guys." He and Fredrik shake hands and he grins. "I hear we got a good mark."

And then to me: "I heard about your trio. About your grandfather retiring. Claudette told me." He looks at me, right at me.

Right at me. "I'm sorry," he says.

It's what you would say at a funeral.

"Thank you." I whisper, but I can't look at him as I say it. I don't want him to see that my eyes are filling with tears.

There's a *cesura* of odd, eyebrow-raised astonishment. I think he's about to say something more. I think he's about to step toward me and offer a hug, but no. Instead, he's taken over by the Hillside contingent, Victoria reaching for his arm and blinking at me, her mouth a straight line.

I don't care. I turn and walk down the hallway with Fredrik, toward the cold parking lot and our bus.

CHAPTER 69

IN SKATING OVER THIN ICE, OUR SAFETY IS IN OUR SPEED, PART 2

Fredrik is hard at work on our film (really, *his* film). The deadline for submission is a few weeks away, in early March.

"I have tons of footage and I can loop your soundtrack with no problem," he says to me in class, a week after the hockey game. "All I need is you to record your speaking tracks."

He's given me a series of questions—*Why did you want to learn to skate? What does skating mean to you? How did Nathan help you with your skating? What was it like that night, skating on the pond?*—and after much editing and rewriting and rethinking, he's finally satisfied. We record my answers. We're done.

He premieres the movie for me and Mr. Norton on a Friday afternoon as the weekend looms. Papa is picking me up on his way from Ottawa, and already I'm longing for a few quiet days at home with him and Père.

But first, our movie.

Fade in, Nathan and me skating on the pond. My voice: "I wasn't allowed to skate when I was little. I think my mother thought it was dangerous." (Oh, the joy it gives me to say those words out loud!)

Cut to a newspaper clipping of Nathan being dragged off Andersson. Even in black and white, there's no mistaking the blood everywhere. The voice of a TV commentator: "McCormick is incensed. The officials need to get him off the ice."

The audio is from the YouTube video.

Mr. Norton is frowning. Turns to Fredrik.

"You realize you need permission to use that audio ...?"

"I have it," Fredrik says. "With a little help from my father's lawyer. There's some video further on that I had to get permission for as well. It's all vetted and approved. Don't worry."

Details like this don't interest me. What does interest me is the story unfolding in the film. My story: the timid skating girl. Nathan's story: the wild hockey boy. The piano girl who rides "on the shoulders of giants" (images from the *Maclean's* article). The hockey boy who just wants to play (audio from the radio interview). He's skating on thin ice and then he's skating with me. And we're flying in and out of the shadows, in and out of the light. Skating away. More newspaper clippings of Nathan's return to the ice. Footage from a 67s game. And clippings of Trio St. Pierre's UK tour, and the announcement that our end of time has arrived. And underneath everything, the sound of Nathan's blades slicing through the ice. And my piano.

And finally, the two of us skating on the dark frozen pond, laughing.

Credits, fade out. A moment of silence in the classroom.

"Good," says Mr. Norton. "Very good."

I'm silent while they talk about the entry process, not sure why I'm so stunned and sad. Maybe it's because I remember just what those moments at the pond felt like. I wish we didn't have to share that with anyone—the Mr. Nortons, the judges, some random audience at the film festival.

But it's a good film, even I can see that. Fredrik has woven it together brilliantly.

I wonder what Nathan will think. I wonder if he will even have a chance to see it.

CHAPTER 70

SAD

Everything makes me sad. Papa chattering about rehearsals with the new Chalmers Chamber ensemble, Père snoozing in his chair with his fingers laced together on his chest. No rehearsal together.

On Saturday afternoon, I work on the Poulenc, with Père sitting nearby, listening and offering suggestions.

"Until you practice with the others, of course, there's not a lot you can do, other than get those notes under your fingers," he says. "Or rather, under your arms. It sounds as if you're weightlifting over there."

I'm resting my hands on the keys and look at him over my shoulder. He's grinning at me. But of course he's right. There's something about this piece that brings out my inner Franz Liszt. I feel like dragging the music out of the keyboard with as much force as possible, showing off, throwing the notes around the room, and smacking the audience with them.

"Too much?" I ask.

He shakes his head. "Not at all. But of course when you hear the others, you will find yourself adapting to the ensemble's voice." He smiles at me. "That is your gift, Imogen, my love"

Adapting myself. That's my gift. I am somewhat tired of adapting myself.

We curl up, we three—Père in his chair, Papa and I on the couch—to watch hockey on Saturday night after supper. The game is exciting (Boston—"those brutish Bruins," Père says) and fast and rough. Penalties, combatants flying at each other, the clashing of weapons picked up by the mics near the ice. The ferocity of it all makes me tired. I drift in and out, sleep a little. Wake up alone in the living room and hear my father and grandfather in the kitchen, chatting as they make our snacks.

It's the intermission, and there's a segment on this year's NHL draft and the "crop" of young players—like corn being fertilized, harvested—whose futures may be decided that day. Nathan is there, one of the names. They show a clip of him skating, throwing a check, scoring a goal—hands in the air, his friend Luc leaping at him against the glass as they celebrate.

"After the year this kid has had, the challenges he's faced up to and overcome," says one of the announcers, "he deserves all the attention he's getting."

"Hardworking, focused, very skilled," says another. "Great hands."

(Victoria, who has been less friendly lately, will like that comment.)

"That's your friend, isn't it?" Papa has just come back with a huge bowl of popcorn for us to share. Père places my tea mug on the coffee table ("Here you go, sleepyhead"), within reach of my lazy corner of the couch, and settles back into his big chair, heaves a sigh of contentment.

"Yes. Nathan McCormick." My friend Nathan, whose kind words after the hockey game almost broke me open.

"Calgary, Edmonton, Pittsburgh, L.A., even Toronto," the announcer is saying about Nathan's possible future in the NHL.

Vancouver, Waterloo, Montreal, New York, London. My possible future.

"Big things for this kid, no doubt," says one of the other announcers, and they all nod in agreement.

Big things for Imogen? At this moment I don't care. I have to get through the Poulenc with Clapperton, consider a possible professional commitment to l'Avenir. I have to make a decision about UBC, currently the front-runner in the university stakes. I have to adapt.

I sip my tea. Eat my popcorn. Watch hockey.

CHAPTER 71

DECISION

Richard Bezic emails me to find out if I'm available for a rehearsal—minus Clapperton—in Ottawa on a Thursday afternoon in early March. Papa picks me up from Hillside just after lunch, and we meet the other musicians at Chalmers, where Bezic has organized space for us.

"So glad you could come." Bezic isn't exactly fawning over us as Papa and I arrive, but his greeting is more enthusiastic than required. Handshakes. I could swear he bows in Papa's direction.

Alain is there. Alain—why?

"Delighted to see you, Genny." He kisses me on the cheek. I haven't seen him since that last media interview Père did, just after we got back from the UK. "Just thought I'd check in on things. Anthony and I have been talking about some possible dates for l'Avenir, so I wanted to hear you in action."

Possible dates. Clapperton. Checking in on us, now that Trio

St. Pierre is *phtt* (insert snap of fingers here).

The other musicians—Alina on flute, Georges on bassoon, and Bartek on horn (last names settle somewhere in my head to be retrieved later)—shake hands, make welcoming noises. Papa sits at the back of the church with Alain for a few minutes, then they wander off to find a coffee shop and make phone calls. We get to work.

And it is work, this piece, this ensemble.

"I don't hear that," says Alina as we stop, yet again, so that she and Georges and Bezic can discuss a few bars in the first movement. She is the nitpicker, the one pulling on the reins. She thinks she's the leader.

Bartek winks at me. He's a veteran already—a young veteran, and a principal with the National Arts Centre Orchestra. It helps. I grin at him and turn my eyes back to the score.

No one criticizes my piano interpretation, which is morphing moment by moment, bar by bar, depending on what I hear from the others. Whether they are being kind to the newcomer, which is unlikely, or just too focused on Alina and her increasingly annoying approach to ensemble playing, I don't know.

I'm adapting, that's all. My gift, says Père, invisibly sitting beside me on the piano bench.

Eventually we hammer through the sextet three times and reach consensus on some of the more difficult issues. Alina of the rhinoceros hide has no idea that Bartek and Bezik are launching spears at her.

I wonder what it will be like when Clapperton—with his oily superiority (there, I said it)—is in the mix.

We set the date for another rehearsal, shake hands, part as friends, colleagues. Papa is waiting at the back of the church and stirs when I sit beside him. No, when I plant myself beside him.

"It sounds good," he says, using his church-quiet-no-eavesdroppers voice.

"I suppose."

"There are always difficulties finding common ground in a new ensemble, of course," he says. I glance at him and he's grinning at me. I wonder if he finds it amusing, watching the Alina Show. Like watching his undergraduates in their ensemble course, kindergartners sorting out their differences in the playground.

"I've made a decision."

He turns to me, eyebrows raised. "Oh?"

"UBC," I say. "I'll let them know tonight."

I'm wrapped up in his happy hug. He's already talking rapidly, excited.

"Excellent choice! A wonderful school ..." and as we sit back again, he starts listing his friends and musical colleagues in Vancouver, the contacts he will let know. A trip—we must fly out and find a place for me to live. Maybe during March Break? Yes. Perfect.

We rise and make our way out to the car. Papa is still talking.

"We must let Vianne know! She has been asking me. And

Père will be pleased, too. Such an excellent music program ... Charles Latimer and Marie-Soleil Bolivar. You remember Missy? You'll have so many opportunities ..."

I let him chatter as we walk arm-in-arm toward the parking lot. I don't tell him that I'm going to UBC because—now that Papa and Père no longer need me—I have to get as far away from l'Avenir and Alain and Clapperton as I possibly can.

CHAPTER 72

IN SKATING OVER THIN ICE, OUR SAFETY IS IN OUR SPEED, PART 3

I'm packing. No visitors this time. Victoria and her posse are keeping their distance since the hockey game.

Which really doesn't matter.

"Man, he's going to be first or second for sure," the rugby boys talk about him a lot, as if he's one of their tribe, the one who got out. They have stars in their eyes, talking about their absent brother.

I'm just happy for him and envious. To be so sure about the future must be bliss.

I zip up my suitcase and look around my room. No bliss here. Tomorrow Papa and I fly out to Vancouver.

My phone buzzes.

Come to norton's room final version of thin ice ready

Fredrik has spent the last couple of weeks getting our film ready to submit to the festival. He recorded me in the chapel playing some crazy fast Scarlatti. He's been adding, changing, reworking it all. I'm half afraid, half amused.

But Mr. Norton wants one final view before we submit.

"You need to see it, too, Miss St. Pierre," he says as I take a seat at the desk next to Fredrik. His laptop is connected to the smartboard at the front of the classroom, with the first black frame already frozen on the screen. "And you've already shared it with Mr. McCormick?"

"Yes, sir. I sent him the link this morning. Thumbs up."

"Right. Let it roll, then, Mr. Floren."

It's a completely different film from the original media studies assignment.

No longer just the shadowy footage from our skating on the pond, with those few small additions. Fredrik has added even more—Nathan doing circles on the Brick Hill Memorial Arena ice and calling to Fredrik: "This good?" Me during my skating lesson, marionette-like beside little Abigail. More clips of Nathan playing hockey. Me playing Scarlatti. (I hate how I look when I'm playing and grimace at Fredrik, but he smiles and shakes his head. "No, you look beautiful," he says. "Look at your hands—fantastic.") And footage he took on his phone at the Ottawa 67s game: Nathan going into the corner below us to retrieve the puck and taking a hit that shakes the boards and the glass, spectators' heads in the way. A squeal from someone that sounds a lot like Victoria. A quick sideways view of me, watching the game. I'm half-smiling, looking spacey.

And then, out of nowhere, as my piano ambles underneath, footage from Père announcing his retirement from Trio St. Pierre.

I make a sound and Fredrik hits "Pause."

"Miss St. Pierre?" Mr. Norton turns to me. "Are you all right with this footage? If you have any reservations, you have only to say. Mr. Floren knows I'm the executive producer here." He gives Fredrik a hard, one-raised-eyebrow look. Artistic freedom be damned. It's a school assignment at heart.

Fredrik is looking at me, asking. *Okay?*

Of course I recover, nod. *Okay. Yes, okay.*

"It's fine," I say to Mr. Norton. "That part just surprised me, that's all."

And then we move on to the scenes from the pond and everything gets simple again. Skating, first Nathan, then the two of us, the cold night, my improvised soundtrack.

And suddenly Nathan's voice over my piano: "Yeah, it's been a tough year. I missed hockey. I missed just skating."

Fade to black and the credits, with just the sound of skate blades on the ice.

Thin Ice

A film by Fredrik Floren, Imogen St. Pierre, and Nathan McCormick

There's more, of course. Thank you's and permissions. Mr. Norton gets a mention, as do the Brick Hill Memorial Arena and Hillside Academy. Mr. Jamieson for help with the lighting.

There are permissions from media outlets for the film clips and audio clips (an unacknowledged shout-out to Mr. Floren's legal connections, obviously). It's a real movie.

"Well, are you both ready for this?" Mr. Norton turns to us when the screen goes black and Fredrik clicks "Stop." "Ready to submit? Have you filled out the entry form properly?"

A few minutes of administrative fact-checking later, a click, and it's done. *Thin Ice* has been entered for consideration by the See Hear Media Festival in the Youth category. We'll find out in April if our film will be screened at the weekend-long event in May.

"I have to go," I say, rising from my seat. "My father will be here soon."

"Well, before you go, I must say congratulations to both of you," says Mr. Norton, who is still seated. "This is excellent work and I think it shows real vision. I wouldn't be surprised to see you going to Toronto in May for a screening. Maybe even to pick up a prize."

Oh, God. All those people watching me and Nathan skate. My mindless noodling on the keyboard. UBC is sounding better and better.

"Off to Vancouver, Genny?" Fredrik asks me as I inch toward the door. "Have a good trip!"

"Ah, yes, I heard through the faculty grapevine that you're heading west in the fall. Congratulations, Imogen. An excellent school and a great fit for you, I'm sure," Mr. Norton says. "What about you, Fredrik? Any decisions yet? What's next for you?"

Fredrik shrugs. "Nothing firm yet. I'm thinking of taking a year off to explore a few artistic options, maybe make some short films."

"Well, if I may offer some advice ..." Norton is launching himself into teacher-career-advisor mode with a tone of voice that tells me Fredrik will be getting the "stay in school" lecture.

I ease my way out of the classroom. Turn my thoughts to the upcoming trip to Vancouver. And my own what next.

CHAPTER 73

VANCOUVER

We're heading east, heading home, somewhere over Thunder Bay and the north shore of Lake Superior, I think, and Papa is sleeping.

My father always smiles in his sleep. I wonder if this is the sign of a happy soul, or if it's just some random response to brain waves and breathing and being in a somewhat prone position.

I'm fairly certain I don't smile in my sleep. The face that I see in the mirror every morning is all about the inner and outer effects of gravity.

"You're going to have such a wonderful time," Papa says as we linger over our after-dinner tea on the last evening in Vancouver.

We're in the hotel restaurant, and his friend and current UBC prof, Marie-Soleil Bolivar—Missy—who could hardly stop talking the whole time we were together, has just left us.

"So excited," Missy says again and again. And again.

She gives us the tour of the campus and the faculty of music and the Chan Centre. She takes me through some of the residences and assures us that as a prime scholarship student, I'll have one of the better rooms. ("A single, of course. Or maybe one of the cute studios in the apartment complex ...") She says the music faculty is thrilled that I'm coming to UBC, since so many of them know Papa, know Père. She introduces me to Dr. Charles Latimer, the Dean, a meeting that turns into an animated discussion of how much advanced standing I should be granted. She drives us back to our hotel by the waterfront and, at Papa's insistence, joins us for supper, where I sit and eat (I'm tired, I'm hungry) while they chat about people and places and musical catastrophes they've shared—both cellists, both ensemble players, the good old days in Montreal.

But now we're on our way home, and the details of the place are starting to blur. Which building were the practice rooms in? Did Missy say I could use the piano in the Faculty of Music concert hall? The residences—they all looked the same.

Papa slumbers. I watch him and think how much he resembles Père. One day, when he's old, he will be Père revisited. Père will be very old, or maybe gone from us. And I will be—also older. Old. Perhaps a professor of music doing ensemble gigs on the side.

We're flying into the night so I close my eyes and try to sleep.

CHAPTER 74

VISITOR

Clapperton is in town.

Town being Montreal. When Papa and I emerge, blinking and blurry, on Saturday morning after our late-night return from Vancouver on Friday, Père tells us we'll be having a visitor for supper.

"Ah, how very Clapperton of him," says Papa when Père explains about the phone call earlier that morning, how he tried to explain that we will no doubt be exhausted, that it's my last few days at home before returning to Hillside.

"He wants to see Imogen, of course, and talk shop," says Père.

The concert at Dominion–Chalmers is three weeks away. Another rehearsal is scheduled next Saturday. I plan to spend the coming week in the Hillside chapel, when I'm not dodging the icy shoulders of the Sirens, who have it in their heads (according to Berit) that I stole Nathan McCormick from Victoria. (As if anyone could steal Nathan from anyone else, or anywhere. Or, let's face it, away from his hockey.)

Talking shop with Anthony Clapperton means listening, mostly, as well as a lot of nodding and agreeing. I'm not looking forward to seeing what happens when he talks shop with Alina.

"I'm sure he wants to see you, too," Papa says to Père. "To congratulate you on your splendid career and well-deserved retirement. Et cetera, et cetera."

They grin at each other.

Père is still playing his violin, of course, and teaching. And no doubt he will be on stage at some point, maybe with the university orchestra. He and I play duets for fun when I should be working on Poulenc—or when I've had so much of Poulenc that my hands fall off the keyboard into my lap and refuse to obey. ("All in your mind," says Papa, but he laughs at me and massages my shoulders.)

So Père takes pity on me and we play duets, sometimes channeling M. Duval and streaking through "Pays de haut" and "La belle Catherine." Père's feet tap out the rhythm under his chair as he does his best M. Duval impersonation. He has to stop frequently, not because he's breathless, but because he's laughing at me sounding like the piano player at the Saturday night dance. Thumping out the chords, dancing a bit myself as I sit on the piano bench. It's raw and exhilarating and freeing. Poulenc be damned.

Clapperton be damned.

But he comes for supper anyway and I'm on my best behavior. I try to remember the boy Tony from the North with his hanky sticking out of his pocket and his nervousness about meeting the Royal Personage. Proud mom and the church auxiliary. Proud dead dad.

I try. I fail.

I fail because he's just so annoying.

"Such a loss to the performing world," he pomps (is that a word? Says pompously?), swilling his wine around in his glass as he tilts his head at Père and Papa. And me. "You will be missed."

"Not dead yet, my boy," Père sips his own wine and winks at me.

Papa and Père desert me to make tea and run some made-up trip upstairs to find an old photo album or something.

"So, I hear the rehearsal went well," says Clapperton. I would call him *Anthony* or maybe even *Tony*, but he's acting so much like a Clapperton that I can't bring myself to soften toward him. I hate that he's even here tonight. "Richard says you ran through it completely four times?"

"Yes, I guess it was about four times." Vague. Disengaged.

"Lots of chat, he said."

"Yes, the winds had lots to sort out."

"Piano score pretty straightforward?"

"Well, no." Poulenc? Straightforward? Are you on crack, Tony? "But I just took my cues from the players. Bartek was very helpful."

"Ah. Yes. Bartek." Obviously some history there. "He's an excellent colleague." Right.

The evening stutters to a close and Clapperton is ready to leave. At the door, he shakes hands with my father and grandfather and kisses me on both cheeks, like a local.

"See you next weekend then, Imogen," he says, pulling his collar up a little and adjusting the ever-present man-scarf, while glancing out the door to check that the taxi is there. "Looking forward to it."

As soon as he's gone, Papa pulls me in for a quick hug.

"You are far too hard on that boy," he says, but I can feel him laughing gently. "Off you go. Your turn to clean up the kitchen."

CHAPTER 75

FRIENDLY SIRENS

"Did you see Friday night's game?" Victoria asks me before the start of English class on Monday morning.

Clearly, Victoria is unable to sustain her hate, and she's once again talking to me, although now it's as if she thinks we're somehow on the same team. Team Nathan.

"No, no, I didn't." I assume she means the Ottawa 67s game. I don't tell her I was on an airplane somewhere over Saskatchewan when that game was underway.

"Awesome game. He had three assists," she says. *He*, not *Nathan*. "We were there." She indicates Polly and Melanie, who are both nose down on their phones, trying to get some quick, pre-class scrolling done before Mr. Norton issues the cease and desist order that rules inside classrooms at Hillside.

"Great," I say, nodding. I wonder if she thinks I'm letting the team down by not watching.

"I can get tickets for this Friday, if you want to come with us."

Wow. Now *that* is a breakthrough, but I have to decline.

"That's so nice of you, but I have this concert coming up, and most of next weekend I'll be in rehearsal."

"Oh, too bad." She actually does look sorry. "Maybe next time. Just ask me."

"Thanks." I'm edging away toward my desk, next to Fredrik at the back by the window.

"New best friend?" he asks under his breath as I sit down.

"She's being nice. It's okay."

But Fredrik isn't really listening. He's holding out his phone to show me an email that has just arrived from the See Hear Media Festival.

Thin Ice has made the long list.

"Knew it. We'll make the short list, no problem," he says. Smug. He's texting. "Better let Nathan know so he can get permission to join us in Toronto that weekend."

Something tells me Nathan is never going to come to Toronto to sit around with us doing the film festival thing, the gala evening, with the short list and winners and prizes.

I'm not even sure *I* want to be there.

"You have to be there, too," Fredrik says but he's grinning, probably because he knows exactly what I'm thinking. "Don't even think about bailing on this."

"Phones away, please," Mr. Norton enters and drops a stack

of books on his desk. “Right. Monday morning. One-act plays. Shall we do a read-through?”

Victoria looks over at me and rolls her eyes, as if we are In This Together. *Norton and his one-act plays!* I smile back at her and shrug in acknowledgement. There are worse things than being friendly with Victoria Hanson-Massey.

CHAPTER 76

FINAL REHEARSAL

I'm curled up on the end of the couch, cocooned in Grandma Geneviève's afghan. There's a cup of tea between my hands and Bach cello suites (thank you, Yo-Yo Ma) on the sound system.

I'm in recovery mode.

Papa and Père are—I don't know where they are. They're giving me some space.

I fell asleep on the drive home from Ottawa, where I spent five hours in rehearsal with the other members of l'Avenir. Several hours on the Poulenc and two other pieces, then another hour alone with Alina and Clapperton, running through accompaniment for their solo performances.

"What? So she's the fucking queen or something?" I overhear Alina saying to Bezic when they don't realize I'm just outside the door of the little kitchen, where we've been escaping for snacks during breaks. Bartek is on the piano upstairs. They must think that's me.

"Shhh! Someone will hear you." Bezic is laughing.

"Well, all right! She's very sweet–and young, for God's sake–and magnificent on that piano, of course, but shit! It's like he's afraid to upset her or something." Alina has lowered her voice as I stand frozen and burning at the same time, just outside the door. "That section has got to go faster. Don't you agree?"

"Well ..." Bezic hesitates.

Clapperton had stopped us, asked us all what we thought, turning to me last. No, the dynamics marked on the score and the flow of the previous eight bars point to *con brio*, but not *accelerando*. That's what I say to them, keeping my eyes on the score (but I can still see Clapperton nodding and Alina squaring her shoulders in preparation for a battle).

Clapperton says no tempo change. Interpretation, Alina says. Making it our own. Creating our own sound. Isn't that what l'Avenir is all about? And on and on. Bartek weighs in, agrees with me. Georges is noncommittal. We all know she wants that section to go faster because she can then showcase her phenomenal fingering skill.

She's very skilled. But Clapperton still makes the call. No tempo change.

"Well?" She's waiting for Bezic to respond.

"I'm okay with the more steady tempo," he admits. It sounds as if she smacks him on the arm.

"Wimp!" she says.

"Hey, everyone? You down there still?" Clapperton is at the top of the stairs and I skitter away from the kitchen doorway, toward the washrooms, as he starts down. He comes along the passageway and I emerge, as if I haven't been standing just outside the door listening to Alina's complaints. "Imogen. Ready to go?"

"Tea," I say and point toward the kitchen.

Hemi-demi-semi-quaver of silence from beyond the door, then Bezic: "We're in here. Ready to go!"

Clapperton steps aside, chivalrous, to let me enter the kitchen first, and I make sure my play-nice mask is in place.

"Is the kettle hot?" Reach for a mug, look around for the tea bags.

"Yes, all boiled up," says Alina, smiling. Smiling *sweetly.* "Here you go." Holds out the box of tea bags.

We all return upstairs and rehearsal continues. Without a change in tempo.

"Good rehearsal?" Papa asks as we leave Ottawa and start the journey down the 417 toward home.

"Yes. I'm tired, though."

"Of course you are, my love," he pats my knee. "It's hard work, pulling a new ensemble together. Put the seat back. Barber or Chatman? Chatman, I think. Good snoozing music."

We sound very good and the concert will be a success, I'm sure. Alain will be happy—and probably busy with business cards and handshakes and his phone, and all the things he does and has done for Trio St. Pierre for so many years. I expect a photo shoot soon.

(I hear the sound of a train engine warming up, an enormous machine creaking into existence, me aboard, looking around, watching out the windows as the world goes speeding by, and wondering why ...)

Why am I doing this?

Too late to think about that now. I reach for my tea and pull the afghan tighter around me. Sip, close my eyes, climb inside the Bach cello suite closet and shut the door behind me.

CHAPTER 77

L'AVENIR

"Brilliant!" Alain is the first to greet us with hugs and handshakes (depending on gender) as we leave the stage. It's Christmas morning in Alain's world.

He's right, though. The audience wouldn't let us leave, standing for almost five minutes in an ovation that nearly brought my hands to my ears. (I wonder if any musicians have ever done that.) We bowed, bowed again. *Bravo! Brava! Bravi!* Clapperton waved us back into position for our encore, a quintet arrangement of the Dvorak *Humoresque*, with me noodling in the background. I had to make it up in rehearsal, as the score didn't include a piano part.

They want more, so we follow up with some Haydn (more noodling). More bows, more cheering, my face starting to crack, and my hand grasped too tightly by Clapperton's during the curtain call, all my willpower in play so that I don't embarrass myself by pulling free. Bow, bow, smile, retreat.

Into Alain.

"Absolutely brilliant," he says over and over. "So proud of you, Genny!" he whispers as he embraces me. "Your father and grandfather will be so proud."

In the green room downstairs, the others pack up their instruments and congratulate each other, me.

"Nailed it," says Alina. She high-fives Georges, hugs Bartek and me. Turns to Bezic and takes him by the shoulders, kisses him on the mouth between each word. "You. Were. Awesome."

Clapperton, who finally lets go of my hand, receives back slaps from Georges, Bartek, and Bezic, and another robust kiss from Alina.

Everyone hugs me, less vigorously perhaps than they do with the others. We're all a bit high still, but I know it won't last. On to the reception, a room full of people I don't know. The inevitable crash awaits, but first, the final post-performance performance.

As I enter the noisy room, I see Papa and Père already swallowed up in the crowd, talking, laughing. Vianne is with them. They don't notice me yet.

"We did it." Clapperton stops me just inside the door before I can move toward the safe corner inhabited by my father and grandfather. He's standing very close to me and I'm sure he's going to reach for my hand or offer another hug, so I turn a little, lift my hand to my hair (worn loose, thank you very much, Victoria). Create some space around myself.

"Yes, we did." I nod and smile at him, trying to see Tony, the nervous boy from the North, and seeing only Clapperton. "The audience loved it."

"Loved it! And we couldn't have done it without you," he says in a *pianissimo*, for-our-ears-only voice, leaning toward me. Oh, God. This is getting weird.

"I'm sure you could have." My voice sounds a little forced and unnatural and I slide a few inches away from him so our arms aren't touching, and raise my hand to indicate Alina and Georges nearby, who are already being embraced by people, offered champagne, laughing in triumph.

"No, when I first met you last fall in Montreal, when we started work on the *Quartet*, I just knew. And I was right. That UK tour was brilliant and this performance was brilliant. Because of you. You're the glue."

He's deranged, of course. Or maybe high.

"I really don't think so."

"No, don't deny it." He smiles at me with his head tilted a little to the side, as if he thinks I'm being modest. His hand reaches out and cups my elbow.

"We were all just doing our job, I think," I say, trying to sound forceful and teacher-like, although inside I'm battling my fight-or-flight response. I need to stem the flow of his crazy talk. What's next? Will he get down on one knee?

"Yes, we were." He nods and looks out over the room. People

have noticed him—noticed us—and are starting to move in our direction. He squeezes my elbow and lets go.

Shiver. No kidding. I shiver.

"Genny," says someone on my right.

It's possible that my mouth drops open a little, because Nathan McCormick actually laughs at me.

"Yeah. Surprise."

Clapperton will soon be swallowed up by some approaching patrons, but he turns away from them and drapes his arm around my shoulders.

"One of your fans, Imogen?" I try not to shake him off too obviously.

"Anthony, *je te présente* Nathan McCormick. Nathan, this is Anthony Clapperton."

I'm frazzled, switch to French and back to English. Also take the opportunity to step out from under Clapperton's arm.

They shake hands quickly and nod at each other. Neither smiles. I can't help wondering who squeezed the hardest.

"Great concert," Nathan congratulates us but he's looking mostly at me.

"Are you familiar with the Poulenc sextet?" Clapperton once again shows what an ass he is.

"No," says Nathan. "All new to me."

"Ah. So you're not one of Imogen's musical colleagues then, Ethan?"

"No," says Nathan. "I'm her skating partner."

Clapperton is still glued to my side. If he puts his arm around me again, I swear I will break his wrist. But no need for violence as it turns out.

"Tony! Bravo!" Clapperton is forced to look away from Nathan as voices rise over the general thrum, as the hands reach out to shake his. The crowd moves in.

I turn to say something to Nathan, but we're surrounded by a mass of people with congratulations and questions.

"Will you be performing at the Chamber Music Festival?"

"It must be such a change for you, playing in this new ensemble!"

"How long did it take you to learn that piece?"

"You should always wear your hair down!"

Alain's training kicks in and I answer, smile, shake hands. I sense Nathan right beside me and see eyes flit up quickly to check him out. The questions unasked. *Who is he?* Not a hockey crowd. He's incognito here.

And then there's a brief lull.

"I need to see my father and grandfather," I say to him. "I haven't spoken to them yet."

"Sure, let's go."

He takes my hand and leads me through the crowd, and I avoid making eye contact with any of the throng, no distractions or detours. Père puts his wine glass on the table behind him and wraps me in a hug while Papa shakes hands with Nathan, introduces Vianne. People around us are watching the St. Pierre Family Show, but I'm edging closer to the crash and am increasingly unaware of anything but the pounding in my head and the thought that Nathan McCormick came to our concert.

"How do you feel?" Père asks me.

"Tired."

"Of course. It's hard work. But satisfied?"

I nod and he nods, too. "You should be very satisfied, Imogen. That was an excellent, excellent performance."

"Exquisite," says Vianne, who has given Nathan the once-over and winks at me.

Papa leans in. "And they are lucky to have you."

Clapperton certainly thinks so.

"What did you think, Nathan?" Papa asks.

"Well." He shrugs and looks uncomfortable. "I'm not an expert and some of the music was sort of hard to follow." Papa and Père nod knowingly, charmed, I think, that he's not afraid to admit that. "But it's always great to see someone you know doing something really well."

He shrugs again, looks at me. "You play the piano really well." Which makes us all laugh.

I am dragged away by Alain several times but swim back at the first opportunity. They seem to be hitting it off. When I return for the third time, I understand why.

"But doesn't it hurt?" Vianne is asking.

"Silly woman! What do you think all that equipment is for?" Papa points out.

"And they coach us on that when we're kids," Nathan says. "How to position yourself, stuff like that."

"Of course, it helps to be enormous like you," says Père. The three of them all lean back and look up at Nathan as if assessing a tree or a high-rise.

Yes, it's true. Here in the wild aftermath of my l'Avenir debut at Dominion–Chalmers they're talking about hockey. Body checking, I think.

I slip up beside Papa and link my arm through his, more for support than anything else.

"Fading, my love?" He rests his chin on my head as I lean into his shoulder. "Let me go speak with Alain and we'll take you home. You've done your part here for today, I think."

"I have to get going, too," says Nathan.

Vianne is very quick. "Genny, why don't you walk Nathan out. Grab your things on the way and we'll meet you in the parking lot. Yes?"

My "things" consist of a hanger and suit bag containing my change of clothes (who cares—I'm going home in my black dress) and my black puffy coat, which is like a blanket wrapped around me in these uncertain early-Spring temperatures.

"That's it?" he asks. "You travel light, don't you?"

The green room is watched over by one of the Festival

volunteers, Mrs. Penny, who is on duty presumably so no one will steal any of the performers' instruments.

"That was lovely, dear," she says to me as I pack up. "You go home and have a good rest. I'm sure you need it after all that hard work."

In my increasingly vague state of crash, I think her kind words might push me over the edge into tears.

Nathan and I go back upstairs and pass the reception room on the way out. I pause briefly at the door to make sure that Papa and the rest have left, see Clapperton glance at me, turn away and glance again, and then I'm out the door.

"Thank you for coming," I say to Nathan when we get out to the sidewalk and pause. It takes a lot of concentration now to make coherent conversation. I can see Papa and Père walking slowly toward the parking lot, Vianne between them, holding Père's arm.

"Alicia wanted to come, too, but Claudette wouldn't let her," he says. "I wanted to see you in action, not just with the school orchestra. Or the girls. Claudette picked up the ticket for me."

"So nice of her. If I'd known you were interested, I could have got you some comps."

"No worries," he says. "I wasn't sure until the last minute that I could make it. Lots going on."

We stand there for a moment, smiling. I'm incapable of conversation but none seems to be required.

"Yeah. Well, I should get going." He pulls car keys from the pocket of his jacket. (He drives?) "That was great. I'll see you. Not sure when."

Something, something, tickling my brain. Oh, yes.

"Hey, our film ..."

"Oh, right, I wanted to mention that. Freddie texted me about coming to the gala thing that weekend. Not sure I can make it."

"Me, neither," I say, and after a moment we both laugh. Freddie and his schemes!

"Well, keep in touch, eh?"

I need to leave soon. I'm going to fall over with fatigue.

He steps into me and wraps me in a quick hug. "Get home. You need to recover from—from all *that*." He steps away and nods toward the church, the concert, Clapperton. He means Clapperton. "Bye."

"Thank you. Really. Thank you so much for being here."

He nods, waves, and walks away, keys in hand, toward a car parked presumably on one of the nearby streets.

When I turn around, I see Papa waiting for me at the end of the sidewalk near the parking lot, and I can't get to him fast enough.

"Let's go home," he says, taking my arm. "What a nice boy."

The car is warm and humming. Père and I share the back seat, both of us dozing as we listen to the voices of Papa and Vianne up front, chatting about—I'm not sure what. The concert. Me, maybe. It doesn't matter.

I'm oblivious. No, I'm empty.

CHAPTER 78

THAT'S THE SOUND OF A ...

Email from Alain:

The reviews are in and they're brilliant! Brava, Imogen!

Invitations already from the chamber music festivals in Montreal (June), Ottawa (July), and Victoria (August). Tony is looking into some possibilities in the UK *for the fall.*

I know you are headed to UBC *in September and haven't committed to l'Avenir yet, but with such an outstanding start, I'm sure we can make arrangements to work performances around your academic obligations. Sound good? Leave it with me.*

I'm working on a photo shoot, possibly within the next few weeks. I will be in touch.

Very exciting next step for you, Genny!

Alain

Listen.

That's the sound of a train starting to roll down the tracks.

CHAPTER 79

IN SKATING OVER THIN ICE, OUR SAFETY IS IN OUR SPEED, PART 4

I'm longing for bed. I don't sleep much anymore, but just to close my eyes and be horizontal would be heaven.

Not yet, though. Too much work to do.

The homework load has increased to crazy proportions as final exams loom. Hillside teachers have apparently banded together and decided we will not succumb to the already-accepted-to-university-so-why-keep-slogging syndrome.

"But, sir!" Victoria protests, when Mr. Norton assigns yet another essay. "We already have five assignments due on Monday!"

"Good training for university, Miss Hanson-Massey."

Maybe he hasn't heard that Victoria will be taking a year off to intern as a marketing assistant for her mother's friend's colleague's PR firm in Toronto. (We've been hearing about nothing else for the past few weeks.) I've started to envy her a little.

The work has piled up, as have the scores I need to learn

for upcoming performances by l'Avenir. I'm up late doing assignments and up early creeping through birdsong to the chapel to practice. In between I sometimes sleep. Badly.

It's a Thursday night in mid-May, and I'm about to abandon my homework for the night when my phone buzzes.

Short list

Fredrik, texting me and Nathan.

May 25-27. talked to norton. my mother will take us. hotel booked in TO. ur coming.

I don't respond right away because I'm trying to find an excuse strong enough to get out of it.

Come up blank.

Me: Have to check schedule

Fredrik: You said first concert in june

I did say that. And Fredrik, being Fredrik, of course, remembers.

Have to check with my father

Like hes going to say no?

Fredrik isn't buying that one, either.

It'll be fun u need some fun.

I used to think playing the piano was fun.

Maybe a break from this place, from the growing pile of piano scores, from writing essays on Margaret Atwood and Canada's role in the Second World War, from solving quadratic equations, and from all that reviewing of past exams—maybe it will actually be *fun* to take the train to Toronto and hang out in a hotel with Fredrik and his mom. And if that means sitting through *Thin Ice* a few times, and having people comment on—judge, actually—the scenes of Nathan and me skating in and out of the shadows on the pond, well, it can't be as bad as some of the things flitting vampire-bat-like around in my head right now: Chamber music festivals in other cities and Clapperton hanging off me like a vine, and leaving Père and Papa for Vancouver, and all that, all that.

Fine.

K. Tell me when, where etc.

From Nathan, no response.

CHAPTER 80

"It's a beautiful spring evening. Come, my love. Let's walk."

Père is standing beside the piano bench and I had no idea he was there. He's wearing his light overcoat and his jaunty hat, his fedora.

I need to keep working on this passage of the Mozart E-flat major quintet, and the Huber *Sextet* is still a train wreck. It's Saturday night of my last weekend at home before the trip to Toronto. Exams and performances loom. Everything looms.

"Come, Imogen." My grandfather lays a hand on my shoulder. "Take a break. I need someone to hold me up."

"Fine."

I hate how my voice sounds but he says nothing, just waits for me to run upstairs for a hoodie, smiles as I thump back down and follow him outside.

The street is filled with birdsong. Robins have taken over the lawns. Goldfinches swoop between the maples and cedars. Two small children with bikes—safety wheels in place—trundle back and forth on the sidewalk across the way, their vigilant mothers holding mugs of coffee (tea? other?) and chatting. They wave as we amble past on our side, my hand safely tucked around my grandfather's arm.

"This is pleasant," he says. Squeezes my hand.

I don't say anything because my head is still inside music and school work. And more.

"You look tired, Imogen. Are you getting enough sleep at that school of yours? Too many late-night parties?"

When someone says you look tired, they mean you look awful.

"No parties, Père. No, none of that. Just a lot of work."

Parties. Ha. Even Victoria has been seen in the lounge in baggy sweats, hair scraped back, no make-up. On occasion.

"Yes, so much work, preparing for exams and for your upcoming concerts."

My stomach gives a flip of—something. Not fear exactly. Concerts don't scare me. But the hours spent with Clapperton do, a bit.

Without even meaning to, I sigh.

"All will be well—don't fret," he says, and that just makes me feel like crying. Am I that obviously hopeless?

We walk. The sun is still quite high, although starting to drop so that beams filter through the fresh leaves and branches. I think I can hear the sunlight.

"I know," I say. Might as well reassure him, and maybe myself along the way. "There's just so much work right now, and the trip to Toronto, and these concerts coming up quickly."

It sounds even worse when I say it out loud.

"And you're not sleeping, are you? I know, I know, I can tell." He pats my hand again when I try to protest. "Your father was exactly the same for years. Until he discovered the secret to being happy."

"Which is?"

"The secret to being happy is to make yourself happy. It's to do what makes you happy."

We walk some more, and I'm not sure if he's expecting me to answer, but I do anyway.

"I don't know what will make me happy. Maybe moving to Vancouver. Maybe l'Avenir."

"Are those your only two choices?"

"I think so, yes. I think I have to choose one or the other, at least for a while."

"Ah."

If he has another option, I'd be happy to hear it, but he doesn't say anything. We just walk all the way to the park and around one of the paths there, then back home, the sun low now and at our back, casting our long shadows ahead of us on the sidewalk.

Me, tall and big-headed with my hair all over the place, and

Père, shorter with a weirdly shaped fedora head.

"We look like monsters," he says, my grandfather, who seems to know what is going on in my head before I do.

"Get some sleep, Imogen. Get some sleep, work on your pieces, write your exams. Meet your concert commitments. Go to Vancouver—although I will miss you terribly. And something tells me that somewhere along the way, you will discover what makes you happy. And you'll do it. And be happy."

Okay, now I'm going to cry.

"That's all your father and I could want for you, my love. We want you to be happy."

We walk home in silence, and I have never been so miserable in my life.

CHAPTER 81

TRAIN

Southern Ontario is looking particularly rough and rocky at the moment as we hurtle past fields and bush, somewhere near Smith's Falls on our way south toward the lake.

Fredrik says something in Swedish and Mrs. Floren replies, nods. Sighs.

"It reminds her of home," he translates for me.

Toronto is about four hours away, and we've spent the last half-hour settling into travel mode on the VIA train, Business Class. Mr. Floren insisted on picking up the tab so that we could travel in comfort. According to Fredrik, he has also picked up the tab for having our accommodation upgraded at the Toronto Hilton, the film festival's host hotel. No dinky little rooms beside the elevator and noisy ice machine for us! We have side-by-side rooms with a view of the city and the lake. I'm relieved I don't have to share. I'm also relieved that what is really a school trip will be as comfortable as one of Alain's Trio St. Pierre tours.

We have our devices full of music and videos, and my earbuds are handy (although I haven't felt the urge to use them yet, which is not at all like me), and exam study notes that Fredrik says we should simply ignore for the next three days. And snacks, which are not required, obviously, because we'll be served a meal and drinks on the train. We have free WiFi and four seats together in a sort of pod, with a table between us, although there are only three of us.

In other words, we are traveling in luxury toward what Fredrik says is our for-sure gold medal.

"How can you be sure?" I ask him on Thursday night after dinner at his house in Ottawa. We'll be leaving from the train station on Friday morning.

"Genny. Come on. Really."

"Humility, my son." Mrs. Floren shakes her head but she is laughing at him, too.

Humility and *Fredrik* are two words that don't go together easily.

"First, it's a good story. Second, people actually know who you and Nathan are, so already we have the audience intrigued. Third," he is counting on his fingers, "it's technically very sound. Fourth, the musical soundtrack is exceptional. In other words, we have a very good film here. A gold-standard film. Just saying."

His confidence makes me laugh at him. Mrs. Floren shakes her head the way a mother does. *Isn't my son awful? Isn't he adorable?*

Mrs. Floren is a restful traveling companion.

"We have lots of time, Imogen, so don't feel rushed," she says at breakfast, where I'm only able to manage a small glass of juice and a piece of toast after a restless tossing-and-turning night in the Florens' guest room. "We'll have a lovely cup of tea as soon as we're underway, I'm sure."

And we do. Tea, in a white china cup. I sip, look at the trees and rocks and farms rushing by. Sip. Feel myself traveling away from that uncomfortable place I was in just a few days ago.

Sip. Breathe. Something is different today. I feel it as I gaze out the window with my companions.

"There is nothing like a train trip, is there?" says Mrs. Floren.

CHAPTER 82

OPENING NIGHT

"I was so sorry to learn that Trio St. Pierre is disbanding," says the rouged woman with the silver hair. One of Père's admirers, no doubt. Her hand holding the wine glass blinds me with its diamonds.

"Thank you," I say, for probably the twentieth time, sounding once again as if I'm at a funeral. I search for something else to add. Come up empty. But it doesn't matter, because she and her two equally blinged friends fill the void with their chatter about seeing us perform at Roy Thomson Hall that time—and remember the fantastic concert at Niagara-on-the-Lake?

It's been like this for the past hour at the reception in one of the hotel ballrooms after the opening-night screening of one of the "big" films at the festival. All the filmmakers and actors have been invited, along with sponsors, and media, and people who bought tickets so they could be part of the opening night scene and are taking selfies at every opportunity.

In his opening remarks, the festival chair mentions a few of the films up for awards—ours included—and my fate is sealed.

"And tomorrow in our youth documentary competition, we have some very fine entries," he blathers. "These short films have been produced by young artists across Canada. Artists like Québec's Sebastien Auger and his visual exploration of his city's artscape. And Dara Lee with her journey following a day in the life of a Vancouver social worker. And Ottawa's Fredrik Floren, who has teamed with hockey player Nathan McCormick and well-known musician Imogen St. Pierre—where are you, Imogen? Ah, yes. Delighted you could make it!—to examine the challenges of skating on figurative thin ice."

Doomed.

It's all familiar to me, this standing in the headlights while people drive straight at you, wanting to talk, wanting to share. So how can you walk away? *Part of the game*, says Alain's phantom voice. But my legs are tired and my smile is becoming forced, and I'm dreaming of retreating to my beautiful quiet room upstairs. (Thank you, Mr. Floren.) Fredrik is here and there with his phone out much of the time, checking texts or email.

"I couldn't believe it when I saw your picture on the poster," one of the other women is saying. "Recognized you right away, of course, with that beautiful hair, and then there's your name in big letters. Can't wait to see your movie and hear the soundtrack you composed."

Composed? Did I compose a soundtrack? If "composing" means closing your eyes, placing your hands on the keys, and letting them find their own way, then yes, I composed the soundtrack.

"Excuse me." Fredrik appears at my side, sleek in his professionally tailored light blue suit, white shirt and striped tie, and (my favorite part) pointy black shoes. "I'm so sorry to interrupt, but may I steal Imogen, please?"

"But of course," gushes first bling lady, obviously charmed by his Swedish accent, which he has cranked up a little for the occasion. "We just can't wait to see your film. Lovely chatting with you, dear."

"Thank you. I hope you enjoy it," I say to them as we move away, and then, "Thank you," *sotto voce* to Fredrik.

"Thought you needed rescuing," he laughs. "Come with me. I have something to show you."

We're heading toward the exit, and I think for a moment we're really going to escape, but no. We've moved out into the lobby and he's leading me toward the reception desk, not the elevators.

The reception desk, where a guy in a dark suit is in the process of checking in, getting a key, turning around, catching sight of us.

"You made it," says Fredrik.

"Flight just got in and I came straight here."

Nathan McCormick, looking as if he just walked out of the dressing room after a game, with a duffel bag slung over his shoulder.

Nathan, here in Toronto.

Nathan.

"But I thought you couldn't come," I blurt.

"I never said that, did I?" He and Fredrik are straight-faced, standing side by side, watching me as I try to process his appearance here at the hotel. Here, tonight.

"Well, no, but ..."

He never responded to the texts, at least not where I could see. The 67s didn't make the playoffs so his season has ended, but he's too busy, not interested, moved on from *Thin Ice*. That's what I thought, and since I never asked Fredrik, that's what I believed.

"Surprise!" says Fredrik, and now they're both laughing at me.

"Couldn't miss seeing Freddie get his prize, could I? Especially since I'm the star. Well, you're the star, too." Nathan acknowledges me, pretending to be the conceited hockey boy that he really isn't.

"Getting *our* prize," Fredrik corrects him. "Come on. Party's in full swing."

Everything gets better after that. We get champagne—no one asks for ID, blind eyes turned—and stand together, watching the crowd.

"Autograph alert," Fredrik says as three girls, probably our rivals for Fredrik's gold medal, zone in on Nathan, stand together whispering, then venture forward. One girl does the talking and I can't help thinking of the Sirens.

"You're Nathan McCormick, aren't you?" she says, ignoring Fredrik and me. "We're from Barrhaven. We're big fans."

"Thanks."

Conversation of a sort follows. Nathan introduces us. We exchange film festival information.

"Your film is *Thin Ice,* right?"

"Yes, and yours is ...?"

Holiday at the Horse Farm or *Magic Mountain* or *The Streets of My Town* or something. Revolving groups pass by and around and through us. I mostly sip my champagne and watch as Fredrik takes the lead. Nathan and I become his background scenery, his chorus.

"Freddie's the mastermind. All I did was skate."

"The soundtrack was easy, actually. Fredrik did the recording and editing."

Later, a short man in a tuxedo (a tuxedo?) stops in front of us to ask Nathan about the upcoming NHL draft.

"Looks like it's going to be Calgary or Winnipeg," he says. "How do you feel about that?"

Nathan doesn't reply right away. Shrugs. "I guess we'll see."

"But do you have a preference?" The man is sweating in his formal clothes, possibly a bit over-dressed and over-imbibed.

Nathan shakes his head. The way he's standing—still, stiff—tells me there's something else going on. Fredrik jumps in.

"You must be media," he says and the man shoots him a look.

"So?"

"Oh, I didn't mean to insult you, sir!" Fredrik is full of

European charm, which cancels out what he just said, of course. (Insult all the way, no doubt.) “Have you seen any of the pre-screenings? What did you think of tonight’s opening film?”

They talk about the film we watched earlier—a bleak look at life in a remote northern community, starring some well-known Canadian actor. The media man doesn’t have much good to say about it and, after Fredrik gets technical, talking about the cinematography and editing and direction, the man moves away.

“Idiot,” Fredrik says.

“Why don’t we just leave?” Nathan asks us. “I mean, do we have to be here?”

We look at one another. No. We don’t have to be here.

Up the elevator and Nathan is already loosening his tie before the doors close. Fredrik has texted his mother that we’ve left the party and are going to gather in his room for a late-night snack.

It quickly turns into a party.

“Room service,” Mrs. Floren announces, so we pore over the dining menu and she orders (and insists on paying) for us.

Nathan is ravenous, apparently, after his flight from Ottawa, so he’s all about a hamburger. Two hamburgers. All I crave is tea and toast, with strawberry jam, the favorite snack Père and I have shared forever. Fredrik and his mother order flatbread and a vegetable tray. Drinks, tea. And cookies for after.

“Go on, you two,” Mrs. Floren shoos Nathan and me toward

the door. "Go change into something more comfortable. Pajamas welcome at this party."

So we do, although I forego the pajamas (so does he) in favor of my new black jeans and Montreal Canadiens hoodie, purchased on a shopping trip with Vianne before leaving for Toronto.

"Geez, are you nuts? You don't wear that in this town," Nathan warns me when we meet up again in Fredrik's room. "You'll get attacked by Leafs Nation."

"And you won't?"

He's all Sens, of course.

"Okay, when we leave the hotel, we'll have to hide behind Freddie."

"Don't worry. I'll protect you both," Fredrik promises. "Viking ninja."

Nathan asks if we can put the TV on, and he finds a sports news show with clips of the Blue Jays and playoff hockey. He and Fredrik are sprawled in two chairs, watching, talking. Mrs. Floren and I sit at a little table near the window while she tells me about a concert she recently attended at the National Arts Centre—the complete Elgar *Enigma Variations* and the E-minor *Cello Concerto*.

"I cried," she says. "Who can hear that piece and not think of Jacqueline du Pré?"

A knock at the door and she rises to greet the server, who wheels a trolley into the room. White linen and serving dishes. The boys pounce. I take my tea and toast back to the table by the window. Toronto is alive out there, a spinning galaxy of lights, while I spread my toast with strawberry jam and sip from a china cup, and chat with Mrs. Floren about rude audience behavior, and listen to Nathan instruct Fredrik on the reason for designated hitters and what "cycling" means during a power play.

And later, "Good night," Mrs. Floren says as she accompanies Nathan and me out into the hall toward our rooms around midnight.

"Have a good sleep," Fredrik calls out to us in a stage whisper before closing his door. "It's going to be a long day."

Of course he's envisioning tons of media attention after our screening in the early afternoon, and then the reception later, where the winners will be announced. People looking at us, talking to us, talking about us.

"It will be a good day, no matter what the outcome." Mrs. Floren gives us both a motherly pat on the shoulder before moving along to her own room. Nathan catches my eye, grins. *Mom talk.*

He has his keycard out already and turns back to me as I let myself into my room.

"*Bonne nuit*, Genny. Sleep well."

"*Bonne nuit.*"

His French is perfect when he talks to me. Not a hint of his neighborhood there.

After brushing my teeth, I catch sight of myself in the bathroom mirror. My eyes are glittering, the ever-present purple shadows underneath diminished by the bright bathroom light, or something else. When I climb into bed, I fall asleep immediately and, for the first time in weeks, don't wake up until my alarm goes off ten hours later.

CHAPTER 83

IN SKATING OVER THIN ICE, OUR STRENGTH IS IN OUR SPEED, PART 5

The audience gives us a standing ovation.

Of the three of us, I think Fredrik is probably the one who is least used to this, but of course he's handling it very well, being Fredrik. He predicted this, after all.

We're in the front row. All the entrants are sitting up front, and when each short film ends, the lights go up and we're supposed to stand up and wave or something while people applaud politely. We're the fifth of eight entries, the first one after intermission.

We've seen a film about dancing, all quick edits of feet, feet, feet, and sinewy, muscly arms and legs up close. One film about dogs in which the soundtrack is people speaking for the dogs—as in a slobbering, jowly mutt saying, "I'm hungry, Sam. You?" to a rat-like miniature creature that might be a Chihuahua (who answers in Chinese, for some reason). A beautiful hand-held camera tour of Quebec in winter during Carnival, with no music, just the sound of crowds and snow and lights, and a voiceover (in French with English subtitles) reciting lyrics by well-known *chansonniers*. Well-known to me, anyway, though maybe not to this Toronto crowd.

Fredrik keeps up a running commentary, but is careful to keep it in Swedish so no one can understand. I imagine he's saying things like: "Amateur. Are you kidding me?" "Learn how to do an edit, please." "Really? You call that a film?"

Nathan elbows me at one point. He can hear Fredrik, too, and I think he's as entertained as I am.

"Shhhh," I warn Fredrik. He turns toward me, face blank.

"No one here speaks Swedish, I'm pretty sure."

"Your mother?"

"She's at least twenty rows back."

And then, *Thin Ice*. An excruciating fifteen minutes of watching myself on screen, hearing my own voice—and my laugh, there at the end.

But it's mesmerizing, too, the final scenes from the pond. I'm back there on that cold November night, feeling my skate blades cutting through the ice for the first time with some kind of power and speed, because Nathan has my hand tucked into his arm. And the cold before that, after the shivery first hour, and the hot chocolate and Nathan's arm like a blanket around me—*Jesus, your teeth are chattering*—feeling warm again inside my puffy parka, while the frozen air slaps into my face. Flying, while the drone captures us from above. In and out of the dark and light.

I forget myself for a moment. Forget that I'm that girl up on the screen.

Nathan's voiceover—*Yeah, it's been a tough year. I missed hockey. I missed just skating*—we disappear into the shadows (oh, God, that laugh!), the credits roll and the audience erupts.

We're the only film so far to get a standing ovation. If the audience were judging, I think we'd be well on our way to a gold medal.

"Fredrik Floren, Imogen St. Pierre, and Nathan McCormick, of Hillside Academy in Brick Hill, Ontario," the MC, Mr. Croydon, from the Festival organizing committee, has to raise his voice as he speaks into the microphone.

The three of us look at each other and stand up to face the applause. I'm not sure what we're supposed to do, so I just stand and smile vaguely from side to side over the audience in an unfocused kind of way, the way I would at the end of any performance. I look at Fredrik and he's smiling at his mother, who is using her phone to video us, the crowd, us again. She gives us a thumbs-up. A quick glance at Nathan, and I see him simply standing and looking at a space somewhere just over the audience's heads.

"*Thin Ice,*" Mr. Croydon says again and the applause continues. Someone gives a whooting-hooting kind of cheer. This is getting embarrassing. The MC looks meaningfully at us. *Maybe if you sit down, they'll stop*. So we do and they do, and the theater is immediately filled with the rustling and thumping of people finding their seats and chattering among themselves.

"Really great film," the girl sitting beside Fredrik says to us. She's one of the dancing people.

We smile, say thanks. Some friendly chatter between Fredrik and others down the row, then he turns to us. Raises one eyebrow.

What did I tell you? Says the speech bubble over his head. Nathan puts out his hockey-boy hand toward Fredrik for a high-five, and Fredrik—who has very likely never high-fived anyone in his life—gets it done. I'm giggling at them. Fredrik leans toward me, takes my shoulders, and kisses both my cheeks, and then Nathan does the same—the sensation of Fredrik's soft blond beard against my skin followed by Nathan's hint-of-stubble chin close to my mouth. I must look surprised or something because they're both laughing at me, and then Mr. Croydon is introducing the next film, and on we go.

And a few hours later, we're presented with the crystal trophy and a check. *Thin Ice* wins the whole thing. Just as Fredrik said it would.

CHAPTER 84

AFTER PARTY, AND AFTER

A girl with blue hair is hanging off every word Fredrik says, but I only catch glimpses because people are flowing in and out of my view, speaking to me, wanting to shake my hand. Fredrik's loving it, though, I can tell. Another girl, tall and dressed completely in black—Goth maybe?—comes up and joins the discussion.

Filmmakers. Tech wizzes. They might as well be wearing signs.

"Great job!" people say to me, floating by. Some stop and want to shake my hand, or (the older ones, the parents, the teachers) just touch my arm, give it a squeeze. Makes me think fleetingly of Clapperton. "Congratulations."

During a break in the onslaught, I look around and see Nathan nearby. Just a moment ago, he was right beside me, muttering a running commentary of the scene into my ear, but the current in this room is very strong. He is cornered by a group of people, mostly girls looking up at him with "boyfriend" in their eyes (so obvious) and boys who want to talk hockey, probably. And the parent-teacher-grown-ups as well. He's not loving it but he's doing a good job of keeping the *Go away* hidden for now.

Somewhere beyond the hundreds of voices simmering throughout the room, I hear music. Jazz, maybe—a clarinet. (Oh, God, Clapperton again.) But it's just wallpaper music, lost in the orchestra of voices filling the reception room. Actually, quite loudly filling the reception room.

I don't mind loud tonight. I'm so happy for Fredrik, so happy to have shared this with him and with Nathan. Happy I had something to contribute, even if I didn't even know what I was contributing, for the most part. Yes, I'm happy. *This is what happy feels like.* I should call Père right now and tell him.

I see Mrs. Floren making her way through the press of people, looking for someone. Her eyes are searching—she finds Fredrik and says something to him and they both turn and scan the crowd. Their eyes land on me at the same time, and I see Mrs. Floren take a deep breath and move in my direction, Fredrik close behind. They're not smiling.

When they reach me, I realize that Nathan has somehow materialized at my side, too. He must have seen them coming our way. The four of us now, and Mrs. Floren takes my arm and speaks in French—"Imogen, my dear, come with me. I have something to tell you. Let's find somewhere quieter"—and we're moving through the crowd toward the exit. People still smiling and offering congratulations, but I can't smile back because my face is frozen—my body is frozen. When someone looks at you the way Fredrik and his mother looked at me across the room, you feel the heat drop out of the air and the freezing start.

We stop in the lobby and Mrs. Floren, in front of me now, takes my hands in hers, speaks to me. I feel Nathan's arm reach around my shoulders, trying to keep me warm because I'm shivering now.

Something has happened. Something has happened to my grandfather.

Père.

I need to get back to Montreal as quickly as possible ... plane ticket ... leaving tonight from Pearson ... Mr. Floren and people at Hillside are helping with arrangements, but I should go pack my things now. She'll take me up to my room ...

Nathan says: "I'll stay with her, Mrs. Floren, if you have arrangements to make."

"Thank you so much, Nathan. That would be helpful. All right, Imogen? Nathan will stay with you while you pack." She squeezes my hands and looks into my eyes. "I will see you back here in the lobby in, say, fifteen minutes? *Bon courage*, my dear."

Then, "Fredrik ..." and she's speaking to him in Swedish, typing a number into her phone and, with a smile of encouragement, I think, Fredrik moves off with her while Nathan guides me to the elevator, trying to keep me warm because I'm just shivering and shivering and can't stop.

CHAPTER 85

PÈRE

Vianne meets me at Trudeau when I arrive just after midnight.

"He is stable." Her first words. Then, "Oh, Genny, I'm so glad you're here."

She wraps her arms around me and we hold each other up. I can feel her trembling and I know I'm still shivering. She might be crying. Yes, I might be crying, too. I'm not sure because I'm so exhausted from the trip—the packing with Nathan sitting on the bed watching me and saying things that I don't even remember now, Fredrik and Nathan hugging me in front of our hotel, and I very nearly ask Nathan to come, too, please, just to keep me warm (silly, of course, and I don't), a short cab ride to Union Station, then the airport train with Mrs. Floren, who helps me navigate the ticketing and the special arrangements. Boarding is nearly finished so I have to hurry. It's fraught and frightening and my luggage probably won't even make the plane, or it will and I won't.

And finally we're at the departure gate and Mrs. Floren hugs me, looks into my eyes and says, again, "*Bon courage*, my dear. I hope all goes well. Please text Fredrik to let us know you arrived safely."

Finally, Vianne and I step back, wipe our eyes, try to laugh at each other.

"It's okay," she says. "The doctors think he will be okay. The doctors say he will be okay. It will take some time, but he will be okay, Genny."

She keeps her arm around me and pulls my suitcase behind her as we make our way to the taxi stand. People look at me, this white-faced girl, and avert their eyes. *Wonder what her story is?*

In the cab to the hospital, we sit close together and Vianne holds my hands and tells me what happened. Watching the hockey game—playoffs, so of course they were watching the hockey game!—and the sudden dizziness and disorientation. Standing up to make tea and then he's on the floor, making noises and then unconscious, and Papa is calling the ambulance, calling Vianne. *We must reach Imogen. She needs to come home.* Poor Papa.

"He woke up in the ambulance and, by the time Maxim saw him, he was telling everyone to let him go home," she says, handing me a tissue. "He wanted to know who won the game, of course."

Of course he did. My grandfather, who can always make me laugh. I nearly laugh now but it's more like a hiccup.

"A little heart attack, they think," Vianne is saying. "Maybe a mild stroke. They have to do tests and see what is going on. But the last word from your father, about a half-hour ago, was that Félix is stable, resting, and in no danger right now. You can relax, Genny. And perhaps check the score of the hockey game, because I am sure he will ask you about it when he wakes up."

And that makes me smile, finally, tears still very near.

Arrived. On way to hospital. My grandfather stable & resting.

Fredrik responds within seconds.

Good!!! Thinking of you.

Please thank your mother for me. She is very kind.

Will do. Take care keep in touch

I put my phone away but it buzzes a moment later.

Good luck. Thinking of you.

Nathan.

Thank you

I can see the three little dots in the balloon, showing that he's typing something. Then it stops, erased. Then it starts again. Then erased again. Then—

Hugs

The hospital is too bright and smells of fear. Why don't hospitals smell of caring doctors and nurses, and people getting well, and new babies? Good things? I smell the fear just walking down the hallway, waiting for the elevator.

Vianne is my guide and I trail along, my hand in hers, as if I'm a little girl. Which is exactly how I feel right now, of course. At the right floor, we approach a nurses station and Vianne does the talking while I glance left and right, trying to see through walls, doors. Trying to find my grandfather.

The hall door to the right swings open and Papa is there, coming toward me, arms out.

They let me go in for a few minutes. Père lying there in the blue hospital gown, with his neck and a few grey-haired inches of chest and beginnings of his bony shoulders exposed, which would horrify him if he were awake. And there are monitors and tubes and needles and all that smell-the-fear hospital equipment everywhere. Père, sleeping. Smiling a little, as if he's relaxing in his chair, listening to me practicing at the piano in the living room. Père, asleep.

I sit in the chair and watch him breathe for a moment, then reach out and put my hand on his arm. I don't mean to wake him—just to feel his skin, alive.

He turns his head and opens his eyes.

"My love," he says in a whispery, sleepy, drug-softened voice. "You are here."

"I'm here, Père."

We sit like that for a while and he closes his eyes again. I think he's asleep now, his chest rising and falling regularly. It's very peaceful. I'm finally warm and out of tears, and mostly out of gas, too, like I am after a concert. My crash is approaching but I think it's okay. Vianne or Papa—or both of them—will take me home, and we'll come back tomorrow and all will be well. That's what I tell myself.

Nurses and attendants swish back and forth and, after a while, Papa comes in and rests his hand on my shoulder.

"We'll let him sleep now. The doctor says he will stay here tonight in ICU, then to a regular room in the morning; then we'll see where we are. He will be fine without us sitting here all night, and you must be exhausted from your trip."

We stay a moment longer, Papa's hand on my shoulder, my hand on Père's arm. Then I rise, take my hand away.

A stirring from Père and, without opening his eyes, he asks: "Your film? Did you win the prize?"

"Yes, we did." It all seems a long time ago. "Rest now, Père."

"Did my Habs win, too?"

That makes me smile, finally. "Yes. A shut-out."

He raises his hand a few inches, thumb up.

"You will come back tomorrow?" No louder than a whisper.

"Of course," I whisper close to his ear. Kiss his cheek, pat his arm again as he smiles and settles back into sleep.

CHAPTER 86

CONCERTO IN EADG

I'm running scales and arpeggios, waiting for Papa to finish with some phone calls before we go to the hospital for today's visit.

Mindless scales and arpeggios so I don't have to think. Which is pointless, really, because I'm incapable of intelligent thought, anyway. Sometimes I'm back inside the See Hear bubble with Fredrik and Nathan, and we're holding our trophy and smiling at a man taking our picture for the news, or for the TIFF brochure, I'm not sure which. I'm back in Fredrik's hotel room, listening to him learning about saucer passes from Nathan, while I share performance stories with Mrs. Floren. Kind Mrs. Floren. I hear Clapperton's email voice asking if I've been staying on top of the Poulenc, because we will perform it three weeks from now, as well as in July at some other concert Alain has lined up for us. Up and down the keyboard until my forearms start to tighten up and I have to take a break. Start over in E-flat Major this time.

"Are you ready, Imogen?" Papa is off the phone, calling to me from the kitchen where he's assembling his computer bag. He'll drop me at the hospital while he makes a quick stop at his office on campus—May is a busy time at the university—then will come back and join us. He is supposed to meet with Dr. LeClair today, too, to find out what is happening, when Père might be coming home.

"Ready."

The hospital is familiar now—after so many visits, it should be, I suppose. I smile at the friendly volunteer at the information desk (her name is Esmé; she's a fan) as I head toward the elevator with my special burden. This is our fifth day of visiting. I should probably be back at school, preparing for exams, but I don't care. UBC has been sending me daily welcoming emails—not all from the same person, of course. Administration, and Missy, and Residence Services, and Dr. Latimer, the dean, and Dr. Jan Larevich, who will be my piano mentor. My teacher, I suppose. They already have me scheduled to perform at the Chan Centre with a trio in November, helping with a master class after Christmas. Do I want to enter the Montreal International Music Festival next spring? It will feature pianists this time round ...

I don't think UBC is going to kick me out if I delay my Grade 12 exams. So I stay home and visit Père every day. Play my piano.

Lie on my bed and stare at the ceiling.

"Ah. You remembered," Père says in his new wispy voice when I come through the door.

He is allowed to get out of bed now, to sit in the chair by the window, but still in pajamas, which makes him look fragile and old. He needs a haircut, and they don't always help him with shaving before I get there, so I've done it a few times myself. Pulled his electric razor from the drawer, checked that it's charged, run the buzzing heads gently over his cheeks and chin, jaw, neck, hold up the little mirror Papa brought from home so that we can do a quality-control check (as he calls it).

"Yes, of course I remembered," I say, not letting my face show that I'm not used to how he looks now, older, more frail. But he has shaved, and his white hair—whiter than it was several weeks ago, I think—is combed neatly.

I lay the violin case on the bed, click the fasteners to open it, and immediately we both breathe in the scent of resin and wood and everything that matters.

"Ah. This will do the trick." His eyes are closed, and then he opens them and smiles at me. "You will have to help me. With my little stroke."

So I do. Lift the precious (and rare, and heavily insured) instrument from its case and place it under my chin, pluck the strings to make sure they're somewhat in tune (they are, more or less; Papa already tuned it at home). Take one of the bows and tighten it to just the right tension (memories of Suzuki String School, many, many, many years ago).

"Perfect." He's watching me from his chair by the window.

"Now, don't drop it, my love. My tired fingers and I are counting on you."

I place the instrument gently on his left collarbone and hold it there as he eases his chin, his jaw, into position over it. Experiments. Sits back, thinking.

"Perhaps we'll take a page from M. Duval's book today."

I know what he means. "Pays de haut." Old style. His arm lies on the arm of the chair and I lay the instrument along it, scroll close to his fingers and the rounded edge of the lower bout resting on his upper arm, just below his shoulder. Make sure it's snug against his chest and let go.

No, it droops over, unsupported. I go to the bed and take a pillow. Stuff it around his arm so that the violin is propped up and safe.

"Ah," he says again, smiles, takes a deep breath, as if inhaling the scent of past performances from the f-holes.

"The bow, Imogen, I'm not sure I can hold it," he says then, and it should sound pathetic and sad but it doesn't. He's grinning, in fact, with his violin resting along his arm, as if he's showing it off, not preparing to play it.

I kneel beside his chair and put the bow in his right hand, cover it with my own so we're both holding it.

"Ready?" I ask.

He nods, winks slowly at me like some aged owl.

Our hands lift the bow onto the open A string and I help him pull it across, making the string resonate with only a little double-stopping on the D as the instrument rocks on his arm.

"Perfect," says Père as we draw the bow through to the tip and then reverse, this time on the E.

He settles the violin on his arm, uses the pillow for support, and grips his fingers a little more tightly around the neck. The wood is resonating, vibrating, singing to him.

"Ah," he says once more. His eyes are closed now and he's smiling. "Who needs medicine and doctors when there is the magic of open strings? Don't you agree, Imogen?"

"Agree, Père."

Back and forth on the open strings. Down to the G. Even I can feel the vibration from that one, and Père laughs a little, eyes still closed.

Our hands are joined on the frog end of the bow, the handle, back and forth, playing through each tone twice before moving on to the next string. Until finally he gives a sigh and releases his grip under mine and we squeak to a stop.

"Enough for today, I think." He leans back in the chair as I rescue the violin and carry it back to the open case on the bed. Collect the pillow. "Thank you, Imogen. That was lovely. The healing power of music, I think."

I loosen the bow, return it to the holders inside the case, and snap the lid shut, then turn and sit on the side of the bed.

Père is watching me.

"You should be at school, my love, not here in a hospital room, playing open string cycles with an old man in pajamas," he says.

"But that was fun. And I'd rather be here than at school."

"Maybe Hillside was not such a great idea. Maybe you would rather have gone to the high school here and then the local CEGEP instead?"

"No, I don't think so. It's been good."

"And now off to Vancouver and the next step in your education. Your father says you have decided on UBC."

"Yes."

"I will miss you," he says.

A long pause because I can't answer. I look away from the window, where I've been staring at sunlight streaming through the glass and no further. Look back at my grandfather, who is watching me with that half-smile and his eyes that always seem to see more of me than anyone else does.

"Time for lunch, I think," he says. "Shall we see if Nurse Amélie will let us eat in the lounge room down the hall? The view from those windows is so much better."

CHAPTER 87

DONE

"Math is the worst," says Victoria, flopping down on the freshly mowed grass near the pond after our last exam. "I'm sure I failed."

The entire Grade 12 class has just emerged from the chapel, where we've been penned up for five days at desks arranged in rigid rows, writing the final exams of our high school careers.

"But WE'RE DONE!" Braedon yells, whoops, and everyone joins in. Cue the celebration.

Berit, William, Fredrik, and I whoop dutifully, but we also drift to the edge of the crowd (because twenty-eight students can be considered a crowd) and settle on the lawn.

My eyes are at the staring-at-nothing stage. On the surface of the pond, the sun creates gentle sparklers, a welcome change from the past two hours of blaring institutional light in the chapel, and page after page of little numbers and symbols.

"It's just not fair that you can't come to the Grad Prom,

Genny," Berit complains. "Can't you get out of it?"

It is rehearsal with Clapperton and the gang all weekend in Ottawa, in preparation for our next concert. Montreal a week from now, at a small chamber music festival. A sort of warm-up for Ottawa in July. I've been living between the chapel and my room. Quick trips to the dining hall, where I avoid eye contact, load up on supplies, and head back to my room to start the cycle again.

"No, I'm afraid not."

"The life of a professional," says Fredrik. "Why are you even going to UBC, anyway?"

I shrug and pull a neglected dandelion out of the thatch.

"I'm still working out what kind of music I want to play, now that I'm on my own." This sounds suitably career-oriented and mature, I think, but Fredrik narrows his eyes.

"And UBC will help you discover that? Wouldn't a good conversation with your grandfather do the job?"

"Maybe. But it will be good to work with someone new. New teachers. Meet other musicians." *Musicians who aren't Clapperton.* I sound a lot like Alain all of a sudden. Like a brochure.

"But it's just so far away," says Berit. She and William have both been accepted at the University of London and will be living in the UK next year. Fredrik is vague about his plans, but I know he's not going to any of the universities who sent him acceptances—and offers of scholarship money. "We'll be scattered all over. Are you sure you can't stay for Prom, Genny? And Prize Day?"

"No. I'm sure."

Tonight Papa will retrieve me and my gear. All my gear—books, clothes, bedding, everything. We'll celebrate with Père, who is still in hospital. And on Saturday morning, first thing, drive to Ottawa for the two-day rehearsal somewhere on the university campus. Home base will be Papa's new condo downtown, his pied-à-terre for his new gig with the Chalmers Chamber Ensemble.

Everything is changing.

"Well, it's a shame." Berit smiles at me. "When will we see you again, Genny?"

"Come to London any time," William says. "Bring what's-his-name. Your clarinetist friend. What was his name?"

"Anthony Clapperton."

"That's the one. Bring him along and we'll get together for a drink down the pub."

Horrors! "I'll let you know."

I take my eyes off the pond and gaze around at my classmates, everyone relaxed and chattering now that the exams are done. It's the tradition, to write the last exam (always Math, because at Hillside, everyone has to take Math and English in Grade 12), and then gather on the grass by the pond for an informal, final assembly. On Prize Day, everyone will peel off their robes and leap into the pond in a final swim of freedom after the diplomas are handed out. I would have done it, too. Well, maybe.

And on Final Exam day, there's another tradition: Mrs.

Clouthier and her staff have just appeared at the door of the school, wheeling a kitchen cart loaded with iced tea and lemonade and her famous cupcakes.

"It's like pre-school," Fredrik mutters to the three of us as everyone catches sight of the approaching entourage and offers up a group cheer. "And way too much sugar. Watch Victoria go nuts."

"But it's tradition," says Berit. "And I think it's lovely."

"Hmm. *Lovely* would be champagne," says Fredrik.

"Beer," William suggests.

I'm going to miss these three. Berit is right: when will I see them again?

"Too bad Nathan couldn't be here, too," says Victoria, from the other side of the crowd, just loudly enough. I expect she's looking over at me.

But I just pretend not to hear and turn my focus back to the sparklers jumping across the uncertain surface of the pond.

CHAPTER 88

VIA SOCIAL MEDIA

Sportsnet.ca:

Who won the NHL *Combine? No easy answers, but surely Kyle Seagram (Oshawa Generals), Peter Linna (Brandon Wheat Kings, Finnish national team) and Nathan McCormick (Ottawa 67s) made the biggest impression, with McCormick—despite missing half the season because of a suspension—making the most significant impact on scouts, trainers, and those of us watching from the sidelines. This kid is big, strong, and determined, and he finished in the top ten in eight of the tests.*

Take a look at the Big Three as they tackle the force plate at the jump station, and then listen to their interviews with Sportsnet's Alex Francis. These kids are smooth. And ready for the big leagues.

Twitter @Sportsnet

Watch McCormick's pro-agility-shuttle-run. Tops right & left #NHLCombine #MeetTheFuture bitly.Kmn843x5p

W. Arthur Boyd, Arts & Entertainment, Globe and Mail

Ask anyone who was part of the enraptured audience at McGill's Pollack Hall on Saturday evening: L'Avenir truly IS the future of chamber music. Featuring the best new "voices" in international classical ensemble performance, l'Avenir is the brainchild of clarinetist Anthony Clapperton, winner of three consecutive Zurich Chamber Music Competition gold medals and a recent collaborator with Trio St. Pierre (Montreal) and Eldermusic Chamber Orchestra (London, UK).

To create this exciting new ensemble, Mr. Clapperton recruited flautist Alina Rolf (Boulder gold medalist), oboist Richard Bezic (National Arts Centre "Artist To Watch"), bassoonist Georges Bertrand-LeBlanc (three-time Riga gold medalist), and principal horn of the National Arts Centre Orchestra, Bartek Król. Rounding out the ensemble, and perhaps Mr. Clapperton's greatest coup, is the teenaged pianist, Imogen St. Pierre, whose muscular, deeply sensitive musicality was one of the pillars of the now-retired Trio St. Pierre (with her father Maxim and grandfather Félix St. Pierre). Miss St. Pierre's expressive and astonishingly unique piano mastery provides the foundation for this dynamic collection of wind players to build on.

And build they do. Their performance of the Poulenc Sextet at Pollard Hall on Saturday evening provided an uplifting and completely satisfying journey through the sometimes murky passages of Poulenc's ....

Twitter @Sportsnet

BREAKING: *2nd pick Nathan McCormick to @NHLFlames #Calgary #NHLDraft*

Twitter @CBCSports

BREAKING: *McCormick picked #2 by #Calgary @NHLFlames #NHLDraft*

Twitter @TSNHockey

BREAKING: *#Calgary @NHLFlames select Ottawa's Nathan McCormick #NHLDraft*

Twitter @OttawaCitizen

"Couldn't be happier." Redemption for tough guy McCormick. #NHLDraft @NHLFlames bitly.hplTY32p

Sydney Hergott, *Ottawa Citizen*

The hype was already tremendous—and growing—before the fledgling chamber music ensemble l'Avenir made its appearance at this year's Chalmers Chamber Music Festival in Ottawa on

Friday night. A pre-Festival performance of the Poulenc Sextet in April gave audiences a taste of what to expect, and obviously the word was out. Sold-out performances, standing ovations, and a steadily increasing buzz in the classical music firmament: l'Avenir is definitely the Next Big Thing.

It's not hard to pinpoint the reasons, either. Anthony Clapperton, the group's founding father—perhaps "big brother" is a more appropriate term, since he's the oldest member at the tender age of 25—is currently one of the best clarinetists on the planet, and his musical vision is both innovative and crystal clear. By collaborating with Alina Rolf (flute), Richard Bezic (oboe), Georges Bertrand-LeBlanc (bassoon), and Bartek Król (French horn), Mr. Clapperton has drawn together the next wave of over-achieving wind players and created magic—thanks to the not-so-secret ingredient: Montreal pianist Imogen St. Pierre. This remarkable 18-year-old, alumna of the recently retired Trio St. Pierre (with father Maxim, cello, and grandfather Félix, violin), demonstrates master-class musical instincts, not to mention virtuosity, every time her fingers touch the keys. Elegant, powerful, nuanced, breathtaking—she is the wind beneath l'Avenir's wings. The future of this ensemble is not just bright—it's very likely to be blinding. Canadian and international classical music fans are in for an exciting ride.

On Friday night at Dominion–Chalmers Church, they showed why, in a program that included ...

Twitter @ClassicalMusicNews

Listen: @CBCMusic playback of pianist Imogen St. Pierre's solo encore at Chalmers Fest. Sublime. #HowDoesSheDoIt bitly. EEmbs8953jp

CHAPTER 89

AND THEN ...

Hey here's something

Fredrik, who is in Ottawa, working on—working on, well, something. Making short films or videos. I'm not sure, but all summer he's been sending me links to some very cool stuff he's done for an art gallery, a fashion designer, an architect.

??

Couple of contracts for short films. Need soundtracks. You can do this in your sleep.

When?

Deadlines in December but need tracks by early November

Kind of busy over the next few months

Fun stuff?

School

FUN STUFF???

I hesitate. Then ...

Stuff that has to be done

Think about it k?

K

CHAPTER 90
WALKING AWAY

The garden around Villa Ste-Jeanne d'Arc is fragrant and fading a bit as the August doldrums creep in. It's been hot and dry, although no one is complaining.

Père and I don't mind. For a month now, since he was transferred from the rehabilitation hospital downtown to this square red-brick relic from the 1920s ("A convent, I'm quite sure," says Père. "Who else would make the doors so huge and heavy?"), I've been walking the half-hour from our house, braving the scorched sidewalks of our neighborhood, to steer him around the massive garden with its trails and trellises, intended to spur healing and offer succor.

Healing, yes, there has been healing. Père's hands will now open and close on command. He can write and carry a book, and he even sat at the decrepit piano in the residents' lounge and played some Bach—slowly but note-perfect—for several elderly ladies at the bridge table. They applauded and he bowed formally. That's something else he can do now—take a bow. And stand, and walk, and not teeter unsupported.

It's been three months. Three busy months. In a week I leave for Victoria. First, a concert with l'Avenir, then off to Vancouver and UBC and the start of school.

The beginning of whatever comes next.

"Ahhh. Smell the roses." Père breathes in deeply as we stroll from sunny patch to sunny patch among the willows and maples. The gardens are full of roses and flowering shrubs and a few slow-moving, placid but always-smiling gardeners, who potter with their fertilizers and wheelbarrows and weeding tools.

"Their names are Théophile and Ovide," Père tells me early on in our garden-walking routine. "Uncle and nephew from Tadoussac."

"How do you find this stuff out?"

"I talk to them, of course, silly girl. We talk about roses and bees, and what kind of fertilizer is best, and when is the best time to prune the shrubs."

We're walking slowly, my arm in his despite the heat of the day. He's wearing a stylish straw hat that Vianne brought him and a short-sleeved cotton shirt. My fingers feel the twigs of his bones right through the papery skin. I know my hand is sweaty and slippery on his arm, but I don't mind and neither does he.

"I didn't know you were interested in gardening," I say.

"I'm interested in anything that grows."

Next to the hours I spend at the piano, this is the best part of my day, walking with Père around the garden paths of Villa Ste-Jeanne d'Arc.

"You'll have to get busy in our little bit of garden when you come home."

"Yes. I will transform it into a floral paradise. Maybe Théophile and Ovide could give me some pointers," he says.

We walk some more. Somewhere, hovering and elusive in the rose-scented and simmering air, are all the things I want to say.

CHAPTER 91

IN VICTORIA

Victoria Summer Music Festival vsmf.org

Second l'Avenir concert! Tickets now available online!

The Victoria Summer Music Festival is happy to announce that due to increased demand, ensemble l'Avenir will perform an additional concert on Thursday, August 22, 7 PM, at Phillip T. Young Recital Hall, School of Music, University of Victoria. Find tickets online at vsmf.org/buy-tickets

Twitter @CBCMusic

UPDATE: second l'Avenir concert sold out. @CBCMusic will be recording for future broadcast @UVic

Hey Genny,

Just wanted to touch base with you before tonight's concert. We'll be in the usual practice room at 4 for a quick run-

through. Exciting stuff, being given an extra slot in the program.

I know Alina has been giving you some strife but, trust me, she really does admire and respect you. I think it's just because you're so young and so accomplished, she maybe feels you're getting more attention than she is. Not to worry. I will speak with her. I know Bartek has also had a word with her and told her to tone it down. I hope that little scene after our Ottawa concert didn't upset you. It was your turn for a solo encore—I don't know what she was on about, to be honest.

We are on a roll! Let's keep it going. Meet out front the hotel at 3:15 for a cab?

Cheers,

Tony

Hey you there?

Hi

Claudette showed me a review from the globe. Sounds like concerts are going good

Going okay. Congratulations on being picked by Calgary

Calgary is good. My mom and sister are happy about it too. Might still be in Ottawa for next season tho. You in BC for good now?

After last concert on Saturday I go to Vancouver

Looking forward to it?

Of course

Hows your grandfather?

Better thanks. When do you know if you move to Calgary?

End of September after training camp

Good luck. Sorry have to go

K. Good luck. When we play canucks maybe you could come watch

Maybe. Bye.

Bye

I don't really have to go, but I just don't trust myself. Texting is so easy—I might accidently send something like, I don't know, like—

Help

CHAPTER 92

OCTOBER

"Can we try my entry again, please?" asks Victor.

"Of course."

I start the section again—Ravel's A minor trio, a piece I've played with Papa and Père hundreds of times—it's fast and exciting and I'm all over the keyboard, and Victor misses the entry again.

"I'm so sorry, Imogen." Poor guy, he's nervous.

"It's no problem. It's hard. You'll get it."

Listen to me, the supportive teammate. The coach. With Papa and Père, I always just followed along and we hardly spoke to each other during rehearsal, sometimes just stopped and nodded and started again, because we all knew what needed to be said, to be done.

It's all different here, with these musicians—my classmates—it's strange. I have to speak when they ask me questions. And they ask me a lot of questions.

"You are something of a celebrity, you realize, Imogen," Missy says to me weeks after I've arrived at UBC and settled into my little studio apartment just off Marine Drive, attending classes, rehearsing with my assigned student trio, avoiding emails from Clapperton, starting to work with Dr. Larevich on expanding my piano repertoire to include some of the big solo pieces. *How do you feel about tackling Rach 2?*

Missy is my minder. She sends me texts asking if I need anything. I have a feeling she also sends updates to my father.

She has taken me out to get some groceries and we're finishing off our Starbucks at my tiny kitchen table.

"I'm not the only musician here," I say. "They don't need to think of me that way."

"But they do, of course. Come on, love, *Maclean's* magazine stories and Juno awards? That's pretty hard to ignore."

Missy has silver-white hair, short and spiky, and she favors bright red lipstick. Today as we walked around Save-on-Foods, I felt like a plodding giraffe next to a sleek thoroughbred. Me, in my jeans and Habs hoodie.

"Does that bother you?" she asks. "That they look up to you, I mean?"

"I suppose not, but I wish they wouldn't."

"You're not used to it," she smiles at me. "Your father and grandfather just treated you like one of the family, I suppose."

"It's just different, playing with people who know you so well."

Missy is right, though. *I'm so thrilled to be in your class!* That's what a girl said to me on the first day of our music history course. I had absolutely no idea what to reply.

"You'll get used to it," Missy says, downing the last of her latte. "And now, my dear, I must dash."

She stands and surveys my little apartment. "Charming! See you soon, love, and let me know if you need anything."

Let me know if you need anything.

After she leaves, I open the email on my phone and read it for the twentieth, thirtieth (I really don't know how many) time.

Hey Genny,

Getting a bit worried here. Alain needs that signed contract right away so we can make the arrangements for the UK *Christmas tour.*

If there's any problem at all, please tell me. I'm here to support you. You know that, right?

Best,

Tony

Also on my phone are twelve missed calls from Alain. Every time I step outside, I glance around, thinking he might be hiding behind a tree and will materialize, contract in one hand, pen in the other. He stopped emailing and started calling about four days ago.

Papa has clearly been enlisted to prod me.

And I understand Alain is having trouble reaching you. Could you connect with him? Something about contracts, I believe.

And two days later: *Alain is pestering me again today. Is there a problem, my love? Can I help?*

I hate that I haven't responded to my father, but I don't know what to say yet.

Victor finds the entry on the fourth try and we get through to the end of the section. A little more slowly than I'm used to, a little ragged, but that's why we practice it, of course.

"Would you both mind if we do it again, from the beginning?" asks Wanda, our cellist. She sounds so timid when she speaks, but her playing is loud—maybe even too loud. But then, I'm so used to Papa's sweet cello. Maybe Dr. Andrews, our ensemble advisor, will point it out. I'm not going to.

"I'd be fine with that," Victor says and they both look at me.

"Fine with me, too," I say.

I think it's safe here, in this practice room but, over on the table, my phone buzzes. A text.

They both look at me.

"Do you need to get that?" asks Victor.

"No, it can wait," I tell them. "Let's go again. Ready?"

CHAPTER 93

MAYBE THIS ...

In vancouver to play canucks fri night. I can get you a ticket. Interested?

CHAPTER 94

AND THEN

Your friend Clapperton being an idiot

A text from Fredrik. He sends another right after.

Don't let it bug you. Ur better out of it.

He includes a link to an article from a UK classical music site, sent to him by William, apparently, in which Anthony Clapperton introduces the pianist who will be performing with l'Avenir for their UK tour this Christmas—Lena Bajorek, a nice girl from Poland; I met her in Dresden once, at a festival years ago. Clapperton goes on to say it's so "unfortunate" that "the level of maturity Imogen St. Pierre displayed in reneging on her commitment to l'Avenir was just not appropriate for a serious professional ensemble like ours."

What? What?

Same article, Alina this time: "I'm afraid Imogen has a lot of growing up to do. Yes, she plays the piano very well, of course, but there's much more to being a respected musician and collaborator. Sadly, she proved herself to be only interested in her own advancement, her own reputation."

Clapperton again: "Well, quite frankly, she's probably just not ready to be part of a more professional ensemble, but what can you expect from a teenage prodigy who was carried along mostly by the magnificence of her father and grandfather, both undisputed leaders in the classical music world?"

Oh.

I text Fredrik back:

I don't know what to say

Leaves you speechless doesn't it? Ignore it. Guy is an idiot.

I feel sick. I feel as if I'm going to throw up.

Three more texts from Fredrik before I turn off my phone:

Don't read the comments

Stay away from twitter too

Call me if you need to talk.

CHAPTER 95

IN THE DARK

I've missed three days of classes and practice because I can't leave my room. *Sorry*, I text Victor and Wanda. *Sorry, I'm sick*, I text Missy when she checks up on me. *Sleeping it off.*

The emails are coming fast and furious now—furious being the more important word. Clapperton is losing his cool, threatening to blacken my name with all the festival organizers, threatening to sic Alain on me, in person. Saying Lena is just a sub and he expects me back at the keys for the next series of L'Avenir concerts. (Series? What series?)

Which doesn't matter, because Alain is also leaving increasingly taut messages about loss of professional standing and getting a reputation for not living up to commitments, and what the hell do I think I'm doing anyway? I don't have the strength to reply. It only takes a couple of clicks to delete, delete, delete.

Papa texts that he wants to Skype with me this afternoon, but I don't actually know if it's morning or afternoon or the middle of the night. He says we must Skype or he's getting on a plane and coming to Vancouver. *You are scaring me, my love. I will have to contact the university and have someone break down your door if you don't respond.*

I am scaring me, Papa.

I'm running out of supplies, too. Drinking tea without milk and sugar is just sad.

The duvet is over my head and I'm curled up in a ball, warm, cozy, safe in my bed, in my little apartment, and as long as I stay here, none of them can reach me.

My phone buzzes again and I ignore it. Buzzes. Buzzes. Buzzes.

All right! Reach out a hand from inside my duvet nest and bring the phone inside.

Know what you need?
You need to come home
And do a couple of soundtracks for me.
Paid gigs
Play anything you want
Make it up even
Think about it k?

Fredrik.

Phone off. Duvet darkness. Later, later I'll check the time and Skype with Papa. Maybe Père will be there, too. Maybe I'll be able to tell them about the way the air around me is so unmoving and heavy and liquid with oily darkness that I can't even find the urge to swim anymore, or breathe, or lift my fingers onto the keyboard. Even my ears are stopped. I hear nothing but my heart beating, and sometimes I think even that has gone away.

Later. For now I'm safe. I'll just stay like this for a while. Later I'll see if I can climb out of my nest. Later. Not now. Soon.

CHAPTER 96

FINE

The teams are coming out for the warm-up just as I arrive at the top of the stairs, so I stand there for a minute to watch, trying to find him among the players (all huge) in their white jerseys, flaming red C on the front.

There. Number 92.

He's circling the ice, along the blue line, down the boards in front of me, around behind the net, up the boards on the other side, along the blue line, and around again. On his own, then briefly with another player, changing speeds, coasting, pushing off, stickhandling one of the many pucks. The effect of all those blades cutting through the ice—his, too, because I'm sure I can hear his above every other—is like hearing an orchestra tuning up.

My seat is in Section 116, behind and to the right of the Calgary players bench. I make my way down the stairs and along the nearly empty row, sit, and take a deep breath. Safe.

It was an ordeal getting here—bus, Skytrain, hordes of people brandishing umbrellas because it's raining again, of course. But now I'm here, and I'm turning my phone off so that Clapperton (two more emails today) and Alain (three missed calls today) can't find me. At least for a few hours.

Nathan takes a shot on the goalie and quickly scoops up another loose puck. He's waiting his turn and, while he does, he looks around, looks up at Section 116. Sees me.

Nods once. *Hi.*

And I nod back at him. *Hi.*

After the game, I've been instructed to stay in my seat and we'll be able to meet briefly before he has to catch the team bus to the airport for the flight back to Calgary. I expect we'll talk about the game (Win? Lose? Maybe he'll score a goal. It could happen, couldn't it?), and he'll ask me about UBC, and l'Avenir, maybe ask how Père is doing.

And then, after he's gone, I'll head back out into the rain and make my way back to my little apartment on Marine Drive and turn on my phone again. And face it all.

The game, once it gets underway, is a terrifying blur of speed, huge bodies crashing into the boards and each other, those blades cutting through the ice. Nathan is there in the middle of it all and, as far as I can tell, is doing everything right. I hold my breath every time he has the puck.

Late in the third period, down by one goal, Number 92 checks a Vancouver player into the boards, sending him crashing to the ice, and suddenly the air is black with booing. No penalty.

"Figures. That's Nathan McCormick." A man's voice from the row behind me.

And someone replies: "Oh, yeah. That kid who was kicked out of juniors because he beat the crap out of that Swedish guy at the Worlds, right?"

I look at Nathan, now sitting on the bench. The player beside him thumps the top of his helmet, hockey's version of a pat on the head, I think. Says something to him. Nathan turns to look at his teammate and, just for a moment, I can see his face. Sweaty, mouth open as he sucks in air, one gloved hand hanging over the boards, his mouth guard dangling. Grinning. Deaf to the sound of the crowd. Blind to anything but his teammate and the ice and his next shift out there.

Happy. That's what happy looks like.

Fine.

I reach for my phone and turn it on, ignore my mail, scroll through my texts to find the last one from Fredrik.

Think about it k?

The same message he sent me back in the summer, during the height of rehearsals and concerts, during preparations for UBC, during Père's slow recovery from that scary night in May.

Fine, Fredrik. As instructed, I think about it. I think about it while watching Nathan McCormick chewing on his mouth guard and waiting for his next chance to jump over the boards.

Fine. I get it.

I get it.

Later, the game over, I move down to the first row of Section 116 and wait for Nathan to emerge from the dressing room. A quick visit, he said. While I'm waiting, I text first Fredrik, then Papa. After that, I turn my phone off.

CHAPTER 97

THE BEGINNING

Tomorrow, Sunday, Fredrik is coming to stay at our house in Montreal, just for one night, so we can do some recording and refining of tracks I've been working on for his latest film project. Père is going to make his famous beef stew and promises to stay out of our way, but I tell him he's welcome to sit in, maybe even add a little violin riff?

"I will stick to making stew," he laughs. "And supplying you with restoring cups of tea."

Papa spends his weekends and non-teaching days during the week in Ottawa, now that I'm living at home again and keeping an eye on Père. The Chalmers ensemble, featuring newest members Maxim St. Pierre and Vianne Courtemanche, is thriving, with concert requests tumbling in. ("They will come home with rings on their fingers, just watch," warns Père. "That would be lovely," I say.) Of course Alain is involved, which means juggling his l'Avenir commitments—l'Avenir, with their new Polish pianist and German horn player and a growing schedule of European engagements. *(Decided I like the NAC more*, Bartek emails me. *I don't miss l'Avenir. Do you? Silly question ...*)

I spend hours at the piano, keeping my hands in shape and the repertoire within reach, because, well, as Père says, you never know. But the concert stage is just a shadowy space in the back of my musical brain now, and I file it gradually into the "just forget about it" section of my memory bank, along with my mother's advice and some nasty tweets from @AClapperton back in October.

There was one conversation with Clapperton, odd and final, before I left Vancouver.

We used Skype, because of course there's no way I'm flying to London to meet him in person.

"Hello, Imogen," he says in a clipped tone of disapproval. He sounds a bit like my mother, and he doesn't ask how I am or how school is going.

But that's fine because it makes everything easier.

His Skype face is pale and distorted, eyes focused on his own image at the bottom, rather than looking into the computer's camera. I feel as if I'm talking to someone who doesn't want to look me in the eye.

"Thank you for making time for this call, Anthony," I say.

"Yes, well, I was happy to hear from you. Finally."

He's angry. This is getting easier and easier.

So I tell him. How I agreed to one concert, how that somehow spun out into four. How the UK tour was never something I agreed to. How things are changing for me and I can't see my future including l'Avenir.

Yes, this is a break-up call.

At first he keeps his face impassive but, as my words sink in, he starts to frown, then squirm a bit. Then he leans back, breathes deeply, leans forward with a smile plastered on his face.

"No, no, no, Genny. I'm sure we can work this out. You surely aren't going to let a few comments from a colleague drive you away from what is an unmatched opportunity for you, now that Trio St. Pierre is done," he says. He's adopting a kindly older brother tone, but of course it comes across in his usual supercilious style.

"Lena has agreed to join us just for the Christmas tour, you understand. This doesn't have to be a permanent arrangement. You do understand that, right? It's just, when I didn't hear from you ..." he trails off.

"This isn't about any comments," I tell him.

"It's about money, then," he says.

"No, no." I thought this would be easier and he's twisting it around, making it complicated.

"What, then? Repertoire? Because if so, I can speak to the group, and I know Alain is on board to negotiate contracts—the best contracts—for performance opportunities. Is that it? What will it take to convince you?"

He actually sounds a bit desperate and, for one tiny, tiny moment, I feel sorry for him.

It passes quickly, though.

He's very still and we spend an uncomfortable moment staring at our screens.

"Genny, you don't think you're just having a reaction to the break-up of Trio St. Pierre? Maybe you just need some time to adjust to being on your own? Responsible for your own career? Making your own decisions?"

"No, I'm quite sure that's not it."

Silence again. He's chewing his lip.

"I do hate to say this ..."

Then don't. Don't say it.

"... but maybe it's time you grew up a little," he says. Big-brotherly again. "Get out from under the shelter of your father and grandfather. Step out on your own."

Echoes of my mother, and I can't find any words that will make him see how wrong he is, so I just shake my head.

"Genny, may I ask you something?"

"Of course."

"Does this have anything to do with that guy? From the concert? Ethan?"

Ethan? Oh, dear. He can see me and I wish he couldn't, because I'm suddenly consumed with a desire to giggle. I don't, of course. I keep a straight face and reply:

"I can assure you my decision has nothing to do with Ethan."

Our conversation is staggering to a close.

"I can't convince you to stay?"

"No. No, Anthony, you can't." Should I tell him that the thought of being stuck in a professional commitment with him fills me with horror? Being on the road with him? Sharing cabs? Sitting across the table from him and Alina in hotel restaurants, fighting over dynamics and tempo changes? Shudder. "I'm sorry. But I wish you all well."

He hesitates, then smiles thinly.

"Well, thank you for being honest." Honest? Maybe not. But I'm not going to lie to him, either. "Good luck to you, too."

And before I can say anything more, he disconnects.

Actually, I think maybe I'm the one who has disconnected, because everything is different now. Now I just play for myself, play whatever comes out of my adventures that day—Père and me on our daily walk when it starts to snow; those kids across the street with their bikes, with a puppy; Vianne and Papa and Père and me jamming klezmer in our living room; a sad ending to a novel I got from the library. Anything that floats through my head is fair game.

I had no idea there was so much unfettered, unattached, unformed music in me. Fredrik knew, though.

I record most of it on some special equipment Fredrik has set up by my piano and send the audio files to him. He has so many contracts for films—marketing and PR mostly, corporate trailers, non-profit groups, and, yes, even an ongoing conversation with the Ottawa Senators—and my piano tracks are now part of his style, his brand, he says. We are partners. Handshakes, contracts, and everything. My own money, which I save (mostly) or spend on iTunes or the occasional shopping trip with Vianne. Two weeks ago, I came home from meeting her for lunch and astonished Papa and Père with my short, sleek haircut. Everything feels new.

Tomorrow Fredrik will come and we'll get to work while Père makes us stew.

But that's tomorrow.

Tonight, right now, at this very moment, I'm sipping hot chocolate, wrapped in my puffy parka, sitting in a seat at the Bell Centre, watching Nathan McCormick skate during the warm-up. Habs versus Flames. His team is staying over at a hotel, so he and I are going out into the city afterward for coffee.

Or, more likely, for hamburgers.

It's already snowing, transforming the streets with their Christmas lights into a fairytale scene. December in Montreal. Christmas at home with Père and Papa, and probably Vianne. Playing my piano for Fredrik tomorrow and eating Père's beef stew.

Watching Nathan McCormick skate in front of me right now, and how he looks up, searching the stands, and finds me.

And nods. *Hi.*

Hi.

Yes, Père. I am happy.

ACKNOWLEDGMENTS

Skating Over Thin Ice features two teenagers whose lives are immersed in the worlds of classical music and professional hockey. I used my own experience with these two worlds as a starting point and relied on research for many of the details. Readers with more knowledge than I have may be shaking their heads at my mistakes, for which I take full responsibility. I hope they will engage their "willing suspension of disbelief" whenever these mistakes pop up, and forgive me for manipulating some details to fit the needs of my plot.

I'm grateful to friends and family who helped me in big and little ways during the writing of this novel:

My former Curling Canada colleague Glenn van Gulik, who offered suggestions about Ottawa malls and neighborhoods; broadcaster and former CFRC Queen's Radio teammate Chris Cuthbert, who provided insights into the daily routine of visiting

NHL teams; my niece, Amy Glynn, who offered advice about the hotels and newspapers of London; writerly friends Heather Wright, Kira Vermond, and Lisa Dalrymple, who offered unlimited positive support and made me feel as if this story might actually see the light of day; and writer Lisa McLean, whose early insight into Imogen's character helped shape the way I portrayed her.

I also gratefully acknowledge the Ontario Arts Council, who provided financial support during the early stages of writing this novel.

To Peter Carver and Red Deer Press, thank you for embracing this project and guiding it to publication.

And finally, carving out a writing life is hard work in this busy world. I couldn't do it without my team: Dale, Elspeth and Derrick, and Tristan—always cheering me on.

PHOTO CREDIT: BY TRINA KOSTER

INTERVIEW WITH JEAN MILLS

What drew you to this story?

This story started in my imagination as a scene: a famous young movie star arrives at the classroom at his new school and all the other students look up, eyes wide, thinking, "Hey, that's [famous kid, the movie star]!" (In my head, I was seeing Daniel Radcliffe, aka Harry Potter, showing up at the door of my daughter's middle school classroom.) What would having a celebrity in their midst do to the interactions between these classmates?

Weird Girl was the working title I gave this story, long before it became *Skating Over Thin Ice*. An unusual girl (a musician?), an outsider without many friends, who connects with a celebrity boy, who everyone wants a piece of – eventually, after many failed attempts, these characters became Imogen and Nathan.

Imogen prefers to be in what she regards as a safe place—yet she constantly finds herself in situations that carry risk. Is that what it's like to be a gifted prodigy?

As this story opens, we get the sense that Imogen feels there is truly only one safe place: at her piano. She runs to the piano when she needs to get away from uncomfortable situations. She wants her future to be built on playing her piano with Papa and Père—but that's impossible, of course.

She's a highly intelligent and gifted individual. Yes, a prodigy. She knows she must grow and change and look ahead, even if that means she must risk facing some new experiences. Does she enjoy it? Not really. The photo shoot. The Hallowe'en party. Skating lessons. Practicing and performing with a new ensemble. It's not all positive, but her intelligence and self-awareness tell her she must step outside her safe place and take risks.

As young people grow into adulthood, it's often the case that they grow away from family, seeking to establish themselves independently. But this is not the case with Imogen. Why do you think that is?

I don't see Imogen's return to the family home in Montreal as a lack of independence. I think she's very independent by the end of the story. She's exploring new professional paths with Fredrik while keeping an eye on her recovering grandfather (not as little Imogen, the granddaughter, but as the person in charge, since her father is now based in Ottawa). She even cuts her hair! And she's forging a deepening connection with Nathan, too. I think these are all signs of her growing independence. It may look different from the independence shown by other young adults, but for Imogen, these are signs that she is taking control of her life.

Throughout the book, you use the present tense. Why do you think that is a mode that works well with storytelling?

I love writing in present tense! It makes the action so immediate, as if the reader is walking beside the characters as the story unfolds. This happens, then this happens, now this happens ... There's no time or distance between the reader and the action, so the story flows, a bit like a movie.

Despite the fact that they excel in very different realms, Nathan and Imogen seem to "get" each other's special qualities. What's that all about?

During the photo shoot, we see Imogen in all her uncomfortable glory: hating the whole process and being pushed by Alain to comply. But when the idea of being lifted into the air by the rugby boys is just too overwhelming, it's Nathan who steps up. Even though he and Imogen don't really know each other, he sees someone being bullied, someone who needs defending.

Later, when she watches the famous video of the fight from

the World Juniors, she sees him defending someone else (his teammate and friend, Luc). She realizes he is someone she can count on.

As for Nathan, I think in Imogen he recognizes someone with talent, accomplishment, and commitment, which are things he admires and pursues in his own hockey life. She's not buzzing around trying to impress him. She's a safe person to have as a friend.

You seem to know a good deal about the world of classical music. What can be the appeal of that interest for young people today?

I've been hooked on classical music since I was a small child listening to my parents' one classical recording: Tchaikovsky's *Nutcracker Suite* and *1812 Festival Overture.*

I think most people are drawn to music in some way, and young people might be surprised to realize how much classical music they've actually been exposed to. Movie soundtracks, television shows, and advertising often rely on classical music: for example, one of Apple's "Shot on iPhone" ads is set to Claude Debussy's famous piano piece, "Clair de lune," and Brahms's "Waltz No. 15 in A-flat Major" (the same waltz Imogen plays for Alicia and, later, Nathan) is featured in *The Hunger Games: Catching Fire.*

I feel I was lucky to be exposed to classical music early in my life, but for someone whose parents didn't play Tchaikovsky recordings after supper and whose only exposure to classical music has been movies and TV shows, this may sound like foreign territory. I think it's territory worth exploring.

You also know about the field of competitive professional athletics. What kind of insights does this experience give you into Nathan's world?

Sports have always played a big role in my life. A number of years ago, my writing and sporting lives intersected, and I landed a job working with Curling Canada as a writer and editor. This means I have the opportunity to work with elite, high-performance athletes and see them in action both on the ice and off it.

For my job, I'm interacting with athletes focused on representing Canada at either the World Championships or the Olympics. What impresses me is how hard they work to achieve their goals. Most of them have been practicing and competing at increasingly more demanding levels since they were young kids, and they've made many sacrifices. But they accept that, because they love what they do.

That's the kind of commitment and character I hope I've shown in Nathan, the hockey player. As he says to Imogen during their chat in the piano room at Fredrik's house about the potential for danger and violence in his sport: "I love hockey so much, I just take that stuff as part of the game."

The unspoken but deep understanding between Imogen and Nathan is expressed in the film project they create with Fredrik. What brought you to deciding this would be a good way of showing their unusual connection?

My original vision for this story was of two unusual teenagers finding themselves thrown together in a school environment. But their interaction needed a catalyst. Why not a school project? Everyone hates group projects (speaking from my experience as a mom and as a college teacher!) so why not throw Imogen and Nathan together this way?

I imagined a school project that would allow both these characters to showcase their individual talents. We have a pianist and a hockey player, sound and motion. A film project seemed to be the perfect choice. Bringing in Fredrik, the tech wiz kid, as a friend and group member, provided a perfect combination of characters to make the film—and the process of creating it—a success.

Why is *Skating Over Thin Ice* an appropriate title for this story?

The title is drawn from a quotation of Ralph Waldo Emerson, the nineteenth-century American poet, essayist, and philosopher: "When skating over thin ice, our safety is in our speed."

Both Imogen and Nathan face an uncertain future, and that uncertainty can be frightening. In Imogen's case, her grandfather's hands are "losing the notes," which could mean the end of Trio St. Pierre. In Nathan's case, he may be banned from playing hockey at a high level because of a violent incident in an international hockey game.

So for both these young people, their "safety" is threatened.

It's Fredrik who has the vision for their group media studies project. He films them skating, because both of them are "skating" over dangers and threats to their professional happiness. And it's during those moments of skating together for the film project that Imogen and Nathan really begin to connect with each other. Thanks to Fredrik and his vision for the film, they find "safety" together.

This is a story of accomplishment, ultimately an optimistic story with no real bad guys, a story in which the main characters find a satisfying life for themselves. Why do you think such stories can appeal to young readers?
Many current YA novels feature variations on edgy teens from dysfunctional families or fantasy/dystopian societies, exploring issues that might include addiction, violence, sex, gender exploration, the battle of Good versus Evil, and all things dark and challenging. I can appreciate that kind of story has an appeal.

I don't always enjoy reading those kinds of stories, so I don't often write them, either. There's certainly a place in literature for the dark side, and I do go there sometimes in my writing, but that's not *Skating Over Thin Ice.*

I believe there are teens—and adults, myself included—who want to read stories with less dark and more light in them, a gentler approach to the young adult journey that doesn't sacrifice any of its challenges or truths. I hope that's the kind of reading experience that *Skating Over Thin Ice* offers.

Thank you, Jean.